THE STONE IN THE ROAD

AUSTRALIAN AT HEART BOOK 2

FRANCES DALL'ALBA

Poinsettia
Publishing

Also By Frances Dall'Alba

<u>Australian At Heart Series</u>
Little Blue Box - Book 1
The Stone In The Road - Book 2
The Silk Scarf - Book 3
Rustic Denim Love – Book 4

<u>Sway Of The Stars Series</u>
The Shooting Star – Book 1
The Glittering Star – Book 2
The Giving Star – Book 3
The Priceless Star – Book 4

<u>Standalone Books</u>
Eight Seconds
Jack & Eva

For my mum, for always being there.
And for Lisa — my critique partner and friend. Your never-ending support
is greatly appreciated.

Chapter 1

With everything crossed off her to-do list for the trip into Winton, Kelly Sheppard tucked it away in the pocket of her jeans and instructed Patrick to start driving home. It was good to connect with the outside world every now and then, even if Winton was a 'big sky, small town' community in outback Queensland. Relaxed in the passenger seat, Kelly settled back. The breeze rustled in from the open window of the old homestead jeep, causing her hair to billow across her face. She tucked the loose strands behind her ear to clear her view.

Three hours later, Kelly checked her watch. Yep, out here in the sticks a watch still trumped a mobile phone. She hadn't bothered to switch hers on after leaving Winton. Reception was unreliable this far out.

With an hour left of the four-hour long drive, she stifled a yawn. It was about this time the drive became wearisome. She would love nothing better than to close her eyes and sleep. Instead, she sat up straighter and rolled her shoulders. Time for a break, Kelly decided, for both her and Patrick, who was only a learner driver.

She raised her voice over the rush of hot breeze. "Okay, Yanko, keep driving for a couple more kilometres, then we'll stop at Leslie Creek."

Patrick Van Der Meeliko nodded, a smile playing along his mouth. "Sure, boss. I can do that." The wind did a good job of whipping his words away, but she caught the teasing in his voice.

Jeez. How had she ended up teaching this upstart how to drive? He was a few years older than her and a bloody long way from home. Why the heck hadn't he learned to drive in a city like Boston?

It was no secret that drugs were the reason he was at Samdarra Station. Kelly didn't need reminding how easy it was to lose oneself to temptations. Luckily, she'd discovered the difference between a bad habit and a true addiction before coming to Samdarra, a cattle station doubling as a rehabilitation and detox clinic. Not so long ago she could've used its services.

Patrick crunched down through the gears as they approached the creek. Used as the homestead's 'get around' vehicle, the jeep had rust around its edges and a lot of character.

"Any objections to parking in the shade?" Patrick pointed to a cluster of eucalyptus trees only metres away from the creek.

Ugh. Where else would you park in this stinking hot weather? She bit her tongue to stop the retort. "No, Yanko. Have a swim, too, if you want. Best way to cool down."

Ever since her first meeting with Patrick, he'd frequently irked her with his smart-arse comments. She'd called him 'Yanko' when she'd been at her most irritated with him and it'd stuck. It was a play on 'Yankee' and his American accent, so alien in outback Queensland. He smiled every time she called him that.

Leaving him to fill his logbook, she opened the jeep door and got out. She stretched her legs, raised her arms above her head and exhaled. Already, she felt more alert.

Secretly, she was pleased with Patrick's driving skills and how he handled the old girl. For someone who'd never turned a key in an ignition before, it hadn't taken him long to pick up the skill.

Was she impressed? *Yes.*

Was she going to share her thoughts? *God, no.*

"Hey, Kelly, can you sign off on these hours?"

She turned, taking in his dreadlocked brown hair and his tall, willowy frame. "Sure."

His hand brushed hers as he handed over the logbook and pen, but she kept her mind on the task, ignoring the temptation to look at him.

She signed before retrieving a small cooler from the back of the jeep. "Sandwich or fruit?"

"Sandwich, thanks." Patrick took two bottles of chilled water from another ice cooler.

A chance meeting with the station's counsellor, Janice, at last year's Winton races had landed Kelly her current job. She was nanny to the station owner's two children and carried out various homestead chores. For a while before that, she'd roamed from place to place doing similar work, making only enough for food and shelter. She hadn't cared where she went; by then, she'd lost direction.

Kelly sat in the shade of the trees, leaving room for Patrick. When he sat beside her, she handed him a sandwich.

For patients, rehabilitation at Samdarra meant working on the cattle station. From what Kelly saw, work was tough and the conditions tougher still. It left people dog-tired by the end of each day, where sleep was a luxury before the morning gong sounded for breakfast at dawn.

For some reason, Patrick was always in her face, doing chores closer to the homestead, as though he'd been put on this earth as an extension of her arm. Being asked to teach him to drive was almost the final straw. If she hadn't liked her station family so much, she would've walked away weeks ago.

She looked at him over the top of her sandwich. "So, tell me, why did you never learn to drive?"

Patrick chuckled. "Haven't I answered that question? You only ask it every time you scramble for something to say."

The heat of a flush crept up her neck. It galled her that he was right. One of her previous attempts at conversation had covered how he'd got around Boston when he couldn't drive. If she recalled correctly, his answers had been dumb-arse ones like, *"My private chauffeur drove me around,"* or *"I'd catch the next flight to the party,"* or *"The guests came to my mansion."*

As if. His replies had only managed to vex her further.

She released a frustrated sigh. On the station he was annoyingly close and constantly invading her space. Once upon a time she had never been shy in front of guys. She could chew off their ear with small talk then start chewing off an arm. Around Patrick, she lost that skill.

"Remind me once more."

Patrick chuckled. "Too much time on my hands, that's why."

What the? That answer made no sense. She shook her head and ignored him, turning her attention to her sandwich. Men with long, unkempt hair never appealed to her, especially when she was forced to spend time with them. How had learning to drive escaped him? Maybe things were done differently in Boston.

"So, tell me," he began, and she shook herself out of her reverie. "With no family nearby, how did you end up in Winton, helping every no-hoper for miles around?"

Fair question, but none of his business.

"Too much time on my hands, I guess."

He burst out laughing and its infectiousness dragged her in too. If she could quit noticing that his dreadlocks and American accent went well together, she would have no problem keeping her promise to boycott men. Today she needed a reminder of why she'd made that vow.

With her hand resting instinctively against her breastbone, she remembered how the pain had sliced through her. It was a loss she would eventually need to overcome and move on from. What she'd done was irreversible. There was no going back.

Stripped down to his boxers, Patrick sank into the shallow creek and lay on his back. Branches from the eucalypts leaned close to the water's edge, brown bark dripping off in strips, their leaves shading his face. *God, this country is hot.*

At the thought, a streak of satisfaction hurtled along his backbone. He loved the dry heat that sucked every bit of moisture from his skin. It made him feel alive in a way he never had before. Boston was a world away, but he was yet to suffer homesickness. That had been another life.

Still wearing his sunglasses, he closed his eyes and floated. It was a relief to cool down and refresh. With a full stomach and feeling proud of his driving skills, he was ready for the final stretch to the homestead. In a couple of months, he'd have accumulated enough hours to sit his driver's test and finally get his licence.

He opened his eyes and angled his face to better watch Kelly. She pulled a t-shirt firmly past her hips and, settling on the creek's bottom, wrapped her arms around her raised knees. He was hyperaware of her closeness, but she showed no interest in him.

Still, he couldn't resist making the lame jokes and irksome comments he knew irritated her, purely so he could get a reaction. He knew it was immature, but he'd never dealt with anyone like her. She was a universe away from the women he associated with in Boston. In this rough outback country, she gave an impression of casual elegance and a hint of something deeper below the surface.

"We better hit the road again, Yanko." Kelly rose, water dripping down her firm, tanned thighs. It was all it took for his body to harden.

He groaned inwardly but rose from the water, loosening his boxers to lessen what might be visible if she bothered to look his way. She didn't, so he prepared himself to deliver a lame comment.

"You know what?" He ran his hands down his torso and legs to remove excess water, before hoisting himself onto the bank and reaching for a towel.

She rolled her eyes. "I can hardly wait for this."

He chuckled at her reluctance to listen. "Of all the Aussie slang I've had to interpret to make sense of what you locals are saying, Yanko outdoes them all. I'm very proud of you."

She burst out laughing and everything about her changed. Her willow-green eyes sparkled, mesmerising him instantly, and her midnight black hair shimmered blue in the afternoon sun.

An elusive thought finally struck home. *Sunlight.*

It was what he thought of every time he was close to her. If sunlight had a personality, Kelly shared it. Whether the day was hazy, scorching, shaded or cool, she exuded it. As he towel-dried himself, his chest expanded with an uncomfortable fullness at the realisation that, for the first time in his life, he was the shy boy. He fumbled with his clothes before settling into the driver's seat.

"Once we get to the gate at paddock one hundred and twenty, gun it. Get up to fifth gear, then work the gears down as you approach Riley's Corner. It's a tight bend and I want a nice smooth drive around it."

They were thirty minutes into the last leg and there'd been no need for conversation. The silence wasn't awkward, just comfortable, with a relaxing afternoon waiting for them at the other end. He knew the corner she mentioned, and now on Samdarra land they were only a couple of kilometres away, with Riley's corner a stone's throw from the homestead.

When the gate at paddock one hundred and twenty whizzed past in his periphery, the last stretch of paved road began. The usual corrugated gravel didn't allow for fast driving, but the onset of paving had a driver naturally picking up speed. This was where he moved up the gears as Kelly instructed.

A thick band of trees huddled around Riley's Corner. They fed off the creek running alongside the steep embankment to the left, giving their foliage an unusual greenness in the dry landscape.

"Okay, start to slow it down soon," Kelly instructed.

He pressed gently on the brake pedal, but his foot tangled with it, finding no resistance. He pushed the pedal all the way to the floor, but the jeep showed no signs of slowing down at all.

"Shit, Yanko, I said start slowing down." Kelly sat up straighter, a hint of worry tainting her words.

The wind whipped against his face. "I'm damn well trying!"

Frantically, he pumped the spongy pedal as they approached Riley's Corner at an alarming rate. His heart boomed. "The brakes! The freaking brakes aren't working!"

Kelly reached for the handbrake, a last-ditch effort to slow the jeep, but they'd already reached Riley's Corner. The vehicle careered off the road. Kelly screamed. The jeep rolled into the ditch and continued tumbling down the embankment. Branches grazed Patrick's face through the open window. The engine finally cut out when the sudden jerk of the handbrake brought them to a stop on the edge of a steep drop.

Pain exploded behind Patrick's eyes. His head had taken a hit each time they'd rolled, but pain aside, he was alive. Not much else hurt that he could tell. Still strapped in, he jerked his head in Kelly's direction and nearly keeled over with pain from the movement. Kelly was conscious but had a gash near her forehead and was rapidly gulping in air. He blinked a couple of times to clear the dizziness, trying to calm his breathing.

"Don't move, Yanko. One breath of wind and this thing could slide to the bottom of this hill. *That* will really hurt."

Shit. How had they managed to stop on the precipice of the rise where Riley's Corner was cut? At least they were sitting upright.

"You okay?" For the first time, concern for him filled her eyes.

Is this what's required to get some sort of reaction from her? He almost laughed at the absurdity.

"I am. What about you?" He wasn't about to mention his sore head.

"I'll live, but when I find out who was responsible for not checking the brake fluid during the jeep's last service, I'll skin them alive. It was only done last week."

Gingerly, she reached for the two-way radio and made an emergency call to the homestead. A small gust of wind buffeted the sides of the jeep and it swayed dangerously. Somehow, it managed to stay put.

"This is my first accident, ever." Kelly blinked back tears and turned away.

Patrick swallowed. He didn't relish the jeep toppling further down the steep decline. "Look, Kelly, I'm sorry. If this thing goes over, I want you to know I'm sorry. I know I say all sorts of stupid things, but I can't help it. I go a little crazy around you."

Slowly, she turned to look at him. "Sit steady and we'll get out of here soon. When we do, you can tell me all the crazy stuff you want."

Her strong and dependable front made him feel inadequate in this crisis. "You're not worried?"

She stared through the cracked windscreen as a sigh escaped. "I'm nervous, just nervous, Yanko. I don't want to end up badly hurt and ... and my parents. I never should've left like I did."

It was hard to miss the wretchedness in her voice. The same aura he always picked up on around her, the one that suggested things went deeper for her than she let on, came through crystal clear. She sounded sad and alone, but he had no idea why. In time, if she let him, he would like to find out. He might be the right person to listen. After all, he carried his own demons.

Before his half-sister, who'd been missing for twenty-five years, burst into his life, he never would've left Boston to come to a place like Samdarra. Things in his family were a long way from perfect, but at least he had family worth living for.

"What happened?" At moments like this, a person could say the dumbest things.

She chuckled wryly. "A lot, and I regret all of it."

How did someone dredge up so much despair in one reply? But he knew the answer before he'd even finished thinking the question. *Easily.* He didn't need reminding.

She turned away and looked into the steep valley. Tendrils of her dark hair gently lifted around her face. Two drops of blood dripped down her cheek, but he didn't say a word. He didn't want to startle her with a sudden movement. If he could have any wish granted at that moment, it'd be to save Kelly. Then he'd capture her image and hide it in a special spot.

His days at Samdarra were numbered and he wasn't sure what road to take next. If he made a list of the people who made him smile, there wouldn't be too many names on it. But getting to see Kelly, who put up with his insufferable humour, was one of the reasons he rose from bed each day.

She turned back to him. "How about you?"

"What?" He'd lost the thread of their conversation. "Do I have family, regrets?"

"Yeah, Yanko." Her eyes latched on to his. "Regrets will do for starters."

He struggled to hold back the deep well of regret surging up his throat. If it exploded, its force would surely topple the jeep down the embankment.

He held it in—now was not the time to break down. "Probably the reason I turned to drugs. It's no excuse, but it seemed the only way I could dull the guilt and pain."

"Fair enough." She gave a reassuring smile. "Since we have about a fifty-fifty chance of this thing toppling further, you go first. I want to be certain I'm about to die before I spill my regrets."

Despite the ache coursing through him, he managed to chuckle. "Okay."

She had a way about her and he'd had plenty of time to relive that twisted day. Since arriving at Samdarra, the counsellor had helped him face what had sent him spiralling. He couldn't talk about the trauma at first, but she'd encouraged him to write about it.

"It goes like this. When I was eighteen, I told my mother I hated her. I called her weak and accused her of being unable to stand up for herself. I should've blamed my bully of a father. He was abusive but not in a way I understood back then. My mother could never bring herself to leave him, but that wasn't her fault. My father made sure it was impossible for her to start a new life elsewhere." He halted for a moment. The pain in his temple increased and pounded against his skull. "She ... she killed herself that day and ... well, I sort of lost it after that."

"Oh," she whispered. "I'm so sorry, Patrick. That's really awful."

He nodded. If he was about to die, at least he'd told her about the burden that defined his life.

They continued to sit in silence. He wasn't going to press her. If she wanted to talk, he would listen.

"I suppose you're waiting for me to talk?"

"Only if you want to."

She peered into the ravine. "If we don't die, I'd appreciate it if you kept this to yourself."

"I promise."

A strong gust of wind howled through their open windows, causing the jeep to wobble.

"I regret—"

The jeep lurched and Kelly yelped. "Oh, Christ!"

The jeep tilted dangerously, and the next breath of air tipped it on its side into the void.

"No!" she shrieked as the jeep cartwheeled downhill, picking up momentum with each rotation, descending in ever increasing tumbles.

Patrick's head smacked hard against the inside panel of the jeep and a scream tore from his lips. There was one final hit to the side of his head and then he felt nothing.

Chapter 2

*T*wo Weeks Later

Kelly's hand shook, causing the letter she was holding between her knees to flap. To still her shaking hands she rubbed at the fading bruises visible on her legs.

Janice put her arm around her shoulder and tutted. "How did they find you?"

Kelly gritted her teeth. She couldn't believe how one weak moment had enabled her parents to locate her. She could admit her mistake.

"I sent one lousy postcard from Winton. I don't even know why I posted it, except there might've been a smidgen of guilt about how I left." The news in the letter had shaken her. "I didn't even sign it. Nothing. So how the hell did their letter find me?"

Janice chuckled. "You forget what a small town this is. You're probably the only Kelly for a thousand kilometres around. Old Marg at the post office would've seen your name and dropped it in Samdarra's mailbag without hesitating."

Kelly pictured the scene perfectly and managed a lopsided smile. Janice knew the whole sorry tale of her life, but that hadn't prepared Kelly for the thumping heart beats that blasted her body, rattling it to pieces, when the station manager had called from his office to say she had mail.

"Here, read it." She shoved it under Janice's nose.

Janice took it and settled more comfortably on the beanbag, which was too small for two people. Kelly rose and went to sit at the table. It crowded the small donga where Janice lived while on the station.

Dear Kelly,

If this letter finds you, your father and I want to express our never-ending love for you. We miss you terribly and look forward to the day you feel strong enough to come back home. We hope you are healing well.

A lot has happened in the past eighteen months and there are things we need to share with you.

Attached to this letter are the details of the property you recently inherited from your grandfather. We know we didn't share in much of his life. We're not even certain if we told you he spent the past eight years in a nursing home with dementia. We didn't realise the property was still in his name and were certain his second wife had sold it and taken the proceeds.

As it turns out, we have no idea what happened to her and were recently informed he expressly left it to you. The solicitor warns us the property is in a very dire state, but the land will always be worth something.

Kelly, my darling, we need you to make contact, or at least make your way up north to sort this out. There are details attached for the solicitor taking care of your grandfather's will and a local real estate agent, who is happy to put the property on the market.

Please, Kelly, if there is something we did wrong, give us the chance to apologise. We never disagreed with your decision and we honestly thought you were happy with it too.

Talk to us. Each day you stay away is tearing us apart. The sun cannot shine on our home again until you return. Come home or phone us. We're always here.

Lots of love,

Mum

"So …" Janice's eyebrows rose when she finished the letter.

"So." Kelly rested her face on her hands, her elbows perched on the table.

"Sounds like they were supportive of you."

Her groan tore along her throat. "That's the problem. They were, even though I knew they were disappointed in me. They had so much hope for my future."

Kelly rose and walked around the small room, bumping a chair on her way. "I still don't understand what came over me when I left. I can't even remember making the decision. What I do know is that the ball of guilt growing inside grows with each day that passes. I should've never left without saying goodbye. How can I face them now, after all this time? They've probably aged a thousand years. Mum used to be so outgoing and social. Beautiful. They were the perfect couple in Sydney's social scene. The darlings of the town. Then along came their daughter who threw it all in their face."

"Shh."

"It's true. They provided every opportunity for me. Sport, music lessons, private schooling, dance training. What else did I need? But in those last few months when I hid from the world, I resented all those privileges and began to hate them. For what? For agreeing with the decision *I'd* made."

Janice slumped back, hesitating before saying, "You know what, Kel? With your body changing so much and your mind barely able to keep up, those sorts of confused feelings were normal. Now that everything has settled down, it's okay to see things differently."

Kelly flopped onto the beanbag and rested her head against Janice's shoulder. Thinking about her parents always opened up a barrage of sorrow and took her back to the day her world had changed. She clung to her memories, wishing she could change her mind and take a different route. The pain clutched at her chest and twisted. The same pain was responsible for keeping her awake on many a long, lonely night and brought back memories of tear-drenched pillows.

Regret was unlikely to leave her in a hurry.

"What are you going to do?"

Janice intruded on her pain, and for a second, she didn't want to leave its familiarity. Her parents' letter represented new, uncertain territory.

She hunched her shoulders, doubt rattling every skerrick of confidence she possessed. "What should I do?"

Janice took her hand and squeezed it. "Okay, let's work through the options."

Kelly smiled.

Janice, the most optimistic person she knew. Janice, who never let her wallow in her sorrow, regardless of whether she might be having a bad a day. Janice was the reason Kelly was now of sound mind. Who knew where her life might've taken her if Janice hadn't stepped in right when she did?

Janice sat up, crossed her legs and forced Kelly to look at her. "First option is to contact your parents and ask them for advice."

Kelly frowned. "Why?"

Janice chuckled. "Yeah, I wasn't so sure about that option. Okay, next one is to go see this property and then invite your parents to see it. That way, you're all away from the memories, all on unfamiliar territory, and you can see whether you can repair your relationship with them."

This time Kelly arched her brows. *Okay, better.*

"So, you like?" Janice asked, her satisfied smile stretching across her face.

"I do, but I'll have to sort some way of getting up there. It's close to a fifteen-hour drive without any stops."

"And you're due for a break, especially after the accident. The station nurse has already told the boss you need another two weeks off duties. By the way, how've you been the last couple of days?"

Kelly rubbed her temple. All her bruises had faded to a light yellowish-purple. "I'm still getting the occasional headache, but I came out of it better than Patrick."

He'd suffered a serious concussion. His half-sister had transferred him from Winton Hospital to Brisbane, where his family could take care of him. If word around the station could be believed, he was due back in a week's time.

She hadn't known he had family in Australia. In fact, she didn't know much about him at all. The less she knew, the better. The last thing she needed were complications with a man visiting the country temporarily.

Images of Patrick, relaxed and floating in the creek, had occasionally popped up in her mind over the past two weeks. Something knotted in her chest as she recalled the conversation they'd shared before the jeep toppled over.

"Does Patrick need to come back to Samdarra?"

Janice rose and put the kettle on. "You're joking, right?"

Kelly sat up. "What's that supposed to mean? He seems to have knocked his drug problem on the head. Now it's time for him to go back to the States and get on with the rest of his life."

"Except *you* don't live in the States. That's what I mean."

She reared back, confused.

"You haven't watched him, puppy dog eyes and all, trailing you? He can't keep his eyes off you, even though you ignore him at every opportunity. I'll give him ten out of ten for persistence."

"What? Stop being so stupid. We irritate each other. Or more to the point, he aggravates me every second of the day when he's here. Anyway, look what happened the last time I let a man come too close to me."

Janice leaned against the kitchen bench and bunched her hands in the pockets of her jeans, clearly exasperated. "Oh, Kelly, look at you. You're young, too bloody young to have gone through what you did. Go up north, get your grandfather's property sorted out, get back on track with your parents, and then look at life again. You have so much to offer the world. You're a strong, brave, independent and very determined young woman. You might be a little cautious and a lot frightened of some things, but hell, have you noticed how damn attractive you are?"

"I don't care. I'm not making the same mistake again."

"Okay, okay, calm down. But when Patrick arrives next week, be nice to him. He's not that bad. Enjoy a little bit of friendship and dare to be young again. I know you won't make that mistake again, so stop worrying."

Kelly slumped back into the beanbag, but when her mind drifted to the huge regret Patrick had confessed, her spine straightened and she made a snap decision. She had to leave Samdarra and leave fast. Hopefully, by the time she returned, Patrick would be long gone, back to the States. She had enough problems; she didn't need to add someone else's to her list.

"How quickly can we arrange a lift out of Winton, heading north?"

Janice tilted her head, her eyebrow twitching. "I'm going to pretend you're not running away, but only this time. And I'm going to keep tabs on you for the rest of your life. I'll overlook it for now, but not forever. Got it girl?"

Kelly laughed. She wasn't stupid enough to throw this friendship out into the wind. Janice was around for keeps.

Chapter 3

Patrick sat in the sterile consultation room at Samdarra opposite Janice, who was reading through his medical notes from his recent hospital stay. The only sound in the small room was the whirr of her desktop computer.

A photo of Janice and her fiancé took up prime position on her desk. Everyone at the station knew of her coming marriage; she was the poster girl for happiness. Years ago, his mother had told him certain colours surrounded people, according to the aura of energy surrounding them. He wasn't one of those psychic souls who could tell the colour of a person's aura, but with dead certainty he knew that black had never tainted Janice like it did him.

He couldn't help the downcast thoughts running riot in his head. It'd been three days since he'd arrived back at Samdarra and his frame of mind had nosedived. The urge to dull his nervous twitch with a fix was strong. A drug-addicted person would always be in recovery, he was told, but would he always be this pathetic? Sighing, he raked his hand through his short, cropped hair.

Waking up in hospital and learning his dreadlocks had been cut off in preparation for surgery had upset him. He'd been proud of his scruffy hair, having grown it to rebel against how he was raised and expected to look. But if he'd thought a haircut was all that could upset him, his arrival back at Samdarra proved him wrong.

Kelly's absence easily eclipsed that.

He'd wanted to rush over to the clinic, barge his way into Janice's room and demand to know where Kelly had gone. Janice would know. They were friends. Instead, it festered like a cancerous sore and a sense of hopelessness assailed him. Was he really this weak? Could one setback like Kelly's disappearance put him back on the road to destruction?

"You look different with a haircut. Fresh-faced and all that. How are you feeling?"

He sat up, valiantly trying to inject some light into his voice but failed when he asked miserably, "Where's Kelly?"

Janice lifted her hand to tuck a wisp of short, blonde hair behind her ear. She closed the folder and rested it on the desk, indecision on her face. No doubt she was debating how much to tell him. Kelly wasn't one of her patients, but confidentiality would be ingrained in her.

"Hell, Janice, I don't even know if she's okay after the accident. The one I caused."

"That's not true, Patrick. She told us exactly what happened and you were not to blame. They found a leak in the old jeep and it's been fixed. It was an accident. She certainly doesn't hold it against you." Folding her hands together, she added, "Kelly came through it relatively unscathed. After a few days she only had bruises to show for it."

He raised his hands, palms up. "Then why has she left if she doesn't blame me?"

"Something personal came up. She has a few issues to sort through."

"Don't we all?" His face fell and his fingers curled as he tried to reason with the strong urge to find her. They had a conversation to finish. She'd been about to say something important.

His gaze lifted. "Do you know what?" He found it easy to talk to Janice now, ever since she'd encouraged him to write things down, when talking had initially been difficult. "The last three days I've been fighting the need for a fix. If I could walk down the road and buy one, I would. I'm not cured at all, and the funny thing is I honestly thought I was. I was so damn certain I'd turned my life around."

Janice swivelled her chair so she faced him. "Patrick, we've had patients who have walked away from Samdarra for that very reason, gotten lost and almost died out there. Your low moments will always be when it's hardest not to reach out for drugs. That you didn't is proof your recovery is progressing."

"How long will she be away?"

She blew out a breath, probably resigning herself to the fact that he wouldn't give up on Kelly. "A couple of weeks. I can't be certain."

"Will you tell me where she is? Did she go north or south?"

Her chair squeaked when she leaned back in it. Joining her hands in front of her chest, she formed a steeple with her fingers while she contemplated his question. "Look, Patrick, I'm worried about where she is." Her gaze pierced his. "The truth is, I trust you. Though you have insecurities, you're a very decent person. Given your history, you had every reason to spiral the way you did. But you will rise above it, especially with the family support you have. Also, I know you genuinely care about Kelly, but if she hasn't returned the attention you seek, she has her reasons."

"And I suppose you can't tell me what they are?"

"Correct, but I can tell you where she is. As her friend, I'd like someone to check she's okay, just in case she needs a hand. Whether she ever tells you her story, well, that's entirely up to her."

Janice paused and straightened in her chair. "What I will say—and Patrick, I won't mince my words ..."

He felt the heat of her gaze and knew by the tone of her voice that what she was about to say was something he better not forget.

"If you ever hurt her or make me regret my decision to tell you where she is, I'll personally tear you to pieces, bit by bit, and that's a promise."

For a second, the intensity of her words stung, her protectiveness of Kelly clear. He would've scaled mountain peaks to feel one iota of something like it from his father. But when Janice's shoulders relaxed a smidgen, he swore there was regret and concern in her expression.

A surge of laughter rose up his throat and he couldn't help lunging across the corner of the desk and giving her a swift hug. "Thanks Janice. I promise I'll never hurt her. I used to be scared that maybe I was more my father's son than I wanted to be, but because of your guidance, I've come to realise that we're responsible for our own actions and being aggressive is something we choose."

This time he didn't miss the relief sweeping across her face. "That's another reason I'm proud of your efforts here and why I trust you. I don't believe you have a mean bone in your body. But"—she tapped her fingers on the desktop—"my threat still stands, okay?"

He flopped back in his chair. "I still hate my father. I don't know how to get over that one. Not even his turning up here out of the blue all those months ago can atone for what he did to my mother. My stepsister Ella gets married in ten days, in Port Douglas and she's accepted dad's offer to walk her down the aisle. It's a long story, but she's the child of dad's first wife, missing after twenty-five years."

Patrick had been speechless when Ella told him of her decision to accept their father's offer. She'd said, "If he wants to walk me down the aisle, he's going to have to earn it." She had a take it or leave it attitude and strongly resembled their father in personality. Since coming into their lives, Patrick and his sister Melita had drawn closer to her, and they were now a close-knit family. Ella was one of the reasons he was in no hurry to return to Boston.

"When did you say this wedding is?" Janice asked, interrupting his thoughts.

"Not this weekend, but the next."

"Well, that's convenient, because Kelly's gone to a small rural town south of Cairns. You could check in on her on your way through. I'm not sure how she's coping without a car, and she doesn't have phone reception.

She called me yesterday from a roadhouse to say she'd arrived safely and promised to ring again in a few days."

Patrick perked up in his seat. "Can you find me a lift to Townsville?"

"Why?"

"I want to buy a car."

"Um ... can you afford one? You need to cover the registration and insurance, too."

He tried to keep a straight face pretending to think through her advice. In truth, he could afford anything, Samdarra included. "I have some savings and Ella's been helping me with budgeting. I should be able to afford something small."

"Okay, well, it sounds as though you know what you're doing. There's a cattle truck headed for Townsville leaving later today, but I expect you back after the wedding. I want to know all about what Kelly's up to. She may call me on occasion but getting all the facts out of her will be as difficult as extracting a tooth. She bottles things up too much and needs to learn to open up. No doubt you'll hound her with your humour and bad jokes. She could use a good laugh every day."

His chest expanded to twice its size and he grinned. "Janice, you're gold. That man of yours is one lucky guy. I'll go pack a bag."

As he left the consultation room, he realised the blanket of despair had been magically lifted. He had a plan, though, and only the anonymity of a city could help him.

◈

Patrick glanced at the used cars in the dealership yard and frowned. Unable to pin his finger on what he wanted, he shaded his eyes against the bright sunshine bouncing off the polished surfaces.

A salesman sauntered over and extended his hand. "Good afternoon, I'm Adam. Looking for something in particular?"

Patrick shook the man's hand. "Well, this is going to sound dumb, but they're all too shiny for me."

Adam chuckled. "You mean we shouldn't wax and polish them before putting them on display?"

Patrick could at least see the humour in his words. "Well, I sort of wanted something with a few dents, some dried-on mud and the colour starting to fade. Know what I mean?"

"Actually, I'm struggling, but you're looking at our lower end of the market. There are some decent bargains among this collection that won't cost you a packet. Have you got a budget?"

"Money's not the issue. It's ... it's just that I want to make a certain impression."

Adam's brow creased. "Ah, well ... that's confusing. You don't want to over impress a person, is that it?"

"Something like that."

Adam massaged his chin. "Well, you could go to a scrap yard and pick something off the heap, but that won't get you a vehicle with a roadworthy certificate. No certificate, no registration. All these vehicles come with one."

Damn. He hadn't considered that. And he didn't have time to search private sales.

"Are you sure there's nothing here that might interest you?" Adam asked.

Patrick turned on the spot and eyed the parked cars, one by one, hoping he might've missed a possible option. He hadn't.

He decided to try his luck somewhere else.

"About the only option I have that's close and handy is my beat-up old Camira." Smiling, Adam added, "By the way, I'm joking."

Patrick perked up. "Can I have a look?"

Adam's smile vanished and his eyes widened. "What? Are you serious?"

"Yes."

Adam shook his head but seemed incapable of moving.

"Please," Patrick persisted. "I need to get on the road."

Adam turned and walked towards the rear of the dealership without looking back.

Patrick spotted the orange Camira, which sported an obvious re-paint job done badly. It was faded in patches with enough dents on it to make anyone proud—or worried about the owner's driving ability.

After a quick inspection Patrick didn't hesitate. "How much do you want for it?"

Adam's eyes boggled. "It's not worth anything, trust me. I'm scraping together enough money to buy something a little more decent."

"Does it run?"

"Yeah, I know a bit about mechanics, so I know how to keep it running."

"What if I offered you $5000 for it?"

This time Adam's jaw dropped. "What? Are you crazy?"

Patrick straightened after peering through the window. "Adam, isn't it?"

"Yeah."

Patrick leaned against the door and folded his arms. "I like your honesty."

"Just doing my job. I can't afford to lose it." He clenched his hands nervously by his side.

"Where's your boss?"

A flicker of worry crossed Adam's brow. He pointed towards a cluster of offices inside the main showroom.

"I need to explain to him that I'd like to buy your car for $5000, plus a $1000 commission for him and an extra $1000 for you to escort me to Cairns, today. I need to get to a town south of Cairns."

Adam spluttered.

"I'm a learner driver, so I need a supervisor." Patrick turned and ran a hand along some of the dents. "I hope you didn't make all these."

Adam laughed. "It looks bad, I know, but I brought this heap of junk as is. I figured there was only one way forward after scraping enough cash for my first wheels."

"So, what do you say?" Patrick pressed. "I don't want to get on the wrong side of the law while I'm in Australia. I'll even organise a return ticket to get you back here."

Adam stood there, scratching his head. As he began to shake it, Patrick wasn't sure if he was speechless or seriously considering his offer.

Adam dropped his arm and shrugged. "Okay, let's talk to the boss. He's going to think you're as mad as I do. All I ask is that you make it clear this was your idea. I don't want to lose my job over this."

Patrick shot out his hand. "I promise."

Adam hesitated for a second and then shook on the deal.

Chapter 4

"Thanks for all your help." Kelly grabbed the last of the groceries, cleaning supplies and gardening implements from the car and placed them near the kitchen door before turning back to Mr Blundell, the solicitor working on her grandfather's estate.

He hesitated. "Are you sure you're okay on your own?"

"Very sure." Kelly rubbed her hands down her jeans and tried to sound convincing. She'd been on her own at lonelier places before.

Mr Blundell shook her hand when she offered it, uncertainty written all over his face. "How about I pop in on my way home each afternoon? You can give me a list of anything you need and I can drop it off the next day."

He was being kind and going way above the normal requirements of a solicitor. He lived and worked in Innisfail, the closest town to Moona Creek, so coming to check on her meant going out of his way.

"I appreciate your concern, but I'll be fine. If I need anything, I'll walk to the roadhouse and call you." Moona Creek, a kilometre away, had the most impressive roadhouse she'd encountered, having seen a few in her outback travels. It consisted of a well-stocked convenience store, post office, public phone, fuel stop—and the restaurant served the meanest hamburger in the country. It serviced every tourist and nomad travelling the coast road between Innisfail and Cairns on their way to or from the Great Barrier Reef.

Mr Blundell ran a hand through his greying hair, tilting his glasses off-centre. "It doesn't feel right. I have a granddaughter your age. I wouldn't leave her here on her own."

Kelly smiled. "The electricity was connected at lunch today. Tree loppers are coming in a day. A skip bin is being delivered tomorrow and the local youth group are arriving to give me a hand for a week, thanks to your efforts. That means I can start cleaning up first thing in the morning. Trust me, it'll be Grand Central Station around here. I won't have a minute's peace."

He straightened his glasses and took a step back. "I transferred the bequeathed monies to your new bank account this morning. You should have access straight away."

"Thank you. I'd like to get this place tidied up so I can put it on the market."

Mr Blundell sighed. "At least the kitchen isn't in too bad a state."

She supposed it wasn't—if you excused the cockroaches, mouse droppings and the possum taking up residence in the pantry.

"Did the fridge crank up?"

"It did. I even managed to give it a good clean."

With indecision still etched on his brow, he said, "Okay, I'll head off, but I'll drop in tomorrow just to make sure everything's fine."

She chuckled. "Okay. I look forward to it. I should be able to offer you a cup of tea by then."

"Well," he said, taking slow measured steps to the driver's side of the car, "goodbye, Kelly. It's been my pleasure taking care of you. Your grandfather was a fine man. I remember him well. In the late 1960's this was the place to be, the social hub for anyone in a one-hundred-kilometre radius. I'm privileged to have taken care of his last will."

He opened his door and settled in. "Your arrival is perfect timing. We can tie up all the loose ends."

Kelly struggled to swallow the lump lodged in her throat. Everyone in Innisfail and Moona Creek remembered her grandfather fondly, yet she had no memories to look back on. It left a streak of sadness that was too late to rectify. How could she have been raised without knowing anything of her grandparents? Why hadn't her father told her stories about his childhood at Moona Creek? She couldn't remember taking a single family holiday this far north.

Mr Blundell backed his car around and Kelly waved as he drove away. She watched as the taillights became fainter and eventually disappeared down the tree-lined drive. When all that could be heard were the crickets in the trees, she inhaled a lungful of pungent tropical air.

It hadn't taken her long to fall into the rhythm of this place, but this would be her last chance to relax. She had an arduous task ahead of her and she needed every ounce of strength she possessed. Plus, she had to find the motivation to make the initial move to contact her parents as she promised Janice. For now, she put it off. She wanted to concentrate on the property first.

The air carried a sudden chill after the sweat-inducing heat of the day. She wrapped her arms around her chest, feeling lonely. Honestly, she'd learned to cope with it in the past and was proud of how she always managed. But this time she really was alone and in the middle of nowhere. The fact that her phone didn't work in this small pocket of rainforest should've alarmed her, but she shrugged off her concern. She'd long since schooled herself on how to be alone.

A tremor vibrated up her spine. Perhaps she was tired. She wasn't scared. She was open to having an adventure, prepared to see where fate took her.

She tightened her arms and raised her face to the sky. By degrees it was slowly turning purple. She'd arrived three days ago but had chosen to stay in Innisfail until she could at least make the kitchen habitable. Moona Creek didn't have schools, banks, supermarkets or any other modern conveniences and without a car she was at a loss. She was grateful for Mr Blundell's kindness, but now it was time to stand on her own two feet and sort the property out. Eighteen months ago, she never would've had the nerve to do so, but she'd learned a lot since then. Working on cattle properties meant she'd developed many life skills she'd never needed growing up in Sydney. She could cook, drive and fix farm machinery. More importantly, she'd learned how to keep regret at bay. Hard work was what you needed when you wanted to escape the consequences of decisions made in the past.

Lowering her face, she turned to take in the front expanse of her grandfather's home. The extent of work required overwhelmed her for a moment. The rainforest vines had been allowed to flourish for so long that the whole top of the building, built into the side of a rain-forested hill, could no longer be seen. Intricately webbed and entwined, their message to Kelly was 'don't mess with us'. The encroaching forest consumed so much of the building, but she was hoping the teens arriving the next day would achieve a lot in the time they were here.

The small amount of money her grandfather had left her would be enough to keep the council rates paid for a couple of years and cover some maintenance costs. It was her safety net if the property didn't sell in a hurry. And selling was her only option. Except ...

Her feet, as if with minds of their own, took her to the most breathtaking view she'd ever witnessed in her life. The vision was a balm to her soul, the endless flow of water a lullaby to her ears. It was hard to believe the property had its very own private waterfall. It cascaded majestically over a ten-metre-high sheer rock face. The water was crystal-clear but shadowed by the overhanging trees. It had been a popular swimming hole in bygone days, she'd been told by Mr Blundell.

She'd spotted, hidden among the weeds, concrete steps leading towards the water. At the bottom of the steep steps, still upright but buried beneath fast-growing saplings, were rounded concrete pillars lining the remains of a pathway. If there'd ever been a chain or rope connecting them, it was long gone, perhaps corroded away. At the end of the pathway were three concrete picnic tables, covered in lichen and veiled by long grass and shrubbery.

Turning back towards the dimly lit kitchen, Kelly kept reminding herself that selling the property was the only option. Moona Creek was no place for her. Alone, with no job prospects and very little money, what choice did she have?

Once in the kitchen, she wrote 'light bulbs' on her list of necessities. The few she'd switched on had cast a gloomy yellow glow. Sighing, she decided to make a sandwich for dinner before snooping in all the rooms to see what they held.

⬦

Kelly couldn't quite work out the structure or design of the building, though she already knew it was two-storey with no backyard. The front yard would make up for that, though, once she cleared it and enticed lawn to grow.

The building was separated into two sections with the middle acting more like an entrance hall. On the left side of the ground floor was the kitchen and living space. On the right was a room that may have been the master bedroom, but it was bare except for her camping bed and sleeping bag.

In the entrance hall, two sets of concrete steps, joined in the middle, climbed in opposite directions. She made her way up the left-hand side. Laced with elegantly carved timber handrails, the stairs led to an empty room. The concrete rendered walls were heavily layered with a healthy growth of mould. One window looked out at the waterfall and another at the front yard. She imagined it as a bright sunny room during the day. Hopefully it would be once the vines taking up residence outside the dirty glass were removed.

She closed the door after noting the light fittings required bulbs.

From this level, there was no access to the right wing, so she made her way down then up the matching concrete staircase on the right. The upstairs room was identical to the one in the left wing. A bare room with two windows that would once again have magnificent views of the not-so-distant rain-forested mountain ranges. They looked close enough to touch, obscured though her view was. She grimaced, realising how much work would be involved in removing the vines strangling the building.

In the dimly lit room, she almost missed the small door hidden in the back wall. She approached it slowly, trepidation making her heartbeat sound awfully loud in the still house. The torch wavered in her hand, sending shadows across the room. The handle showed signs of corrosion, but the door swung open easily for her and revealed a small space, no larger than one square metre. The only item it contained was a timber crate. She lifted the handle on the side closest to her and it squeaked on its rusty hinge. Pulling it out of the storage room, she struggled with the weight of it and the torch, so she slipped the torch down the front of her jeans, hoisted the box up and took it to the kitchen where the lighting was better.

The box had no lock, so there was nothing keeping her from opening it. Her heart continued to beat loudly, though she wasn't certain why. The crate was only small. She brushed away nerves and pried the lid open. Its rusty hinges squealed in the quiet kitchen.

She grabbed her torch for better vision and her eyes feasted on what looked like diaries. The one lying on top was dated 1965-1968. The smell of old paper and ink rose to meet her. She inhaled and, picking up the book, carefully began turning the fragile pages.

She stopped on a page that had a hand-drawn picture of a building with two turrets and thick forest behind it. The caption read: 'He Built Me a Castle'.

Kelly sucked in a breath, sat down and placed the diary on the rickety timber table.

Then she got it.

It might've become clear when the vines were removed but the design of the building was now obvious. The two sections were turrets. Her grandfather had built her grandmother a castle.

Chapter 5

"Tell her Yanko's here to check on her. Strict orders from Janice. I'll walk the one kilometre from here, giving you plenty of time to make sure it's okay with her. She won't know who Adam is, but you can explain why he's here."

Patrick had met the lawyer Mr Blundell, earlier that afternoon at his office in Innisfail—Janice had given him his contact details—and he'd agreed to meet them at the Moona Creek roadhouse. He'd been happy to arrange Adam's return to Townsville, but now he didn't look too certain about anything and might actually be regretting his hasty decision.

Patrick ignored Mr Blundell's obvious reluctance and wrapped his hands around a massive hamburger, Moona Creek's claim to fame, and bit into it. His hunger had reached the point of no return hours ago and he was now starving. Adam had already demolished his.

Warily, Mr Blundell made his way to the driver's side of his vehicle, his shoes crunching on the gravel in the car park of the roadhouse. At the open door he pointed to an obscured road entrance on the other side of the highway, "There's no other property on this road. When it ends, you're there."

Adam was reclining against the Camira, which looked in even worse condition than when it had sat parked in the bright Townsville sun. Patrick stifled the grin threatening to escape. No wonder the solicitor was having second thoughts.

Mr Blundell turned to Adam. "Take care of the potholes. The overhanging trees make them hard to see." His jaw tightened. "You don't want to cause any more damage to the vehicle."

A chuckle escaped Patrick, but he managed to make it sound like a cough. Adam kept a straight face and slid into the driver's seat. No doubt he was excited about getting his next car and was more than happy to hand this one over. He'd turned out to be a relaxed travel companion and Patrick had decided to keep in touch. Adam's life was so far removed from his and their personalities so different that there hadn't been a dull moment. They'd laughed and joked for much of the drive. A lifetime ago Patrick never would've connected with someone so out of his sphere so quickly.

As he finished his hamburger, he watched both vehicles disappear down the road, swallowed up by the dense rainforest. He was delaying, just for a moment. It wasn't the one-kilometre walk worrying him. He could do it in fifteen minutes. But thinking about how Kelly would react to the news of his arrival had his heart pumping uncomfortably in his chest. Ella's wedding was a little over a week away, and Mr Blundell hinted at there being plenty of work available at Kelly's to keep him busy until then. If, and only if, Kelly agreed he could stay. He'd promised Mr Blundell he wouldn't make a scene and would leave immediately if she didn't agree. Except, this far north, he had nowhere else to go.

He hoisted his backpack on and ambled across the main highway. He took a moment to look up at the rainforest canopy. Tree branches weaved intricately together so only patches of sunlight reached the ground. Dappled shadows danced before him as the late afternoon sun penetrated the foliage. He filled his lungs with a good dose of rainforest air. So different to anything he'd ever experienced. Apart from the smog and fumes of Boston, he'd only ever experienced the dust and heat of Samdarra.

For the first time, it hit home. There was so much to life he'd yet to experience. Why had he limited his choices? Finances had never been a problem—he had enough money to drown in—so why hadn't he escaped the clutches of his restrictive life in Boston and the father he could never please before now?

Ever since his mother's death, depression had always hovered. He'd fought against it when he'd returned to Samdarra and found Kelly gone. Normally he could handle it, but some days he struggled. He understood that in order to move forward he had to make peace with how she'd died. For some strange reason, his stupid brain kept telling him Kelly was the key. She'd told him that if they survived the crash, he could tell her all the crazy stuff he wanted—and there a lot of shit he wanted to share with her. She might even reciprocate and finish the sentence she'd started that day.

Will she even remember our conversation?

He remembered every word. Their lives may've hovered on the brink, neither of them certain if they would live to see another day, but every word was seared on his brain.

He followed the road, stopping every so often when a rock jutting out of the gravel caught his attention. He had a fascination for rocks and as a kid had collected some when the opportunity arose and identified them. His mother had always encouraged his interest. *Where is my rock collection now?* He couldn't remember if he threw it out after *that* day. Anything reminding him of his gentle, loving mother hurt, so along with turning to drugs, the only thing that'd helped was destroying everything that had kept his memories lingering.

After he'd collected five interesting-looking rocks, a streak of sun broke through the canopy and concentrated squarely on a shiny one on the ground. He stooped to remove the gravel around it and noticed what looked like old leather or fabric near it. Having loosened it enough, he picked it up. It was covered in dirt, but there were obvious green shades shining back at him and some smooth surfaces. He rubbed some of the dirt off onto his jeans. The rock had an unusual shape, even with the hardened dirt removed. He turned it over in his hand. The sun suddenly dimmed and darkness shrouded its shape, turning it into a dark blob on his hand.

He grunted into the surrounding quiet, and not wanting to waste any further time, he put the rock in the side pocket of his backpack with the others he'd collected. Hoisting his bag back on, he increased his pace. He would never see Kelly if he kept stopping every one hundred metres.

⚜

Kelly expected Mr Blundell at any moment, but she stretched her weary back and was glad of the peace and quiet for a few minutes. A small bubble of delight grew inside as she thought about the work she and her helpers had done. They'd made huge inroads in removing the vines strangling the house. Although from where she stood it didn't really show. She eyed the piles of foliage ready for the skip bin's arrival the next day and grimaced. They'd be adding to the pile for days—who knew how many times the skip bin would need to be emptied to clear it all.

She rubbed her tired eyes, probably streaking more dirt onto her face. God, if only she'd slept more. But the diaries were like a drug, her grandmother's in-depth entries of the life they'd carved out more addictive than the potent party drugs she'd once experimented with. She imagined the delighted crowds that had once played tennis and cricket in the large front yard. The parties and special occasions hosted here, and the fun and games had down at the swimming hole.

She'd come across some photos of her father when he was younger and frowned every time she thought of them. What she couldn't understand was why she'd never been told about this place. There were so many questions for her father piling up in her head. The reasons for making contact with her parents were snowballing.

She looked up at the sound of an approaching vehicle then remembered the promised cup of tea and hastily retreated to the kitchen to put the kettle on. Coming back outside, where the sky was slowly darkening, she saw Mr Blundell's car and another parked beside it.

A fair-haired young man stepped out of a badly dented orange vehicle and leaned against it. He appeared shy, his hand rubbing through his dishevelled hair as he glanced towards the road.

"Kelly, how was your first day here?" Mr Blundell approached with a shopping bag. "Some light bulbs. I noticed yesterday a few were missing."

She took the bag, smiling. "You must be a mind-reader. They were the first things I wrote on my list." She swung an arm out wide to encompass the pile of foliage. "I thought we had a great day until I stepped back and realised how much there's still to do."

"When did the teens leave?"

"About half an hour ago. You didn't spot them at the roadhouse?"

"No, we didn't see them there."

"We?" Kelly gazed over at the young man.

Mr Blundell turned towards the orange car. "Adam, come and meet Kelly." When he turned back, he added, "He won't be staying. He's on his way to Townsville but drove here with a friend of yours who wants to visit."

"A friend?" She couldn't imagine any friend of hers coming this way. Janice was too busy with her work and wedding plans. Who else knew where she was?

Mr Blundell introduced them and then asked, "Is that cup of tea ready?"

Unease settled in the pit of her stomach. Mr Blundell was holding something back.

She folded her arms. "No cup of tea until you tell me what's going on. Are my parents about to arrive?"

His eyebrows rose in surprise. "No. Why would I call them your friends? I remember your father well and thought he might've come here with you. I know it's not my place to ask too many questions, but I do know they struggled to locate you when your grandfather died, so I understand things may not be great between you."

"Then who the hell's about to arrive on my doorstep?" Her impatience made her sound rude, but her lack of sleep wasn't helping her keep calm.

His shoulders dropped, but his hands stayed knotted. "Everything about leaving you here alone has sat uncomfortably with me. A young man calling himself Yanko told me to tell you that Janice sent him to check up on you."

Yanko. Relief poured out from the tips of her fingers. She could handle him in small doses. Heck, she could set him to work for as long as he wanted to stay.

"When's he arriving?"

"You know him?"

"Yes, I do." Feeling contrite after her earlier comment, she added, "Thanks for looking out for me."

"He insisted on walking here from the roadhouse. Said he wanted enough time for me to warn you, so if you objected in any way, I could send him packing. His gear's in his car." Mr Blundell pointed back to the orange bombshell. "And he's prepared to work."

"His car?" Her interest piqued even more.

"Apparently so. He bought it from Adam in Townsville on the condition Adam acted as his driving supervisor."

She burst out laughing. *God, that sounds so like Yanko.*

The sound of whistling emerged from the trees. *Yanko?* She almost didn't recognise him with his hair cut shorter. *Ohhhh.* What'd happened to his dreadlocks? She quickly put it down to the surgery he'd needed after the accident. The smile she remembered so well, and had ignored for so long, hadn't changed though. It stretched across his face.

"Hey, Kel," he drawled in his strong accent before looking her up and down. "Looks like you dressed up for my arrival."

He couldn't have missed her messy ponytail, more out than in—no doubt with bits of twigs and leaves caught up in it—or that her face was streaked with dirt and her clothes were clinging to her sweaty body.

Heck, he was a pain in the arse, but he was a familiar face and she was more than ready to see one.

She thrust one hip out and stuck her hand on it. "I hope you're here to work hard, Yanko. That's the only way you'll get a free feed from me."

When he bowed informally, his backpack fell off his shoulder and his laughter echoed in the cleared space. "Those are the sweetest words I've ever heard, boss."

Chapter 6

Patrick was barely off his camping mattress the next morning when Kelly thrust a plate of scrambled eggs and toast in front of him, telling him to hurry.

As he shovelled down the delicious breakfast, a couple of carloads of scruffy teenagers turned up and within minutes were hard at it. Together, they didn't stop all day, except to eat the snacks and lunch Kelly threw their way. The only instruction Kelly gave him was to remove all vegetation from the building and he quickly learned this was no small task.

All the teens had caught onto Patrick's nickname, Yanko, very quickly. A little awed by his accent and the fact he was Kelly's friend, they kept their jibes low-key and friendly. They worked well together and Patrick found himself taking on a supervisory role whenever they looked to him for further instructions.

By about three that afternoon, after many second glances, he thought the house began to resemble a miniature castle. He hoped Kelly had a wild imagination, otherwise he was going to sound like an idiot when he shared that observation with her.

He sat on an old tree stump and, resting his hands on his knees, took a well-deserved rest. His long-sleeved khaki shirt clung to his sweaty body, as it had for most of the day. It had been a long time since he'd worked himself this hard. He glanced down at his willowy frame and wondered how long it would take for this sort of physical work to bulk him up. As a growing teenager he'd always wanted to look muscular, but gyms bored him.

He could hear the others squealing and laughing behind him. They'd climbed down the steep concrete steps for a swim in the cool water. They were due to leave in minutes and a small selfish part of him was eager to have Kelly alone.

There'd been no time the previous night for any interaction. Kelly had declared she needed to get to bed early and catch up on sleep. He'd refrained from thinking of her, sleeping in the room below. In fact, he tried not to think of her at all. It was probably better that way.

He looked up and spotted Kelly walking over with two big mugs and what he hoped was the container of mud cake she'd offered around earlier. He could do with a sugar fix.

As she approached, he rose and pointed to the stump. "Allow me, Your Majesty."

She chuckled and handed him his mug of tea. "What's with all the formality?"

Patrick sat on the grass and crossed his legs, his body creaking at every joint. He took the cake container from her and helped himself to a sizeable piece. "Well, it might be my imagination, but this thing we're trying to uncover looks like some sort of castle, or is it just meant to resemble one?"

Tea dribbled over the edge of her mug. "How the hell did you work it out so quickly?"

"What do you mean?"

He went to reach for her mug before more hot liquid spilled. She steadied it, but emitted a loud groan and started to swear.

"This frickin' building belonged to *my* grandparents, but I had no bloody idea what it was. Not one idea and not a single clue about anything to do with their lives. Can you imagine that, Yanko? My father never once told me one damn story about his childhood. Nothing. Zilch. I get here and all I see is a mess of rainforest and a shitload of work to do before I can put it on the market. You, on the other hand, have barely been here five minutes, take one frickin' look at the place and work it out straight away."

He realised his mouth was hanging open. He'd never witnessed 'Cool Kelly' lose it before.

Her hand started to shake again, so he took hold of her mug and placed it on the cake container, worried that one more uttered curse word would have the tea ending up in both their laps.

He let her stew. She deserved to. He silently finished his drink and demolished another piece of cake. He understood why she was upset. Hell, he knew every damn piece of his family history, right back to the day his ancestor had first set foot on American soil. It had been drilled into him from an early age by his father. Apparently, it was meant to make him appreciate everything he had.

Except it hadn't. It'd left him wanting to do things differently. To branch away.

It made sense, though, that Kelly wanted to learn *something* about her grandparents. Christ, they'd lived only one generation ago.

He looked up when she unexpectedly burst out laughing. Her body shook and the echo of her infectious laughter vibrated around them. Luckily, he'd already taken control of the hot drink because now he could only stare.

There it was. Sunlight. It poured over her, highlighting the black in her hair and twinkling in her irises. Today she smelled of rich soil, honeyed sweat and freshly cut timber, more overpowering than when the hot midday sun blasted through the opening of trees they'd created, allowing sunlight to touch exposed foliage and limbs for the first time in years.

When her laughter became a chuckle and she turned her magical willow-green eyes in his direction, his stomach clenched.

"Sorry about the language," she said. "I didn't realise how annoyed I was by it all."

As if reacting to something she saw on his face, she became serious, then reached for her mug, took a sip and lowered her gaze.

"You're right, you know," she said, sombrely, "I found my grandmother's diaries and she wrote about my grandfather having built her a castle. I had no idea. They were the reason I barely slept the other night. I couldn't put them down."

Patrick nodded and gazed over at the crumbling building. He had a thing for historical buildings and this one intrigued him. His father always claimed he had no interest in anything, but he was wrong. There was a story here and he wanted to learn more.

He turned to Kelly and asked, "Will you let me read some of them?"

"Yeah, sure." She rested her elbows on her thighs and cupped the mug with both hands. "Apparently, this place was magical in the sixties. Talk to anyone old enough to remember and they'll tell you it was the place to be. Visitors played tennis and cricket out the front, parties were catered for, bands played and people danced, and there was an outdoor screen and projector for movie nights. On weekends there were water activities and picnics by the falls. My grandmother detailed so much in her diaries I wish I'd been around to experience it."

What would it take to bring a place like this back? Hell, it was perfectly positioned off the Bruce Highway, which was jam-packed with tourists, young and old.

"Hey, Kel, you could make it a tourist attraction. With the history surrounding this place, tourists would flock to it."

She tipped her remaining tea onto the grass, rested the mug on the cake container and rose. "With what, Yanko?"

She stared towards the castle, but he could tell she wasn't seeing it. She was looking beyond it, at the possibilities, and the lost opportunities that a lack of money foretold.

"You're a hard worker, Kelly. Anything's possible."

She turned back, her gaze piercing his. For a heartbeat he saw something in her expression resembling respect, or a new understanding between them.

But she lowered her chin and uttered, "It'd take millions. I wouldn't raise that sort of money in a lifetime." Despondent, she squared her shoulders and added, "Nope, putting it on the market is the only solution."

There were so many things he could share with her, but instead, he said, "Glad I can be of some help. I have nothing better to do. Offer me a bed and a meal and I'm here for as long as you need."

"Thanks, Patrick. I really appreciate it. I won't knock back your offer."

He wasn't Yanko this time, he noticed.

"By the way, you were great with the kids today. I couldn't have managed them like you did."

She paused, and the way she looked at him made him think she was seeing him for the first time. It was enough to make his heart jackhammer behind his ribs and his breath to jam somewhere down his throat.

"So, how long can you stay?"

As long as you want.

Instead of blurting that out, he took a deep breath, filled his air-deprived lungs and put everything on the line. "Actually, I have a favour to ask?"

She groaned and, rolling her eyes, perched a hand on each hip. He knew she was thinking there was always a catch with him. He did his best to curb his smile by biting his bottom lip and feasted on the sight of her.

Then her gaze pierced his. "Heck, Yanko, do you always have to say something bound to irritate me?"

He burst out laughing.

Irritation glared back at him. "Are you going to tell me what the hell it is you want from me?"

He wiped his face with his sleeve, no doubt smearing it with more sweat and dirt. "I'd like you to accompany me to my sister's wedding next weekend in Port Douglas."

"What the?" she spat. "Is that the reason you're up this way?"

"Yes and no."

"Dumb answer, Yanko."

Patrick dropped his arms by his sides. "Look, when I told Janice I was going to Port Douglas, she suggested I check up on you. Before that I had no idea where you were and no one was telling me anything. We'll only be away for one night and I promise I'll work double time next week."

Her face relaxed, masking any further irritation. "Thanks. So how *did* you worm your way around Janice?"

"It took a damn long session with her." Managing a smile, he added, "But I did it. Anyway, she was worried. You've got no car and no phone reception, only now you have me and the use of a car."

She grunted. "Are you sure that car's safe?"

He raised his eyebrows. "I'm willing to overlook that comment because I still need a supervisor when I drive."

She tugged on her hair, pulling some of it out of her untidy ponytail. "God, I thought I got out of doing that."

Acting affronted, he cried, "Hey, my driving's not that bad."

She finally broke through her mood and chuckled, surprising him. "Okay, okay, it's not bad, but I can't accept the wedding invitation unless you're happy for me to turn up in jeans and riding boots. I can't afford a decent outfit."

Patrick rose and stretched his stiff legs. He could hear the volunteer workers coming up the bank. "Is an outfit the only requirement you have?"

She turned towards the youths reaching the top of the concrete steps. "I'd say it's fairly important."

He grabbed both mugs and the cake container. "Great, that's a 'yes'. Daddy dearest is paying for everything, so we'll put it on the tab."

He wasn't about to give anything away. It wasn't necessary to reveal the truth yet.

A frown etched her brow. "I thought you hated him."

"I do, so we'll be sure to spend big."

Chapter 7

Kelly dipped her toes in the water and shivered. As she hugged her t-shirt closer to her chest, she decided that the contrast between the air and cool flowing water was too great, so she submerged. Even then it took a good half a minute for her body's temperature to regulate.

Coming up for air, she floated on her back and mentally listed the chores for the next day. The youth group had spent their final day helping but there was still so much to do.

The plumber had promised the toilet and shower would be functioning by the end of the day. As it hadn't been working she'd taken to washing away the day's sweat and toil in the natural pool beneath the falls, and although she was coming to appreciate the experience, putting the property on the market meant the plumbing had to be in reasonable order.

Her heart wrenched at the thought that one day, very soon, she would have to give all this up. The more of her grandmother's diary entries she read, the harder it was to separate details of the lives her grandparents had created here from her actual reality.

Five days ago, Yanko had insisted they buy beanbags on one of their shopping trips into Innisfail. It'd been his idea, so he'd paid for them. Since then, they'd settled into a comfortable routine. Each night after dinner they'd head up to the top left turret, snuggle down into the beanbags and read interesting entries from the diaries. She couldn't remember the exact moment it'd happened, but Yanko no longer irritated her.

The skin on her hand still burned where his fingers had brushed against it. They'd joked about something in a diary entry, she couldn't remember what, and he'd pointed it out. When she'd looked up, his gaze had latched onto hers and her breathing had sounded loud in the room.

She'd dismissed it—or had at least tried to—but she couldn't ignore the subtle shift in the way she reacted each time he was near.

Yanko had taken control of the youth group and kept them engaged, happy and hard at work. As long as she made sure they had enough refreshments, no one complained. Occasionally, Yanko caught her staring at him. In her eyes he was changing in stature faster than his hair was growing back. He was standing, walking, even smiling differently.

She was worried about tomorrow. The youths weren't coming back and only the occasional tradesman would be around when she could afford it. She tried to still the flutter in her stomach as it strengthened, but her mind tortured her with the knowledge that it'd only be her and Yanko here.

The current was slow today and caused her to drift away from the falls. Frustrated with her body's refusal to obey when Yanko was nearby, she rolled onto her stomach and swam freestyle to the falls.

In two days, she would accompany Yanko to his sister's wedding. The thought of it brought another rush of nerves. She was about to meet his family but didn't even know his last name. Not that she'd ask what it was. The last thing she needed was for him to learn her surname and the can of worms that would open. One minute spent stalking on the Internet, available at the Moona Creek Roadhouse, and he'd swiftly learn who her parents were. And she didn't need to be reminded that she hadn't contacted them yet.

Yanko had insisted she go down to the falls and refresh while he helped the plumber finish up. The sound of the falls blocked everything else out, so nothing prepared her for the moment his face glided out of the water right before her. She gasped and her heart missed a few beats. In fright, her arms floundered.

Shoot. It took five years off her life.

She mustered her scariest scowl, but he laughed so hard she couldn't hold it for long.

"Swim to the falls with me, Kel."

She splashed water into his face and shouted, "I almost had a heart attack. I'm probably dead right now."

He smiled his gorgeous smile. The one she was having trouble ignoring lately.

"Not my fault you're deaf. I made the biggest splash possible. Most scientists would have called it a tsunami."

"Yeah, sure," she smirked, gently treading water. "This is me you're trying to fool." Her leg rubbed against his and a shot of chemistry warmed its length.

"Come on, there are rocks we can rest on. You won't regret it."

She hadn't been near the falls yet, but Yanko and the young kids had done so. Swallowing her pride and annoyance, and promising to keep her eyes off his naked chest, she followed after him with clumsy strokes towards the cascading water. They covered a distance of a mere fifteen metres, but the noise increased tenfold, making normal conversation impossible. She squinted to keep the spray from her eyes and lost sight of Yanko until he grabbed her upper arm and tugged her closer.

He pointed heavenward and as she looked up he towed her deeper into the falling water. She gasped at the wonder of a million diamonds showering over her, shutting her mouth and closing her eyes only when they passed through the heaviest part of the falls.

Once clear of the falling sheet of water, Yanko hauled her onto the black rock ledge jutting out of the jagged face. With her hand comfortably settled in his, she looked up and couldn't remember anything more spectacular in her life. Diamonds continued to rain down, the afternoon sun glistening on their fiery edges, the flow never ending.

With all this spectacle, she hadn't noticed the way Yanko tucked her in towards his chest, his strong arm now firmly around her waist. The rocks were wet and slippery, but the natural ledge was large enough to seat them.

When she became conscious of where his hand was she twisted to face him. This was the closest she'd been to his alluring blue eyes.

A colour she didn't see often.

A colour holding her captive.

A mouth moving inexorably closer.

A mouth she invited.

A mouth so soft and warm, there was a chance her moan might have been heard over the falling water.

The kiss went on for a lifetime.

Yanko was the first man to break Kelly Sheppard's long-time ban on men.

⁘

Awkwardness crippled her ability to act normal. She tucked her towel around her waist and slipped her feet into her thongs. She didn't resist Yanko's hand when he led the way up the steep concrete steps.

At the top he halted and she walked into him.

"If you want me to leave I will."

What? She gripped his hand harder—an involuntary reaction. For a split second she wasn't sure if she'd heard right. His naked and wet torso was only centimetres away and the steep climb couldn't be blamed entirely for the way she was struggling to breathe.

She shook her head. "No. God no."

At her reply, worry eased from his face and he reached out to cup her chin.

"Oh, Kel," he murmured, right before his mouth found hers again, smothering every sensible thought in her head.

Patrick tried to ignore the unease jittering around his body. He'd crossed a line and now there was no telling what would happen. Would she still come to Ella's wedding? He shook his head as they made their way back into the kitchen. That should be the least of his concerns.

Dinner preparation was something he usually left to Kelly, given his extremely limited culinary skills. Instead of heating up frozen pizza every night, Kelly cooked while he continued working outside. Except tonight, he found himself in her space, offering to cut vegetables and make a salad. They worked well together.

Wracking his brain for some sort of sensible conversation, he mulled over bringing up the possibility of turning the property into a tourist attraction again. The more he considered it, the more attractive the idea became. He just didn't know how to approach the subject of finance. *Christ*, his petty cash could fix the place up in a flash, but he didn't want her to know who he was yet. The last thing he needed was for her to recognise his surname and judge him because of who his family was. Having Kelly attend the wedding concerned him a little, but Ella assured him the Van Der Meeliko name was not printed anywhere, and although their father would be walking Ella down the aisle, that was where it ended.

Finally, he settled on a safe topic. "I found a leather suitcase full of projector reels in the shed today."

She glanced up as she stirred noodles in boiling water, though her eyes didn't quite meet his. "You did?"

With the salad done, he leaned against the old kitchen bench and folded his arms. "They look in very good condition, though the same can't be said for the old projector."

She chuckled. "Let me guess, another victim of rust?"

He nodded, having quickly learned no metal lasted long in the tropics. "Do you want me to have them transferred to new media?"

Mild annoyance flickered across her face before she turned back to the stove top. "No, Yanko, you know I don't have the budget for that."

He wasn't giving up. All he had to do was get her to take small steps. Hell, he didn't care how tiny they were as long as she had a plan. And he was prepared to spend his money without her knowing, then when the time was right, he would tell her the truth. Just not yet.

"What if I talk to Mr Blundell and the historical society? They might have some funds for historical preservation." He tried for a cheerful tone when he raised his hand and added, "I bet they're important to Moona Creek's history if your grandmother's diaries are anything to go by. It'd be a shame not to preserve them. Just think, when all the tourists come streaming up the drive, you'll have it playing in the background. They'll order cake and tea and ... and—what do you call those chocolate cube things covered in coconut?"

"Lamingtons."

"Yeah, those and what else do Aussies love?"

"Scones with jam and cream."

"See, now I've got you thinking."

Flustered, she waved him away and turned back to her task. "Forget it, Yanko. In a couple of weeks, this place will be on the market. Let someone else do it."

He hesitated for a fraction then damned the risk.

Coming up behind her, Patrick wound his arms around her waist and pressed his cheek against hers. "You can do it, Kelly. I see the passion in your eyes every day when you look at the progress we've made. You're in love with the history, the idea of it and the romance your grandparents had. Everyone will fall for the story. Use it and the tourists will come in droves. Baby steps. That's all you have to take for starters."

She sniffled and his heart clenched. "Shh, oh my God, Kel, are you okay?" He turned her around. "What did I say?"

Tears trickled down her cheeks. "Nothing," she mumbled against his chest, "only that I've ruined my life. Finally, I feel like something is going right for a change. Everything you say is true. I do feel a connection to this place, but there are so many things I have to fix first, before I can even think of moving on."

He lingered over her face, the saltiness of her tears touching his lips. "Do you want to talk about it?"

She sniffled. "I've only ever told Janice. You might not want anything to do with me after I tell you."

He doubted it. Nothing could eclipse what he'd done. "Try me, Kel, I promise I won't desert you."

She nodded, dinner almost forgotten when his mouth found hers again and her arms wrapped around his neck.

Chapter 8

K elly tried to still the heavy thumping in her chest. What had she promised?

Dinner was a quiet affair, the clean up even more so. Now she stared at her reflection in the small mirror that barely functioned as one, and brushed her teeth with sharp, agitated strokes.

Janice had been easy to open up to. She'd asked all the right questions at the right time, and Kelly had spilled her secrets. Easy as. But this situation couldn't be any farther removed from the one with Janice.

The connection growing between her and Yanko was no hopscotch template—they couldn't just move from one numbered square to the next. Feelings were involved, and for the first time in what felt like forever, she was okay with that. It'd been a long time since she'd been so giving.

After rinsing her mouth, she wiped her face and forced her feet up the stairs to the left turret. With all the turmoil raging through her head, she hadn't realised what Yanko had been doing. Her feet froze when she saw the beanbags pushed aside and Yanko's camping mattress in their place. On it were two pillows—her cloud pillow beside his.

With eyebrows arched, she met his gaze. He stood by the open window, the full moon visible above the treetops. The overhead light was switched off and only a bedside lamp emitted a dull glow beside the mattress.

"Uh, Yanko, I ... um ..."

He was beside her in a flash. "It's not what you think."

She tried to keep the annoyance out of her voice but failed. "Then what is it?"

He placed his hands on her shoulders and gently massaged. "I want to hold you in my arms. You're about to tell me something that's had a huge effect on your life and I want to be there for you. I promise, Kel, that's all. I wouldn't do anything at such an inappropriate time."

She dropped her gaze.

"I remember our conversation the day I ran the jeep off Riley's Corner. I promised I wouldn't tell anyone what your biggest regret was."

She lifted her face.

"That promise still stands."

Looking into his sincere eyes, fear zapped across her chest. He must've read her thoughts because he clasped her shoulders tighter.

"Look, Kel, I know you're hesitant to trust me even one little bit. After all, I was at Samdarra to battle my drug habit. I'm no role model but ... my feelings for you *are* real."

The tension eased from her shoulders. She had no right to condemn anyone until they were tried and convicted.

Her feelings for Yanko had changed faster than a speeding train blurring past a station. Today she learned it was possible to look to the future again. Hope blossomed where no rain had fallen in a long time.

He led her towards his camping mattress and they both lay down.

Cradling her against his chest, he stroked her hair away from her face. She inhaled the smell of flowing river water. It permeated his skin and clothing and invited an intimacy that wrapped them together in the semi-darkness. She regretted having to spoil it with all she was about to say.

Letting the repetitive beat of her heart fade to the background, she licked her dry lips, gearing herself up.

"Take your time, Kel."

His words were a balm, just as her nerves threatened to make her clam up.

She took a deep breath. "Eighteen months ago, I had a baby girl and ... and ..." Her voice broke on a sob. "And every day since I've regretted giving her away."

"Oh, Kel, I'm so sorry." Patrick wrapped her even closer and squeezed tighter. When he pulled away, he took her hand in his. He stroked the top of her knuckles, lulling her into a welcome cocoon of security, where she was happy to remain.

"Did your family support you?"

Pain threatened to erupt. She closed her eyes and instructed her heart to stop hurting long enough for her to tell Patrick her story. She kept her eyes shut and tried to concentrate on the stroke of his thumb on her sensitive skin.

"Growing up in Sydney," she said, "I had the best family life an only child could ask for. Private schooling, music tuition, dance lessons, a legion of friends and all the sport I wanted to play. My parents are both doctors and they live a very social life. Parties started when they got there and they were always invited to important events. I never had a problem with that. I grew up around the socialites and mingled with their children."

Patrick cupped her jaw and turned her face to his. She opened her eyes and welcomed his closeness. He leaned in and kissed her eyelids, one at a time, with the softest of touches.

She bit her bottom lip and took a moment to curb her tears, swallowing once before continuing. "I started to experiment with party drugs towards the end of my HSC year. It was stupid, I know, but one night I was so out of it I had unprotected sex. I never would've done that if I was thinking clearly. It took a few days for the implications to sink in and three weeks to learn I was pregnant."

He placed a kiss on her forehead and didn't move away. "How did your parents take it?"

A tremor rattled along her spine. How could she explain something she didn't understand?

He must've sensed her reluctance because he rubbed her arm and soothed her with his words. "Take your time."

Grateful for his understanding, she rested her face against his neck and lightly kissed him.

"Thank you," she managed to say through a thick throat, "but that's the part I've never been able to reconcile with. Right from the moment they learned the news, they were supportive. We went through the options, the choices I could make, and like the modern-day parents they are, they let me make the decision. I was okay with this, so the process was put in place."

She paused, remembering the morning she woke when something inside her changed. It might've been the flutter of movement in her stomach, or, as she liked to think, it might've been her little girl tugging on her heartstrings, begging her not to give her away. Whatever it had been, she'd known the stakes had changed.

"I remember beginning to hate my parents for letting me make the final decision. I hated them for agreeing that adoption was my best option. My God, Patrick, I was a kid, but that baby was something I'd created. At the time I couldn't pinpoint why I was so angry, but after everything had been arranged, I realised deep inside that I didn't want to give my baby away."

Patrick continued to leave gentle kisses over her face, consoling her in a way that no one else had been able to before.

"I held her once." Her voice cracked. "How am I supposed to forget that?"

Dark hair had framed the smallest face. Her eyes, when she'd briefly opened them, had been blue. Her own heart had stopped beating when she'd looked into her daughter's eyes and it had never beat normally again.

"The night after she was born, my parents had to attend a charity function. They couldn't get out of it. I discharged myself, made it home and gathered a few of my possessions. You know, passport, purse, phone and some clothes. Then I went to the closest ATM and withdrew all my money."

She sought his eyes and begged for his understanding. He seemed to comprehend her need when he tucked her hair behind her ear.

"I haven't been home or talked to them since. I have no idea why I left. I couldn't even explain my reasoning when I told Janice my story. All I know is, the more days that passed, the harder it was to pick up the phone and call. I couldn't do it. I blamed them for everything. I wanted my baby but it was too late. My muddled brain reasoned that they should've argued with me, made me keep the baby whether I wanted to or not. But they didn't and I can't seem to forgive them."

She didn't even bother to stop the slow march of tears down her cheeks. Patrick gently wiped them away.

"All I think about is whether my baby's family is taking good care of her. Do they love her, like I was loved? Will she get all the opportunities I received as a child? It torments me so much not knowing. It should be me teaching her. Do you get that, Patrick? Am I making sense?"

"A lot." He wrapped his arms around her and tucked her head beneath his chin. "I take it you learned about your inheritance from your parents. How did they find you?"

She grimaced against his chest, her shock at receiving the letter still fresh in her mind. "I was having a bad day and sent them a postcard from Winton. No message, just their address written in square block letters. Two weeks later I received a reply addressed to me, care of the Winton post office."

Patrick chuckled and the sound vibrated against her hair. "Small towns, hey?"

She tried a crooked smile. With Patrick's warmth surrounding her and his legs tangled with hers, she could at least see the funny side of how it happened. "That's what Janice said. I was probably the only Kelly for a thousand kilometres around, so old Marg at the post office wouldn't have hesitated to put it in Samdarra's mailbag."

The screech of a rusty hinge reverberated around the turret.

BANG!

They came apart with a start. A gust of wind slammed shut the old casement window and they both turned towards it. Mentally, she added oiling the rusty window hinges to her long list of jobs needing to be done.

Patrick drew her back into his embrace. "Where to from here?"

The enormity of what she'd undertaken with the property overwhelmed her all of a sudden. To have her parents near, to support her emotionally and financially was what she needed.

"I promised Janice I'd contact them. I can't keep hiding forever and they need to know I'm okay. They didn't do anything wrong and I want them to forgive me one day. I just ..."

"Just what?"

"Well ... I want a bit more time."

"Hmm ..." Patrick's grip tightened over bare skin under her loose pyjama top. The contact on her skin sent many flutters flurrying inside her chest. "Look, Kel, I don't want to rush you, but, ah ... in case you're not aware, I'm scared as hell of Janice. My advice would be not to take forever to make the move. She'll be on your case before you know it and will turn up at your front door demanding to know if you've done so. In fact, you'll hear her hollering from the roadhouse."

Kelly chuckled. Unburdening her deepest regret somehow managed to lessen its burden. It felt good to share it with Patrick and doing so took her one step further in the gruelling race of life.

He smiled down at her. Her smile froze on her lips and so did his. The intimate setting could easily be blamed, but hell freezing over couldn't stop the burning heat between them. When his mouth reached for hers, a moan escaped. The kiss deepened and went on for a long, long time.

There were moments when they might've taken a break, a pause when they might've slept, but every waking moment that night involved his lips against hers. She felt secure and free of all the hurt that had assailed her for so long. Only when she woke to the first touches of daylight did she sense something was different.

Chapter 9

Perched on an elbow, Patrick watched Kelly sleep. The heavy rain falling outside screened them from the rest of the world and isolated them together. It seemed fitting that he should wake to the sound of it. He'd never experienced anything like it. Then again, he'd never lived in this part of the world before. His lack of travelled experiences always managed to touch a section of his brain at unexpected moments. This was one of them.

Kelly's cotton pyjama shirt had ridden up, and in the light of the slowly waking dawn, he could clearly see stretch marks. It only just occurred to him that each time they'd swum together, she'd worn a t-shirt over her swimwear. His desire to see her wearing as little as possible had always been at the forefront of his mind, so he'd never understood why she kept it hidden. With a body worthy of praise and appreciation, it hadn't escaped him either that other young stockmen at Samdarra had noticed it too.

Mesmerised by the regular rise and fall of her chest, he recalled their conversation from the night before. He thought he'd known a little about her, but really, he had no idea.

With no change in the intensity of rain since waking, he momentarily considered the river and how close it ran beside the castle. Had it ever broken its banks and flooded the property? If they were stuck indoors all day, he might ask Kelly if they could read more of the diaries in case her grandmother mentioned any prior flooding.

Kelly stirred. Her eyes opened lazily and latched on to his.

"Morning, Sunshine."

She smiled, languishing beside him, until she glanced down at her exposed belly. Now that he knew of her telltale scars, it didn't surprise him when she immediately grabbed hold of her shirt and tugged it down.

"Don't, Kel."

She froze. Her widening eyes resembled those of a startled animal caught in a vehicle's high beam. He lowered his face to her belly and with his teeth tugged her shirt up. She gasped when he found the soft edges of the red marks and kissed them tenderly.

When he looked up, she watched him, moisture glistening in her eyes.

"Don't be self-conscious, Kelly." He cradled her against him. "Don't ever be ashamed of your beautiful body."

She clung to him, the last shred of evidence of all she'd suffered finally exposed. He would do everything in his power to help her heal and began by holding her tight, trying to show her she wasn't alone.

The deafening torrential rain was cathartic and almost lulled them back to sleep, but it didn't stop the booming sound of his hunger.

"Would you like some breakfast?" Kelly asked, pulling back.

He couldn't refute that the sounds had come from his body. "I'm starving. How about I cook this time?"

She smiled. "Sure. Except I don't want to risk dying today."

Patrick harrumphed. "We might get swept away if this rain keeps up. Now how would you rather go?"

Laughingly, she took his hand and kissed it, surprising him with her affection. "Rain this heavy is probably normal in the tropics."

"Have your grandmother's diaries mentioned flooding?"

"No, not yet. I think we're up to their tenth wedding anniversary, where Granddad promised her a surprise."

He held her face and gently outlined the shape of her mouth with his thumb. How many surprises could he bestow on her over a lifetime?

Reluctant to leave the warmth they'd created, he rose, covered her with the blanket and went to the window. Nothing outside was distinguishable. The world beyond their castle was a blur.

He turned back to Kelly. "You stay put. I'll be back in a flash with breakfast, then I want to know what your grandmother's surprise was."

He could learn a thing or two about how to keep a relationship alive for ten long years. His father certainly hadn't taught him how.

⁂

They lay on their stomachs while Kelly gently turned the pages of the fragile diary.

"This is it, Patrick, the moment she learns of the surprise."

Kelly snuggled closer when Patrick rolled onto his back and sidled up beside her. As she read the entry, each word was etched into her subconscious.

Early yesterday morning Paden handed me a small package. It was our tenth wedding anniversary and as the sun rose, we made love before William awoke. He's growing into a beautiful little boy.

We are money poor but love rich. We work hard and deserve all the good fortune that occasionally comes our way. Finances are not so tight; I can afford the occasional new dress. I thank God for my good fortune and pray we have many years left to share.

I unwrapped the small package and realised it was jewellery. Paden has never been able to give me jewellery before. My wedding ring, a plain band and dearly cherished, was the only thing he could afford before we left our beloved Scottish shores for the last time.

Naturally I was eager to see what Paden had chosen. I will never forget the beauty of what lay on the cushioned velvet when I opened the box. A smooth heart-shaped gem, the size of a penny, glistened when the morning sunshine streamed into the bedroom and rested on it. Paden told me it was made from a genuine piece of jade a friend had collected off a beach in New Zealand. As payment for a favour, the friend gave it to Paden, insisting it was meant for someone special. Paden told me it was crafted by an expert lapidary in Cairns.

When I turned the jade heart over, my heart turned over too. 'All my love, P' is inscribed on the back, etched by skilled hands. The gold necklace attached to it is the finishing touch to an exquisite piece of jewellery. I wear it today with pride and love. I never wish to be parted from it.

"So, you have Scottish blood in you?"

Kelly bookmarked the page, turned on her back and secured Patrick's hand in hers. "My mum's Spanish. Dangerous combination if you ask me."

Patrick rolled towards her and kissed the side of her neck. "I wonder what happened to the necklace."

She reached up and combed through his short, spikey hair, surprised at how long it was already.

"She could've been buried with it. She mentioned never wanting to be parted from it."

"It's strange, but this property has remained empty all these years, but it's stayed in the family. What happened to all their belongings? You'd think there'd be some books or keepsakes lying around, frames and photos still nailed to walls, that sort of thing."

"I know my grandfather remarried in his later years. I don't know anything about his second wife, except that my parents didn't like her."

Patrick started to probe beneath her shirt, distracting her. "She probably took everything when he was put in the home."

The light touch of his fingers had her breath catching in her throat. "My parents have no idea what happened to her."

His eyes searched hers. She gulped in a lungful of air. "In the letter they wrote to me, my parents said they'd thought she'd taken this property, too, but somehow my grandfather managed to keep his will unchanged. He left it to me as I'm his only grandchild."

"Hmm."

Kelly could feel his hardness against her thigh. "You know what? The whole time I've been here, not one person in Moona Creek or Innisfail has mentioned Granddad's second wife. I'm curious as to who she was and I want to find this woman. I'm sure if I ask the questions, someone will talk. She might even be somewhere close."

His hands moved to her back, but she managed to slide back a fraction.

He looked up. "You sound very determined. I'm sure you'll find her."

She attempted to chuckle but it came out sounding like a groan. "And you're one very persistent man."

He raked a hand through his hair. "A man that needs to take a cold shower."

She chuckled at his pained look. "Plenty of rain falling outside you could use."

Patrick rolled onto his back and sighed. "You don't play fair."

"Oh, Patrick," Kelly wailed, "I just need you to be patient."

Suddenly alarmed, Patrick scrubbed a hand over his face and smiled sheepishly. "Of course. It was the promise I made you. Since we're stuck indoors all day, I have an idea of something we can do. Give me a second."

He rose from the mattress, trotted down the stairs and was back in less than a minute. Curious as to what he was up to, she sat up. He held a sketchpad and a small container holding coloured pencils.

He sat down and casually flicked to a clean page.

"Hang on a sec." She put her hand out to halt him, took the sketchpad and sat it on her lap. Slower this time, she turned each page and her eyes widened at the raw talent she saw in each of the landscape sketches. "Is this your work?"

"Ah ... maybe."

"Wow, Patrick, you're pretty darn good."

Drawing his knees up, he loosely wrapped his arms around them. "I've never been so sure. My mum used to tell me I was." He wasn't fast enough to hide the hurt that flickered in his eyes for the briefest of seconds. "My father didn't say much."

Oh no.

Putting the sketchpad down and kneeling beside him, she wrapped her arms around his neck. "Well, I think your talent is incredible." When his gaze met hers, she added, "And before we leave for Port Douglas, you and I are going to have a little powwow about your father and the rest of your family. I want to know what I'm up against."

She managed to make him smile.

"You're fast becoming very bossy." He straightened his legs and took hold of both her hands, which were still wrapped around his neck. She straddled him and he pulled her up against his chest. "No, I take that back, you were bossy from the first time I annoyed you. So, about five seconds after we met."

Laughing was easy to do around him and she had to face facts—he had a point. She did exude bossiness and didn't hold back with him.

"Okay, okay, whatever. Now tell me, what's your plan here?"

He picked up the sketchpad from where it'd fallen beside them and went to the first clean page, while she removed herself from his lap. "Okay, it goes like this. You have to use your imagination."

Ugh. Already she didn't like this game and it probably showed in the wry twist of her mouth. She wasn't sending him any good vibes. She knew that much.

His brows rose. "Imagine you had a spare million dollars in your bank account and—"

She harrumphed. "So, this really is going to need one hundred percent of my imagination?"

"Just listen first. What would you do to this place if money wasn't a problem?"

She fell back and stretched her arms out wide. She knew the answer. As if she hadn't dreamed up what she would do here. She'd concocted so many ideas. They reached out to her, streaming from the pages of the diaries, demanding someone pay attention.

She sat up again and looked at what Patrick was doing. She gasped. In the minute her thoughts had turned inwards, he'd sketched the castle with the waterfall to its left and the view when you reached the end of the driveway.

"Come on, woman, I haven't got all day."

She didn't waste another second spouting her ideas. Water features, fountains, an additional building to the right, a brand-new commercial kitchen, a small private hidden cottage, suspended lights, outdoor dining in front, indoor dining everywhere else, a café during the day and …

She wasn't aware how talented Patrick was until she ran out of words and breath, and realised he'd sketched everything she'd mentioned.

With downcast eyes, he hastily added the final touches to the drawing then put the pencil down. He tore the page from his sketchpad and handed it to her.

Neither of them spoke. What could she say? The rain continued to pelt down. It hadn't eased up at all. Never wanting it to stop, she looked down at the sketch again. The details were so precise. He'd brought her imagination to life.

Then she spotted the words scrawled along the bottom. *'Dreams do come true.'*

I wish.

She curbed the desire to let her shoulders sag, refusing to acknowledge defeat in front of Patrick. It would spoil what was a very special talent.

It was a good reminder that it didn't hurt to dream. Until he suggested his next idea.

"I think we should drive into Moona Creek and have one of those famous burgers for lunch."

She snapped out of her reverie. "What?"

"Come on, lazy bones. Get changed and come with me. When we get back, I promise to tell you all the sordid stories you've been waiting for about my family."

"But ... driving in this rain for a burger?"

"It'll give me a chance to check my emails and make sure everything is still on track for the wedding. And we can ask the locals if they think this rain is likely to clear up. We have to leave for Port Douglas first thing in the morning. By the way, my sister Melita has your full schedule pencilled in, so I probably won't see you until the ceremony."

She groaned, rolled away from him and buried her head in the pillow. Sure, the intent was to have that burger for lunch, but when Patrick joined her on the mattress, Kelly wondered if they would make it to the Moona Creek roadhouse before the lunchtime menu was over.

Chapter 10

"**H**ere you go, two Moona Creek burgers with the lot."

"Thanks, Paula," they choroused in unison.

Patrick didn't waste another second. His growling stomach reminded him that breakfast was many hours ago. Kissing all morning built up an appetite apparently because Kelly didn't hesitate either.

Before Paula had a chance to retreat to the kitchen, Patrick asked, "Hey, Paula, is this rain likely to hang around for a while?"

"Not this time, darl. It's only a tropical low and hasn't decided if it'll turn into a cyclone yet. It's moving quickly down the coast, so there's a good chance you'll wake up to bright sunshine in the morning." She collected dirty plates from a nearby table, the roadhouse surprisingly busy for such a wet day, then made her way back to them. "Make sure you pair don't go swimming for a few days. The water will be fast flowing and full of debris. We don't need the excitement of setting up a search and rescue. Stay indoors. Got it?"

Patrick bit off another mouthful. He managed a smile and a nod, taking on board Paula's advice. She knew them both by sight now. It wasn't the first time they'd driven up in his dented orange Camira to use the free internet service provided with every meal purchased.

He was working on a few projects but hadn't shared them with Kelly. The first was organising a communications tower so Kelly could access phone and internet services at the castle. It was taking longer than expected—apparently, no amount of money could fast track the process. And before the burgers had arrived, he'd purchased a new washing machine, which was to be delivered and installed the following week. He didn't quite know how he was going to explain that one, but Kelly had been washing her clothes—and some of his—by hand. She had enough work to do as it was.

Kelly flicked her still-damp hair off her shoulder before again securing her burger with two hands. "Did you check in with your family? Is everything still good to go tomorrow?"

He put his burger down and wiped his mouth with a serviette. "Melita says they all arrived in Port Douglas yesterday. She can't wait to meet you."

A blush coloured her neck and face. He didn't doubt she was nervous.

Patrick leaned away from the table and rested his hands on his thighs. He watched her carefully. "You can't believe you're meeting my family, can you?"

Even he couldn't believe he was taking someone to the wedding. In all truth he was probably more anxious than she was.

She choked on her food. Hastily putting her burger down, she covered her mouth with a napkin and coughed to clear her throat. "You're making me nervous, Yanko. You haven't said much that's good about them."

With relief, he grinned at her use of his nickname. He liked it, never having had one before. It gave him a warm, fuzzy feeling, and he missed it when she called him Patrick. He shook his head and reached for his burger, letting another of life's mysteries swirl around his head. How could one miss being called by a nickname?

"Well? It's true. You haven't said a single good thing about anyone in your family."

Oh shit. He hadn't even been thinking of them.

Somehow, he managed to keep the need to laugh out loud in check. God, how his dating skills had changed since landing in Australia.

"Sorry, my mind was elsewhere. And you're right. When we get back, I'll tell you all the good things about my family. Might only take five minutes but at least you'll know before we arrive tomorrow."

She grimaced, no doubt getting worked up again. But he couldn't help her; he was going to be agitated enough.

Deciding to dismiss all thoughts involving his family, he tangled his wet feet with hers beneath the table.

She couldn't suppress a giggle. "I can't believe I'm dining out barefoot." Her troubled look vanished and he laughed along with her.

They'd left their thongs—still hard to call them that instead of flip-flops—in the Camira and used an old newspaper as they ran inside the roadhouse. They'd hunkered under it, managing not to get too drenched. His standards were dropping and he was loving it.

When he put the last mouthful of burger in his mouth, he had to fight to keep the smile on his face. He could already see the frown his father would be wearing and he wasn't even in the same room yet. If he walked inside the roadhouse right now, his features would be laced with bitter disappointment. No son of his would dare dress this way or be seen eating at a diner or roadhouse.

Was this what he had to contend with tomorrow? Would he ever please his father? History told him not to bother, but every time he saw his father, he once again became the little boy who desperately craved the man's approval. His father's mantra, 'all that wasted money', rang around his head.

"You okay?"

He looked up, startled that his thoughts had spiralled downwards. He tried to school his features. Had he spun away to that place he sometimes went to, when his sadness overtook everything?

"Sometimes I'm not sure."

He regretted his words instantly. He *was* in a much better place when he was with Kelly and the last thing he wanted to do was scare her off. He needed her and he sternly reminded himself of that.

Having finished her burger, she reached across for his hands and squeezed them tight. "Let's go back. This time I'll wrap my arms around you."

He looked into her willow-green eyes and his moistened the more intense her gaze became.

"It's magic, Patrick," she whispered, "when you unburden the heaviest part of your heart. Thanks to you, I'm different today. I want you to experience the same thing."

Though he needed more time on the internet, he refrained from suggesting they stay longer. He still wanted to find someone who could transfer the old film reels to modern-day technology, but he let it go and accepted that Kelly was right. He wanted to talk. Wanted her arms around him. He had all the time in the world to deal with the old reels and was fast learning that everything in this far-flung place took time. For now, he wanted the opportunity to heal some more. He had Kelly on his side and arriving in Port Douglas with an ally would boost his confidence and make confronting his father a lot easier.

Patrick parked the Camira near the castle's kitchen entry and turned off the ignition, but both he and Kelly were reluctant to leave the dry safety of the car. Within seconds, the windows had fogged and the rain falling outside was a blur. An idea eddied around his head as they sat in quiet contemplation.

"Want to hear a crazy idea?"

She smiled and shrugged, as if to say, 'Sure.'

"I want to see the waterfall, and—"

An instant frown appeared on her brow.

"Yes, I know, I heard Paula. Don't stress. I just want to see how it looks after all this rain."

"Okay, no big deal."

"And we'll get drenched."

Her eyebrows rose at his stating the obvious and he could tell she was trying not to respond with a smart-arse comment.

"But there's more. You ready?"

Again, she shrugged.

He took a deep breath. "No thongs"—which wasn't a big deal, but when her brows rose further, he chose to ignore them—"and we leave as much clothing as we can in the car."

Now her eyes grew round, her face skewed and she looked at him as if she wasn't sure whether he was crazy or just a pervert.

He stalled at her expression, then registered what he'd suggested.

Oh, shit. Now I've done it. Did he always have to talk like an idiot around her? His suggestion was so stupid. He scrambled for some sort of damage control before blurting, "Have you ever danced in the rain before?"

"Have you?"

"No." He held his breath, believing for the first time that maybe he was a little crazy or depraved. What could he say?

She shook her head and his heart dipped. The expression on her face told him she couldn't believe what she was getting mixed up in. What if she jumped out and ran all the way back to the roadhouse and called the police? What if she demanded he left now and never came back? What if—?

"So ... um ... you want to dance in the rain?"

He jerked his attention back to what she was saying.

"We could save on washing." Kelly suggested.

His breath hitched in his throat when she drew her shirt up and over her head. Her shorts came off next and still he didn't dare to breathe. If he died from lack of oxygen ... well, big deal.

The notion she was going along with his stupid idea, paralysed him. In a matter of seconds, she'd unclasped her bra, had flung it onto the back seat and in the next instant was out in the rain. He was a breath short of death before he'd realised what had happened.

Her knock on his window startled him enough that he scrambled out of his t-shirt and board shorts, and then he was out on the front lawn with only his boxers on.

Fat drops of rain soaked his skin, but no amount of falling water could blur the image of Kelly, twirling around and around, her arms floating out wide, water dripping off her toned body, her underwear and down her heavenly legs. With her head flung back, she embodied freedom at a whole new level.

He'd never done anything like this before. If only his father could see him now— drenched in his underwear, with a half-naked woman doing the same thing. Patrick hadn't needed his father in a long time. Being around Kelly made him bolder.

Kelly spun closer to him, his body still paralysed until the touch of her skin set him off. The falling water was no saving grace. Nothing could put out the burning fire between them. He caught her to him, pressing her against his chest, then kissed her while her blue-black hair plastered itself around their faces.

Eventually, she pulled back. Her mouth hung open as she gulped in air, trails of water dripping from her face, over her chin and down to her breasts. Patrick couldn't resist and gently cupped one. He toyed with the dark-plum nipple, its tiny size stretching with his ministrations, before lowering his mouth and finding a sanctuary for the blossoming bud.

Her fingers tightened in his hair and her mouth rested near his brow, her warm breath a welcome change on his wet skin. He pulled away, his feet squelching in the soggy lawn, then he placed both her hands in his and took his fill of her. He soaked up her natural beauty; her willow-green eyes were sparkling emeralds that made up for the sun hiding that day.

With one hand gripped firmly in his, he turned and led her towards the concrete steps. At the top they watched wild Mother Nature at her best. Dark, muddy water swirled and eddied below, with debris caught up in its vortex. With the river's level higher than normal, the falls fell only three metres. The rock he and Kelly had kissed on only days earlier was now hidden behind the heavy volume of tumbling water. Paula's wise words thrummed in the back of his head.

He turned away from the vision when Kelly squeezed his hand. With a slight tilt of her head, she indicated she wanted to go indoors. Like tiny children at play, they ran for the kitchen door. Whenever their footing slipped and squelched in the muddy and drenched lawn, they gasped, laughed, giggled and held each other up.

Patrick swept the door closed behind them, dulling the sound of the falling rain.

"Right, don't move, Yanko. I'll get a couple of towels."

He stood on an old potato sack they kept at the door, a doorstop for mud and dirt before they entered the kitchen. Rivulets of water ran down his body and were sopped up by the hessian.

Kelly returned from the small adjoining room where she kept the towels, and without stopping, she threw one in his direction then headed towards the room where she slept. "I'm going to get changed and then I'll make us a hot drink."

Patrick removed his drenched boxers and dried himself. He wrapped the towel around his waist and wrung out his boxers in the kitchen sink. In the small adjoining room, he pegged them on the makeshift line installed earlier that week.

I'll make the hot drinks. Kelly loved Milo, the malty chocolate drink he was fast getting a taste for. He put the kettle on and found some chocolate chip cookies. He wouldn't have any problems fitting them in, even after the huge burger he'd eaten.

With drinks in hand and the cookie container secured under his arm, he turned, and there she was, waiting by the doorway, leaning against it.

She wore navy blue track pants with a white loose-fitting shirt and all he wanted to do was clasp her face in both hands and bury his face in her neatly combed hair.

"Here, let me."

Could she see all the emotions whizzing around his face? Had he been talking to himself? He couldn't remember. He *had* been whistling an early millennium song he remembered from his teenage days that had been playing at the roadhouse.

She took hold of the mugs and cookies. "Go get changed, then we can talk."

He led the way out of the kitchen to the hallway where the two staircases met.

"And hold onto that towel, because I can't be responsible for what might happen with two hot drinks in my hands."

Oh, hell. He'd been in love with this girl for ages. *Should I tell her, now?* He swallowed, hoping to dislodge the thick lump in his throat.

At the bottom of the staircases, and clasping the ends of the towel firmly together, he leaned in towards her. He found the crook of her neck and tenderly placed his mouth on it. When he pulled back, he found her eyes and locked his gaze on them.

"Thanks, Kel. Thanks for so much."

Nervous boulders, the size of small trucks, tumbled around inside him. How did he tell this hard-working girl he loved her? He had so many issues and nothing to offer her, other than a screwed-up life and a messy family to go with it.

"Hey," she whispered, "we'll get through this. One day at a time. Thank *you* for so much." She started up the staircase. "You're not so bad, Yanko. You're growing on me."

He smiled stupidly, reminding himself of a dog being praised and showered with rewards. But soon it'd be his turn to talk, his turn to spill the beans, and he had no idea where to start. He didn't want to be vulnerable.

For Kelly, he wanted to be strong, supportive and man enough to stand up to his father.

"The drinks are getting cold, so don't be long."

Bemused, he shook his head. She'd always had a way with words. Resigned to his fate, he went to get changed. The thought of being wrapped up in her arms was more than enough motivation.

Chapter 11

"**M**y mother was my father's second wife."

After drinking their hot Milo and eating a few cookies, they'd snuggled under the covers of his camping mattress. True to her word, Kelly folded him in her arms. She'd suggested they move to her end of the castle, where her camping bed was more comfortable, but neither of them could be bothered. Besides, this end of the castle was the designated counselling room.

"I knew about his first wife, Catherine, and their baby girl, and how they'd disappeared without a trace, but by the time I was old enough to understand, no one spoke of them. The case had never been solved, though murder was the suspected cause of their disappearance. There was certainly no evidence of anything else."

Kelly ran her hands through his hair and tucked his face against her chest.

"Then late last year, twenty-five years after she'd disappeared, Ella, the baby girl, turns up out of the blue, alive and healthy. Ella hadn't told Catherine she was looking for her father."

Kelly pushed back. "Holy shoot. Why not?"

"Every time Ella brought up her father, Catherine got upset. And for good reason. Ella just didn't know why. Anyway, let me go back to the start, when Catherine, her best friend and their one-year-old babies disappeared without a trace ..."

Patrick's chest ached as he retold the story as he knew it, memories of his mother crowding in. If only his mother had left before it was too late, like Catherine had. He steered the pain away before it threatened to shroud him.

"So, something happened?"

He grimaced. "Did it ever. Catherine had never told Ella the truth. She'd made up a story about how Ella had been conceived and never wavered from it. Ella, though, found a small box holding some clues hidden in her mother's cupboard."

Patrick paused, debating how much he should tell Kelly? She had no idea of who he really was and that was how he wanted it to stay. For now.

"Yanko, don't stop. My heart's thumping just wondering what happened next. This story sounds like a suspense thriller."

He chuckled and wrapped his arms around her, hugging her tightly before smacking a big kiss on her mouth.

"Ella went to a private investigative company in Brisbane, and this is the weird part, or the bit you're not going to believe. It was as if fate threw its hand in the ring and said this is the direction your life's going to take."

She frowned.

Patrick smiled. "The person assigned to look after her case was Zane, the son of Catherine's best friend and the other one-year-old baby who'd gone missing."

Disbelief was written all over Kelly's face. "No way. You're lying."

"Believe what you want, but I'm telling you the truth. Of course, neither of them knew who the other was at the time. Not until Ella showed Zane the few items in the hidden box, including a photo of their mothers. Zane recognised it immediately, but his mother had told him that her friend in the photo had died. Instantly, he knew his mother had lied because Catherine was very much alive."

"Oh my God, lies everywhere."

"And it gets worse.

"Don't keep me in suspense. Keep spilling!"

He smiled and ran his hands down her arms, resting his leg over hers. How he found it possible to smile he had no idea. Because lying beneath all the words he spoke were hurt, lies, violence and a toxic man with a shitload of money and uncontrollable power.

But there was no need to disclose all of that.

There was so much he'd rather be doing with Kelly. Talking about his screwed-up family was the last thing he wanted to do. But the show must go on and he was keeping her enthralled. The story had captivated her imagination like some warped movie, where events were so bad they were hard to believe.

"Yanko, you better not have gone to sleep on me. You weigh a ton and I want to hear the rest of the story."

He chuckled and moved his leg. "Zane took himself off the case but started his own private investigation."

"Really? What happened next?"

"Well, unlike Ella, Zane had no idea his father wasn't his biological one."

"Are you serious? His mother kept it from him?"

"Yep. To cut a long story short, by the time Zane worked out who Ella's father was, they were madly in love. They lied to their families and made a quick trip to the States to meet Ella's father. *My* father. The minute they returned to Australia he activated an old court order. Even though it had been put in place a long time ago, it was still valid, and under American law Catherine had broken it."

"What was it for?"

"Oh, something to do with Catherine being unstable and incapable of looking after her baby. You only have to meet Catherine to know it was all bullshit. When Ella and Zane arrived back in Australia, Catherine had been deported and was sitting in a Boston jail."

Kelly looked dumbfounded, her eyes wide open in disbelief and her hand raking through her hair. "No way. No freaking way. That doesn't happen in the real world."

"Yes freaking way, it did. And when I met Ella for the first time, I was at my worst. But when she returned to the States, she set the world on its edge, prepared to fight to the death to have her mother released. She used social media, radio stations, TV talk shows. She was a bit of a celebrity while she mounted a challenge against our father."

"And?" she demanded when he paused again.

"On the first day of the trial our father withdrew all charges. He handed over the family business to his nephew and decided to travel around Australia. He's been doing that ever since. I think Ella swapped him with an imposter."

"Holy frikkin' shoot." She gazed past his shoulder, clearly in shock.

He watched the play of emotions on her face, desperate to kiss her again but prepared to give her some time to absorb the worst of what he'd said.

She startled him when she asked, "So how did you end up here?"

"Good question." And he leaned in and kissed her long and hard before continuing. "Ella was relentless in her pursuit of both Melita and myself. She wouldn't leave us alone. During the weeks leading up to the trial she managed to convince us to travel to Australia. I was here barely a day when Ella's half-brother, Luke, drove me to Samdarra. Melita was instructed to help Ella's half-sister, Victoria, with her chemo and do whatever was required to make her cancer treatment easier. There's a younger sister, Lily, but without Catherine at home, things were pretty tense."

"How did it all work out for Melita?" She gave him a light punch on the arm when she added, "Obviously I know how it worked out for you."

Sassy minx.

He let his hands roam under her white t-shirt and managed to make her gasp. "What, you mean you know how intolerable you made my life?"

She giggled.

"Melita's learned how to cook. Luke's teaching her to drive and she works part-time at a clothing boutique."

"What happened in the end? I assume Catherine came home."

"They got out of the States as fast as they could. Zane and Ella are madly in love and they tie the knot tomorrow. The end."

"Wait, wait, what about Zane?"

"What about him?"

"Did he find out about his father?"

"Oh, yeah, he did. His father died in prison. I don't know all the details, but his family had connections with the mafia. He'll never meet his father, but he did meet his grandmother. She's making her first trip to Australia for the wedding."

"Wow. Is he okay about it? You know, the lies about his real father and all that?"

"Apparently so. You'll have to read the book to learn more about the juicy bits."

"Except you haven't written it yet."

He smiled, wrapped his arms around her and rolled so she was lying on top of him. "So that's it. I think I've mentioned everyone you'll meet tomorrow."

Enjoying her weight, he gazed into her eyes and his body hardened against her stomach. He tried to lift her away, noticing the worry in her expression, but her arms tightened around him and she rested her face in the crook of his neck.

"What about you and your dad, Patrick?" she asked quietly.

He remained still, despite his heart beginning to thump louder and louder in his chest. When she pulled back, she looked at him questioningly.

They stared at each other but didn't move.

A huge sigh escaped him. "I ... I hate him, Kel. I really hate him. I can't stand being in the same room and I can't forgive him for how he treated my mother." Tears pricked the back of his eyes and he swallowed hard. "For years I tried hard to please him, but nothing I ever did was enough. By the time I was a teenager I didn't care and I sure as hell didn't try. My ... my mother's death made any reconciliation between us impossible."

"So ... um ... okay." She was clearly choosing her words carefully. "If you hate your father, and Ella and Catherine do as well, how the hell did he get invited to the wedding?"

Damn, another good question.

The tension eased from his shoulders and he tickled her sides until she squealed and squirmed. "Stop, Yanko, please. I hate being tickled."

"Well, stop with all the smart questions. For crying out loud, I couldn't believe it either when Ella told him he could give her away, but that's probably my fault. Dad dropped by Samdarra a few months ago and we spent a few minutes together. I didn't say much, but he wanted me to pass on the message to Ella that he'd be honoured to walk her down the aisle. I must've made him sound half human when I told her, because a few hours later, she agreed."

"Maybe the fact he'd dropped all the stupid charges helped?"

"Nah. Ella's a smart cookie. She didn't do it lightly. Part of the deal was that our father pay to have the wedding in Port Douglas. Ella has always wanted a wedding in a chapel by the sea and this place has one."

"Did Ella have a good life with Catherine?"

"Yes, she did. She had a great stepfather who treated her like his own. He died last year in a workplace accident, so it's been a rough time for the family, especially with Victoria's diagnosis. I hope for all their sakes this wedding is a happy occasion. They deserve it."

"So, how long have you got until you return home?"

Such an innocent question, but one look at Kelly and he knew it wasn't asked lightly. Heck, this thing between them had already been running well below sea level and now it was getting deeper.

He rolled onto his side and let his eyes draw level with hers. Getting lost in their comfortable depths, he cradled her face with both his hands. "Ella, Melita and I have become a close family in a very short time. At this point in my life, I've got nothing to go back to." He tenderly touched his lips to hers. "Now I have even more reason to stay."

He lingered, kissing her eyes, her cheeks and gradually finding his way to her neck. They had all the time in the world, cocooned as they were.

"Well," she said, "I can sure keep you busy for as long as you want."

Patrick chuckled. "I knew you'd find the right words to convince me to stay longer."

They laughed as they clung together, and as the afternoon gradually faded to night, they talked more, laughed again, kissed and touched.

Only the grumble of their empty stomachs roused them to rise.

Chapter 12

"Perfect!" Melita clapped her hands, clearly satisfied with the dress she'd selected for Kelly.

It was the third Kelly had tried on, and even she loved the soft, floaty lines of the light-plum material. It had a halter neck and the back fell to nothing, but its layered lengths draped from her waist to the floor and had slits cut into them so that her legs flashed as she walked.

"At least Patrick got your size right."

Kelly did a catwalk spin, jutting her hip out and resting her hand on it before facing the pretty and petite Melita. "Did he now?"

Melita slipped on her shoes and rose. "Sure did. He told me your curves were in all the right places. That your legs went on forever and he may have mentioned breasts."

Kelly chewed her bottom lip, finding it difficult to stop the warm spread of her blush. *He said all that?*

A concerned Melita stepped closer to help her out of the dress. "Is he in trouble?"

Kelly released an exasperated sigh and kicked off her borrowed shoes. "Maybe. I'll clobber him next time I see him."

"Clobber?" A momentary frown etched Melita's brow when her hand automatically reached up to her bronzed highlights.

Kelly tried to maintain her composure but fell into a fit of giggles.

"You're joking, aren't you?" Melita asked.

"No, I'm not." Kelly stepped out of the dress. "That brother of yours has to learn not to talk about my breasts with anyone."

Now Melita started to giggle as she gathered up the dress. Kelly wrapped her arms around her body, hiding her exposed breasts as they shook embarrassingly with her laughter.

It wasn't until the owner of the boutique gently reminded Melita they needed to wrap things up if she wanted the dress dry-cleaned before lunch that they managed to get some control back.

Melita shared her packet of tissues and Kelly wiped the tears from around her eyes. She dressed quickly, putting on her jeans, bra and t-shirt, before slipping her feet into her comfortable, scuffed thongs.

"Okay," Melita said, "a quick coffee and croissant before the shoe stores open." Regimental in her schedule for the morning, she marched up to the boutique's cash register. Kelly couldn't believe she'd allowed for any snacks at all.

She and Patrick had left Moona Creek at six a.m., pushing the dented Camira as much as they dared. When they'd arrived in Port Douglas, Melita met them at the exclusive boutique after arranging for the owner to be there before the normal opening time. So, yes, Kelly was starving and would have more than a croissant now that the opportunity was offered to her.

She went looking for her handbag. Patrick had strictly instructed her not to ask any questions or offer to pay, which was certainly a change from how she'd lived for the past eighteen months. It wasn't foreign to her—she'd been raised buying only the best, and this boutique couldn't hide that it catered only to the wealthiest travellers to the little tourist town—but the last thing she wanted to do was spend someone else's money. Of course, she had no idea how wealthy Patrick's father was. He must have some money to be able to pay for a wedding in this lavish location, but one look at Patrick and it was hard to tell. Anyway, it was none of her business.

There was one thing she *was* certain of—spending eighteen months away from the life she lived in Sydney meant she'd forgotten how to look and feel pretty. Not that she cared. So what if her nails were chipped and broken? Their condition had already upset Melita, but Kelly had refrained from saying anything. Good Lord, the days when she'd worried over the way her nails looked were a lifetime ago, in a time and place she could never return to.

She bunched her hair into a loose bun and wrapped an elastic tie around it to keep it off her shoulders. According to the plan for the day, after shoe shopping came a hair appointment along with a manicure and make-up booking. She was going to enjoy this, even if a thin sliver of guilt over spending someone else's money kept intruding on her conscience.

◦◦◦

Kelly twirled in front of the tall mirror in her single room at the Port Douglas Sheraton Mirage. Her dark hair was a mass of curls cascading down her back. Her rescued nails were now even and perfectly painted in dark plum. Her heeled, nude shoes enclosed her sheer-covered legs. She kept picking up the many layers of her dress and letting them fall and float through her hands. She'd never looked this striking. Ever.

She moved towards the large glass window with the view of the sprawling resort. In every direction she glimpsed the sky-blue water of the swimming pool. It lapped at the lower-level rooms and covered the vast expanse of the entire front of the resort, as far as the eye could see. She'd never seen a pool so large. All the buildings sat nestled comfortably in tropical rainforest, a short walk from the town's famous Four Mile Beach.

Port Douglas, she was fast learning, was famous for this strip of beach and for its access to the Great Barrier Reef. If she had her way, tomorrow she'd step into the tranquil waters of Four Mile Beach. So different to the beaches she'd surfed in as a teenager, with their dangerous rips.

She waited in her room for Zane's mother, Tilly, to fetch her for the short drive to the chapel. So far, Kelly had only met Zane and Ella, separately as instructed by Melita, and had eaten lunch with Melita and Luke. No one said anything, but she wondered if something was happening between Melita and Luke. It wasn't obvious, but she sensed a spark there.

She shrugged. Had she missed sparks between her and Patrick? Was her annoyance with him all those weeks ago part of how chemistry worked? She had no experience and no idea. That was how she summed up the extent of her knowledge of men. She couldn't help frowning, reminded her of her naivete.

With Melita whisked away for bridesmaid duties, Kelly was left alone for a couple of hours after lunch. She hadn't seen Patrick since their early arrival and wouldn't see him again until the ceremony, as he was also part of the bridal party. She hoped for his sake he wasn't stuck somewhere with his father. Having to kill time with someone he detested wouldn't leave him in a good frame of mind for the wedding.

She bit her bottom lip, even though she risked ruining her lipstick. She couldn't steer her mind away from her own parents. How would her relationship with them fare when she took the plunge and made contact? Guilt twisted in her gut. Their concern and worry at her sudden disappearance was always at the forefront of her mind. She stared out the window, unseeing, and resolutely made a promise to phone them soon. Her estrangement from them had gone on long enough. She needed them, and no doubt they needed her.

A knock sounded on the front door, causing her to jump, but as she was expecting Tilly's arrival, she picked up her clutch, switched off the light and went to open the door.

Two men, formally dressed in black suits and white shirts, waited outside. Their ties were covered in cartoon characters.

"Kelly, I hope?" the taller one asked.

She nodded.

He stretched his hand out in greeting. "Alex."

She shook it. "Hello."

The other man extended his. "Trent. We're Zane's brothers."

Kelly shook his hand and nodded again. She could vaguely see a resemblance. Not too strong, but she knew the story, so it made sense.

"Mum's not quite ready, so we've been instructed to escort you to the waiting limo," Trent announced. "She also advised us not to bother hitting on you as you're already taken. But, jeez, you're the only pretty girl for miles. Please tell me it's not true."

Kelly burst out laughing at the way Trent haggled for her attention. Deciding to take matters into her own hands, she closed the door, wound an arm through each of theirs and led the way down the steps to the pebbled path. "I don't see any reason why I can't enjoy the night and dance with each of you. What do you say?"

She chuckled at their wide grins.

"Yes, please," Trent replied.

Oh boy, what happened to boycotting men forever?

"So, who's the lucky man?" Alex persisted. "And please don't say the brother of the bride."

This time her laughter carried around them and mingled with the shrubbery lining the path. "Sorry, boys, but it *is* the brother of the bride."

"Drats," Alex exclaimed.

As they walked off as a trio, Trent told a joke that kept her laughing all the way to the chapel.

Janice's words rang in her ears. *Dare to be young again.*

Chapter 13

P atrick had made a point of avoiding his father for as long as possible. He couldn't dodge him forever, but was determined to remain calm and not get pissed off until after the ceremony. After that, he'd be unable to escape his presence and all bets would be off. So, he'd kept busy and out of harm's way. After leaving Kelly in Melita's care, he ran last-minute errands for Ella and Zane and made it through the morning without any sighting of the old bastard.

Only minutes earlier, he and Zane had arrived at the chapel. Trussed up in a straitjacket—the term he used for a suit and tie—he was at his most uncomfortable. God only knew how many times he'd been required to wear one throughout his life, and each time he'd resented its restrictions. If only he could've convinced everyone to dress in boardshorts and a comfortable shirt. But no, he didn't want to be the guy who ruined Ella's day by complaining. No doubt his father would fill that role.

Patrick switched off for a few minutes as Zane and the celebrant compared final notes and the organist did a last-minute check of the music.

Looking up, he eyed the stained-glass windows. Their greens, oranges and reds were a strong contrast against the stark white of the high-arched interior. The afternoon sun streamed in from the western-coloured windows and danced in a path the whole twelve metres to the front door. It really was a tiny chapel. The gloss lacquered timber pews featured the only other dominating colour, their ends awash with huge pink silk bows to match the bridesmaids' dresses. A large window positioned behind the altar opened to the serene blue of the ocean. It would frame Ella and Zane as they spoke their vows. Ella had got her wish.

His gaze fell on the image of a suffering Jesus carrying his cross. Religion hadn't crossed his path since the age of about twelve, but something about the way a man was forced to carry his own cross, knowing he would die on it, touched a raw nerve. Did everyone have to suffer in some way to overcome life's adversities? Was the outburst with his mother the day she died his cross to bear?

A commotion at the chapel's entrance had him forcing his attention away from the image and his mind from the maudlin thoughts connected to his mother—and not before time. This was supposed to be a festive and happy occasion and he needed all his wits about him. He expected the guests would start to arrive soon, as Ella was due to make her entrance in about fifteen minutes.

Kelly arrived, entering the chapel laughing and smiling with Zane's errant younger brothers, who also formed part of the bridal party.

Jealously sluiced through him and he didn't hesitate. Leaving Zane's side, he covered the length and breadth of the chapel in seconds, and in the next two, he had his arms around her. It only took one second for his mouth to find hers and he savoured every second thereafter.

A day without her had hurt. To be able to hold her this close forever was a chore he would relish.

He pulled back when he cottoned on that the hollering in the background, by Zane's brothers, was directed at them. His gaze didn't leave her face though, and even with make-up on she blushed brightly at the attention.

"Sorry, I might've messed up your lipstick." It was the only apology that came to mind.

She shrugged and leaned in to whisper, "The more you remove, the less annoying it becomes. I've never been a big fan of gunk on my lips."

Patrick chuckled and took a step back to view Melita's handiwork. He took Kelly's hand and twirled her so he could take in her entire outfit. He let out a soft whistle meant only for her, causing her to blush again. Zane's brothers added their own wolf whistles to the mix.

That secured the deal. He wasn't taking his eyes off Kelly for the rest of the day.

She reached up and rested her hand on his cheek. "How'd your day go?"

The strings holding his heart together constricted. He knew what she was asking and a long time had passed since anyone had cared enough about his welfare to do so. It wasn't like she was asking, 'What did you have for lunch?' Or, 'Did you go for a dip in the ocean?' Or, 'What did the boys and groom get up to?' Nope, none of that. She was asking how things had gone with his father.

He reached up and laced his fingers with hers. "So far, I've been lucky enough to avoid him." He smiled wryly before adding, "My luck has to run out some time."

Worry etched her brow. "I'm here now. I won't leave your side."

Jeez, why did tears have to prick his eyes now? How the hell did he get so lucky to find someone who wanted to watch his back, to stand side-by-side and weather the storm that was only around the corner? Actually, it was only minutes away.

All he wanted to do was tell her he loved her. To tear out of this place and head back to the crumbling castle. He could stay there for the rest of his life, if only she remained by his side. Christ, there was still so much to tell her. How did he begin?

"Thank you," he managed to say through the thick lump in his throat.

The guests began arriving and were crowding the small chapel, so he relinquished his hold on her. Kelly took her place in the pew reserved for close family and he didn't once take his eyes off her.

With the formalities over, the wedding was in full party mode.

"I'll be back in a few minutes." Patrick removed his jacket and draped it over his chair, then he loosened his tie and placed a quick peck on Kelly's cheek before going in search of the men's room.

The music gradually dimmed as he left the elegant reception centre at the Sheraton Mirage. A faint pulse throbbed at his temples, but he hadn't drunk anywhere near enough to cause the onset of a headache. A few minutes away from the music would do him good.

With his head down and shoulders hunched, he dragged his feet instead of lifting them. It was always this way when he expected trouble, and with his father in the same room, it couldn't be far off. He'd nodded once in his direction, acknowledging his presence, but that had been the extent of their interaction.

He was tired of the same old tirade. He'd heard it all before. What didn't his father get? He didn't want to be stuck in one of Boston's high-rise buildings making more money for the family. They had a stack of it already, the greedy bastards. He had lots too, and it multiplied year after year, thanks to the intricate web of trusts his great-grandfather had put in place. It was mind-boggling how little of it he spent and how the numbers continued to double. What bothered him most was that he hadn't earned a single cent of it.

He scowled, not wanting to believe his father's accusations that he'd wasted a lot of time over the last few years. Should he have done things differently? Maybe gone to college? Taken a job elsewhere? He was skilled at nothing, with very little to show for his existence, as his father loved to remind him. But it was too late to regret the wasted time, which his father didn't seem to understand. He sighed, anticipating a re-run of past conversations about his failures when his father eventually found him.

Years earlier, before his mother's death, his father had always spoken about how Patrick would one day work with him. He was twenty-three in a few weeks and still couldn't bring himself to do it. It had always been expected of him, but as he'd developed his own opinions, he'd come to view his father's so-called work as aggressive and unethical. He wanted nothing to do with it.

"Son."

Patrick swivelled around. Dread descended over him. Their chat was going to happen sooner rather than later. He looked longingly at the door to the men's room, only metres away. He didn't want to deal with his father now—or ever.

"Father," he managed to utter through a clenched jaw. At least he wasn't drunk. That was one positive that might impress his father.

"We haven't had a chance to catch up yet."

Which was his way of saying, 'It's time to talk. Time to sort out your future'. It was always the same discussion, always the same result. Never leaving anything but anger and resentment boiling inside.

"I don't think tonight's the time or place."

"You're right."

I'm right? Had the old bastard taken too much sun lately?

"Maybe over breakfast in the morning?"

Those same Ulysses butterfly blue eyes studied Patrick. Were their edges a little softer or had Patrick consumed too much alcohol after all? Lines etched his father's smooth face. Were they new? His father's tall and willowy frame mirrored his own except for brown hair that carried more streaks of grey than Patrick remembered.

They stood in silence, one young and the other old, assessing, both prepared to defend their ground.

"I'm not here to upset you or ask you to come home."

Patrick quirked an eyebrow. This was a bloody change, but he wouldn't fall for the human act. It was too late for that.

"Breakfast, maybe. If I make it." If he could convince Kelly to share his room tonight, he may well not make it. Inviting her to his room was definitely on the agenda.

"Patrick?"

He turned towards Kelly's voice. Wisps of material floated around her legs and her image overtook all his senses. His heart thumped inside his chest. Kelly had come to stand by his side. He took her outstretched hand and grinned stupidly before leaning in and placing his mouth on her slender neck. He inhaled her scent. All the attention to her grooming couldn't compete with the light she radiated. Being near her made fighting his way out of dark places feel easy. She wore the sun on her shoulder like he wore a shirt every day. Everything about her brought him warmth and joy.

He took a step back when he remembered his father. "Kelly, this is my father, Thomas."

Kelly pasted a beautiful smile on her face and extended her hand towards his father, ready to take his. Let him try to manhandle her. At least she was armed with plenty of background information. He almost laughed out loud with the direction his thoughts had taken.

Hmm ... Would he try to manipulate her? Good luck, Daddy dearest.

"I'll be back in a few minutes." Patrick turned away and made his way through the door to the men's room. Once it shut behind him, he allowed himself a small chuckle. This might turn out to be very entertaining. All the tension that had slowly built up over the day eased its way out. With Kelly beside him he could finally loosen the shackles his father had tied around him.

This was his life. He'd do it his way.

It was time his father understood that.

Chapter 14

"Ten minutes," he'd said. "Grab a couple of towels," were his parting words.

Reluctant to end a fabulous night, Kelly removed her floaty dress and cuddled it to her heart, hugging the memories of the dancing and laughing that had ended only minutes ago. When she'd watched Patrick walk to his room to change out of his finery, she'd fallen a little more in love.

There! She admitted it. She was proud of him and he was so good-looking she couldn't help being drawn to him.

After her introduction to Thomas, she'd done everything possible to take Patrick's mind off his father. They'd danced every dance, and she might've drunk two drinks more than her usual.

She smiled and let out a huge, satisfied sigh. Still holding the dress, she fell onto the bed. He'd suggested a walk on the beach when the bride and groom had made their departure, and though she was unsure of what would happen next, she was keen to keep the night alive, so she'd agreed. She should be weary after their early start, but realising how she felt about Patrick and admitting it for the first time pushed common sense to the background.

Kelly hoisted herself up and removed her stockings, jewellery, hair pins and bra. She scrambled around in her bag and pulled out a simple summer dress. Pulling it over her head, she straightened the thin straps. The tropical night was sultry enough that she wouldn't need a jacket, but she grabbed one just in case. She found a hair tie in her toiletry bag before rushing to the bathroom to brush her teeth.

The knock on the door sounded and she remembered the towels. They were strictly for use around the pool, so they were being naughty using them on the beach. She made a promise to clean them on their return.

When she swung the door open, Patrick lounged against its frame, a lopsided smile on his face. Without hesitation, she dropped everything and wrapped her arms around his neck.

He wore a loose cotton t-shirt and what looked like comfortable shorts. She understood his need to escape the suit he'd worn for most of the day. His comment at dinner that 'a person could suffocate and die in one of these' had made her laugh. She liked his sense of humour. To think, once upon a time it had irritated her. What had she been thinking?

He tucked the towels he carried under his arm and they nudged her breast when he lowered his face towards hers. She inhaled when her mouth touched his, their matching peppermint breaths mingling. Relaxing against his tall, willowy frame, she enjoyed the softness of his mouth. Kelly loved the way his stubble gently rubbed against her skin. Tired or not, her newly admitted feelings changed everything.

"Ready?" Patrick rasped, reluctantly pulling back.

She nodded, stooping down to collect her towels and the jacket she'd dropped. "Very."

Clearly more organised than she was, he took a torch from his back pocket and quietly led the way along the pebbled pathway, the slap of their thongs blending in with the sounds of night animals scurrying in the trees. His hand tightened around hers, its security a comfort as they slipped through the strip of forest that separated the resort from Four Mile Beach.

Once past the trees they found a small group of people to their left, laughing and chatting, so Patrick turned right. With no glimpse of the moon, the inky blackness of night was only broken by the torch's light. "Thanks for agreeing to come this weekend."

She glanced at him but his face was a shadow. "I had a fabulous night. You dance extremely well."

"Learning to dance was a prerequisite for my life in Boston. It was expected."

He sounded bitter. There was so much she didn't understand about his early years, but she didn't want to spoil the night by asking.

"It was a very nice change from the skill level I'm used to in my dance partners. How many times did I trip over your feet?"

He chuckled as his hand tightened around hers. "Not enough."

That was better. Her goal was to keep him happy and laughing. They were both damaged. Maybe they could work their way through it together.

They continued walking in silence. A slight breeze caressed her skin, the sultry humidity from earlier manageable now that it was past midnight. Patrick stopped when they were about a hundred metres from the resort. He passed her the torch and laid out the two towels he carried. When he took hers, he rolled them up to use as pillows.

He took back the torch and switched it off, then tugged on her hand and lay down, taking her with him.

"You looked so beautiful tonight," he said as he wrapped his arms around her and held her close.

Heat suffused her skin and a tingle spread across her body. Luckily, he couldn't see her blush. "Can I say how delicious you looked?"

He chuckled again.

To prove her point, she pushed aside the neck of his loose t-shirt and gently bit the top of his shoulder, nibbling until her tongue got involved and she licked and sucked the spot she loved best.

His arms tightened around her and he answered with a groan.

She rested her face against his neck. "Your father said he's never seen you looking so healthy and happy."

Patrick stiffened for an instant. She hadn't meant to blurt it out, but there was no way he'd ask her what she and Thomas had spoken about for the few minutes they'd been left alone together.

"He said a few weird things to me, too, before you came along."

She snuggled in closer. "Like what?" She sensed his hesitation.

"Um ... said he wanted to talk over breakfast in the morning and that he wasn't here to ask me to come home."

"Does he always ask you to go back?"

"Well, I've never left before. He makes no secret of the fact he wants me to work in the family business."

"What sort of business is it?"

"Finance, banking, that kind of thing."

"It would be a bad thing?"

His groan vibrated against her skin. "Stuck in a high-rise building full of assholes every day *and* wearing a suit? Jeez—"

"You'd die and suffocate," she finished for him.

He laughed and she smiled in the dark. With his fingers gently massaging her scalp she could easily fall asleep.

She asked the next thing that came into her head. "What's your surname?"

Was it her imagination or did he stiffen again? Hesitate?

"I could ask you the same thing." Any sign of laughter was gone now.

She lifted her head. "Er ... I'm sorry." Things had turned awkward all of a sudden. "If you'd rather not tell me, I understand. I must admit I've been reluctant to say too much about my family."

"Do *you* have something to hide?" he asked.

Ugh! Were they at a stalemate? Not once had she thought he stressed about the same issues she did. She didn't want him to find out who her parents were. Didn't want him to know they were famous in Sydney for many things. He knew they were doctors, but it wasn't unusual for their faces to appear in magazines and online. Not that she'd looked recently. She had no idea if news of her disappearance had made it to the public arena.

"I'm just not ready for you to know. That's all."

"The same goes for me."

Well, things were past awkward now. What next? Two people were supposed to learn about each other, but she wasn't prepared to fully open up. Neither was he, considering the direction their conversation was going. She had good reasons and could only suppose he did too.

"Would you rather we went back now?"

He rolled to his side and held her closer. "No, Kelly, I'd rather not, and I'm sorry for being so short. My family, many of whom you've now met, are not perfect. Yes, there are a thousand things I need to tell you, but I honestly don't know where to start." He reached up and cradled her face. "You're the first person to ground me in a long time. My mother was the first to try, and Ella was the only other person to make an attempt."

While she couldn't see much in the dark, she heard the anguish in his voice and knew he struggled to speak.

"I need you, Kelly, like you have no idea. I need you to show me what it's like to live a normal life. I sensed it the very first time we met."

"But ... what makes you think I've lived a normal life?"

"I'd know if you'd been raised in a dysfunctional family."

"But you don't know my family."

"From the few things you've told me, I don't need to. I just have to look at you."

He was right. Her childhood had been perfect—she'd only stuffed up recently—but how different could his upbringing have been? She'd met his father and hadn't recognised him as anyone famous. Had he been abusive? With a family history of suicide, wives fleeing, violence ... God, how damaged was Patrick?

While this thought should've scared her, instead it did the opposite. Something stirred deep within. She wouldn't be able to let him go easily if it became necessary.

"Can we stay out here a little longer? Will you hold me in your arms and kiss me senseless?"

This brought back his chuckle. "Gladly."

His hands roamed over her body and found their way underneath her dress. He found her breasts and she told him of the clobbering coming his way. He laughed and she laughed with him. They whispered things in the still of the night, using words to connect their minds and souls. No more talk of family but of dreams and hopes. Eventually, they shared one rolled up towel and draped the other over their entwined bodies, as night, too quickly, raced towards dawn.

Patrick came awake with a start as a rush of cold water rushed up his thighs and dampened the bottom of his shorts. He sat up in alarm and Kelly squealed beside him. Neither had thought of the morning tide. Hours ago, the ocean had lapped the sand metres away, but with the first tinges of pink sky peeking through the clouds, the water rushed towards them again with its next surge. They scrambled backwards and grabbed the towels, just missing getting wet again. The torch was floating nearby, but Patrick pounced on Kelly's jacket that had been left behind, only he was too late; it was soaking wet. He held it aloft as water dripped off it and Kelly groaned.

He turned to look at her beautiful face. Her cheeks were zigzagged with creases from his shirt and her morning hair was perfectly disarrayed. She reached for her jacket but let it drop to the sand and burst out laughing. He couldn't help but join her. He hadn't planned to sleep on the beach but had no regrets.

Early morning walkers turned at the sound of their laughter. What thoughts ran through their heads? Two scruffy people sleeping off too much alcohol? A few years ago that would've been the case, though sleeping on the beach hadn't been an option. Instead, he'd often wake up on someone else's couch or in a stranger's home with no idea of how he'd ended up there. He cringed at the stupid things he'd done.

Last night, he and Kelly had been sober but drunk on each other. Hell, he'd do anything to sink into her depths and share exquisite pleasures with her—except something held him back. Some premonition warned him that if they did, it would spoil everything. That day could wait. It wasn't like it was the first time for either of them.

When the incoming tide threatened again, they scrambled back even further.

"Must be time for a shower and breakfast," he declared as he stumbled to his feet.

Surprise crossed her face as he helped her up. "I thought you might do everything possible to miss breakfast this morning."

Holding her hand tightly in his, he gazed out at the gentle roll of the waves and contemplated her words, then turning back he asked, "Will you come with me?"

She nodded.

"Well, then," he mock scolded, "what are you waiting for? A man can only starve for so long."

They laughed easily together and gathered the towels and the torch that might never work again. He hid his anxiety well, which had nothing to do with the wet torch. What was the worst his father could do? He couldn't force him onto a plane. Since turning twenty-one, he'd inherited full rights to most of his wealth, and now was the time to start using it for good.

It's time to become the man I want to be. His father couldn't hurt him any more than his mother's death had.

Chapter 15

Kelly squeezed his hand momentarily, as he was about to push open the glass door that led into the breakfast buffet restaurant.

He looked down into her worried eyes.

"I know you're nervous this morning," she said, "but you're not alone. I'm here. Use me if you have to."

Strong emotion, not unusual for him these days, rallied around inside him. His life since leaving Boston was full of new experiences. Or was it that he was simply growing up?

"Thank you." He leaned down, his hand tangling in her semi-wet, dark strands, and kissed her. Closing his eyes, he fortified himself, not daring to let any tears show. Christ. He needed to be under control in less than thirty seconds, or else!

The person behind them cleared their throat, so Patrick manoeuvred himself and Kelly out of the way, enough to enable the guests to enter the restaurant, then with a firm hand on Kelly's shoulder, he reached forward and pushed the door open. "Okay, time for breakfast. After you, my Queen of Karradmas Castle."

He managed a smile but hadn't meant to spill what'd been playing around in his head.

"Karrad what?" A confused frown marred her beautiful face.

"K for Kelly and then Samdarra spelled backwards." He loved playing with words. A mite embarrassed, he raised his eyebrows, daring her to question it.

When she burst out laughing, his smile curved for real and heads turned as they entered. His father, sitting alone, noticed their arrival and waved them in his direction.

"Good morning, Patrick. Kelly."

No casual handshake or slap on the back. Did the man ever relax? Patrick didn't want to reply formally, so he said nothing and just nodded.

Kelly was having none of it. She placed a hand on his father's shoulder and greeted him with a kiss on the cheek. "Good morning, Tommo. Did you manage a good night's sleep after the party?"

Patrick almost choked.

"Don't mind us. The morning tide caught us unawares after a terrific sleep on the beach, so we had a quick shower before brekkie." She reached up to disentangle the wet strands of her hair still clumped together.

His father's eyebrows shot up. This was a first for him. No one had ever greeted him that way. You spoke to him with respect or you didn't dare open your mouth.

Patrick did everything possible not to laugh at the outrageous way Kelly was settling herself in. He gave her free rein to do whatever the hell she wanted. Who was he to hold her back?

Waiters hovered once they were seated. His father must've insisted they be waited on. Patrick frowned. Some things never changed. No 'help yourself' buffet for them this morning.

Once their coffee had been poured, Patrick came right out with it. "So, Father, you wanted to discuss things?"

His father straightened his tie and tucked the tail in neatly. "I was hoping we could do so in private."

Patrick added milk and sugar to his coffee and avoided eye contact. "This is as private as it's going to get, so fire away."

Kelly was busily buttering warm toast that had just been served but glanced up at his father. She smiled, acting too well, and waved her hand in the air. "By all means, talk away. I'm just here to listen."

Patrick choked on a mouth full of coffee. His father was probably regretting not having any of his personal security guards close by. Kelly would be kicked out on her rear faster than it would take his father to nod his head to give the order.

"This is private family business between father and son. I'd rather it was only the two of us."

Kelly stopped chewing. Her eyes narrowed and Patrick swore he could see warfare etched in them. His father was not getting out of this lightly. Kelly was on the war path.

"Thomas," she began, "private family business usually occurs between people who care about each other." She paused, long enough to get his father's full attention. Her words were clipped and perfectly pronounced. No Aussie slang this time. "*You,* from what Patrick has told me, haven't given a shit about him for a long, long time."

She paused again.

His father scowled.

"Patrick has spent his entire life trying to please you with no success. But you should know that fathers build up their sons rather than always pushing them down. So maybe you should consider yourself an uncle or an acquaintance until you get that sorted out."

Her glare never wavered from Thomas's face. When she placed her folded napkin beside her plate, the bread knife slipped and clattered to the tiled floor. The sound resonated as Patrick leaned down to retrieve it and Kelly smiled her thanks when he handed it back.

"The sad truth is," she said, "you don't know your son. You know nothing about the way he thinks, what he feels or how hard he works. To request a discussion between father and son, you have to be more than the guy who passed on his genes."

Patrick stared at her in astonishment. No one—and he meant no one—had ever stood up for him as Kelly had just now. His mother had been too scared and others too in awe of his father's position to dare say anything. Yet, here was Kelly, saying exactly what he should have said years ago. He was grateful, but he feared the worst was yet to come.

In front of his eyes, however, his father deflated, as if someone had rammed a big sewing needle into his arm and let out all the air. His ramrod back buckled and he all but collapsed over his breakfast. Then he coughed, clearing his throat, and said, "Thank you, Kelly. I appreciate you telling me exactly how it is."

What the?

Hang on. This was *not* his father. No flaming way. Patrick wanted to spin out of his chair and yell to the waiter to bring back his real father. This man was an imposter and had somehow stolen his father's identity.

Tartly, Kelly picked up her spoon in readiness to eat her breakfast and faced his father squarely. "No problems at all. I just want to make sure you understand how special Patrick is. It's about time you knew it."

Patrick was so spun out by the conversation he hadn't eaten a mouthful of solid food yet. Certain he was sitting with a stranger, he jumped when his father addressed him.

"Patrick, I've made some decisions lately and I wanted you to be the first to know."

Patrick froze.

"I'm taking more leave from the business to do some voluntary work in Asia with organisations that are desperately in need of support. I'll be donating money, too, but I want to personally deliver it so I know it's going where it should."

Kelly nudged Patrick with her elbow. "Your toast's getting cold."

He hadn't noticed she'd buttered it. Robotically, he took a bite before his father spoke again.

"I'd like you to join the business, but the decision is yours. There's no expiry date on the job offer."

No way. His father wasn't even bothering to justify or apologise for his behaviour over the years.

The cold toast in Patrick's mouth sat like a soggy lump. He couldn't swallow it, but as he forced it down his chest exploded with emotion. He hissed through clenched teeth. "Is this your way of redeeming yourself after what you did to Mum? My God, you bastard, you all but killed her."

He managed to contain his anger, even though the accusation ran around his head and spun with deadly speed. He couldn't hide the truth forever. But was he being entirely truthful? His father hadn't led his mother to her death. *He* had. Despite years of his father's verbal and emotional abuse it had been his own cruel and heartless words that had driven her over the edge.

Still, he wanted to lash out and hurt his father. Hurt him as much as he'd been hurt during his lifetime. But it probably wouldn't make any difference. Why would his father care? He thought that voluntary work would excuse the bullying and aggression he'd resorted to over the years. Wipe his slate clean.

"I'm sorry, Patrick."

His father kept his voice to a low whisper, so others nearby couldn't hear. There was enough movement and bustle in the breakfast room that their conversation could be contained between the three of them. Kelly rubbed his arm.

"I've a lot to repair and a long way to go. I hope one day you can bring yourself to forgive me. I *was* terrible to your mother and Ella's mother." He leaned forward with his hands knotted. "I'm grateful that you got your mother's attributes, not mine. She would be very proud of you."

What about you? You're not proud of me?

Christ, he was working hard to keep it all in. His brain buzzed so loudly he confused it with the hubbub around him. This was not a conversation he'd ever had with his father and soon he'd wake up and realise it was some weird dream. That the nightmare was still to come.

"If this is your way of using some reverse psychology shit on me, it won't work."

His father scraped his chair back and rose. "It's not. I'm sorry this conversation didn't quite go as planned. I'm in Australia for a few more months and I'd like to see you again before I leave. I'll contact you."

He picked up his jacket, turned and walked away.

Patrick's heart jolted into action. Kelly winced beside him at the noise his chair made when it scraped back, but he ignored her. His only goal was to reach his father before he disappeared.

He rammed his way through the glass door and yelled at his father's retreating back. "Don't you dare make me feel guilty for not wanting to forgive you."

His father halted and spun around.

Patrick's vision honed in on him. They were the same height as each other as they faced off. His father's brow was etched with a deep frown.

"For years I desperately wanted five minutes of your time," Patrick spat. "Five minutes where you'd act like you wanted to be my father. My friends went fishing, skiing, took vacations, even ate meals with their families, but I was never worth the trouble for you to put your work aside and do something with me."

Patrick wheezed as his voice threatened to break. Years of pent-up disappointment and neglect fought to be released.

"And Mom. You were such an asshole to her. And don't think I didn't notice. You should be sitting in jail right now, but you're too bloody rich for anyone to touch you. No one would dare question the almighty Thomas Van Der Meeliko."

Guests walking past looked their way, but this was too important to stop. For too long he'd bottled up his feelings, always afraid to say his piece. Now was the time to let his father know the truth. Except his father didn't argue back, didn't try to blame someone else. There was no fight in him.

"Son, I can only apologise and say I'm sorry. Everything you're saying is true. If you want to put me in jail, I won't stop you."

Guilt piled onto Patrick's shoulders, made him feel as though he should accept his father's apology and start afresh. So much had changed since the day Ella turned up on their doorstep. Her arrival had certainly changed the course of his life. Was her influence also leaving its mark on their father? Some days Patrick wished there might come a time when he and his father could enjoy each other's company. On most days it was hard to believe it would ever be possible.

He didn't get a chance to vent any more of the emotions jumbled up in his head because his father turned and walked away. Patrick shrank, his body filling with sadness that a proper reconciliation would probably never happen. They would go their separate ways and God only knew when they'd meet again. Wretchedness threatened to close in. Futility surrounded him. Only one voice broke through the fog.

"Patrick."

He didn't turn. Couldn't move.

She must've heard most of the conversation, but she wrapped her arms around him. "Let's go back to the castle."

They were the words he needed to hear.

Chapter 16

O *ne Month Later*

"What the heck? I didn't authorise this!"

"Look, all I know is that the costs have been covered and I have to erect it wherever you tell me to put it."

Kelly eyed the young tradesman in the fluoro yellow work shirt. "What's it for?"

He continued to remove tools from the back of his utility. "It's a telecommunications tower. This property is in a black spot, so it'll give you better access to phone and internet."

Coming back from an early morning swim, Patrick reached the top of the steps. As he dried himself, he asked, "What's going on?"

Kelly rested her hands on her hips. Something was afoot but she couldn't quite put her finger on it. The early morning sun rising through the trees behind Patrick distracted her for a second.

"Someone has organised a telecommunications tower for the property."

Patrick shrugged and wrapped the towel around his waist. "Might be Mr Blundell again, or the historical society."

"What? Like the washing machine that turned up a few weeks ago?" Disbelief brought out her sarcastic side.

She'd appreciated the washing machine but suspected this went beyond Mr Blundell and his historical cronies. This smacked of her parents and added to her guilt, as she still hadn't phoned them. But, of course, there was no proof. All she knew was that things were being paid for and conveniently delivered to the property. What could possibly be next?

"I just need to know where you want it installed."

Kelly turned back to the tradesman.

Patrick tapped her shoulder. "You go and have breakfast. I'll take care of it."

He slipped his cotton t-shirt over his head and went to assist the tradesman with getting the tower off his roof rack.

Kelly made her way to the kitchen where she plugged in the kettle and placed two slices of bread in the toaster.

Did she want better phone and internet access? She and Patrick had closed themselves away from the world since the wedding. She'd forgotten her promise to phone her parents, letting Patrick heal without any further drama. When his father had walked away, it had broken him and the effects reached deeper into his soul than anything Kelly had ever dealt with.

But slowly, day by day and with lots of hard, physical work, he was coming out of the trance his father had left him in. At the end of each day, they slept like the dead. There was no need to extend their relationship beyond what they had. Their time together wasn't about being intimate. It was much, much more.

She settled at the table with yesterday's newspaper, munched on her toast and sipped her black tea. Skimming over the articles, she reflected on all she and Patrick had achieved over the past weeks. The state of the castle left a lot to be desired, as it would take too much money to fix, but the lawns and encroaching forest were immaculate. Last week Kelly had instructed the real estate agent to put it on the market. Now it was just a waiting game.

Besides working, she and Patrick had talked a lot, too. For fun, they discussed a complete renovation of the castle as if she had the money. Talk of it always left her a little wretched about how a person's hopes and dreams could easily be squashed when you lacked finances. They delved a little deeper into Patrick's early life and the differences between growing up in Australia as opposed to the States. Patrick refused to call tomato sauce anything but 'ketchup', and for some silly reason they laughed plenty over that.

What they didn't talk about was the future. No mention had been made of Patrick leaving to work for his father. Zero words were wasted on what they would do once the castle sold and zilch was wasted on whether they had a future together. Patrick worked for meals and a bed and Kelly provided both.

But each day their attraction flared brighter and their movements grew with more intimacy. In the safe bubble they'd created, she lived for the next day. There was never a dull one and the weeks since Ella's wedding had flown by with alarming speed.

She stopped chewing when she heard a vehicle but assumed Patrick had the tradesman under control and they were moving his utility, so she ignored it.

How would she ever find the strength to leave the castle and the memories she and Patrick were creating together?

She paused at an article about a recent crocodile attack, refusing to ponder life away from the castle—or Karradmas Castle, as they often jokingly referred to it. Her adopted family at Samdarra were happy for her to return when she was sorted and she wanted to go back but … there were too many 'buts' in her head lately.

She heard footsteps approaching the kitchen door so wasn't surprised when Patrick hugged her from behind. She swept the newspaper closed and pushed it towards the other side of the table before taking another sip of her tea. "Where did you decide the tower should go?"

His fingers pinching into her shoulder and his hesitation to respond had her rising and turning to face him. Worry creased his face.

"What's up?"

"You've got visitors, Kel."

"Yeah?"

"Do you want to come outside?"

"Who are they?"

This was stupid. Why had fear wavered across her chest? If it was Janice and her fiancé, why would Patrick look uneasy? Patrick knew them both. If it was Mr Blundell, well, he would find his own way in like he usually did.

Patrick tucked an errant strand of hair behind her ear.

Now her chest pounded. She had an inkling of who was waiting outside and she'd been dreading this day for a long time.

"Your parents are here."

She gulped a lungful of air and held onto it. In their own loving fashion, they'd given her all the clues she'd needed. She'd already put two and two together and had known it wouldn't take long for them to show up. The arrival of the washing machine started the first niggle in the back of her mind, and the appearance of the telecommunications tower was another big spoiler that her parents would soon be turning up. So she shouldn't be surprised. Anxious? Yes. Worried? Hell, yes. Ashamed of her past actions? Absolutely.

Mr Blundell knew her father from their school days and Kelly had wondered if they were still in contact. Now she had her answer.

She looked up into Patrick's face and garnered the strength he offered. Telepathically he spoke back. *You helped me, now it's my turn.*

"Are you sure it's them?"

"You look like your mother. Does that count?" His lopsided smile told her it was an unnecessary question.

She blew out the air trapped in her lungs and straightened her shoulders. "Okay, I can do this." She was talking to herself more than Patrick, but he'd figure that out.

"Of course, you can. They don't look scary."

She chuckled wryly. "I look nothing like the girl who ran away from home. They might not recognise me."

Patrick steered her towards the door. "Relax and take a deep breath."

Before she took the final step outside, he reached in and kissed a spot on her neck. "Use me if you have to."

She chuckled and that was the first expression her parents saw.

They stood only metres away and when Patrick's hand fell away, her smile vanished. The time had come to deal with this. On her own.

"Mum, Dad." Her voice quavered as a tidal wave of emotions swept over her. How could she have done what she did?

Her mother's hands were twisted in knots, the uncertainty and hurt on her face clear as day. She was their daughter, their only child, and she'd denied them a place in her life when she'd disappeared. Her behaviour had done untold damage.

She ran the last few steps. She had to.

Oh, what a mess! Emotion choked her throat and nothing could stop the backlash of tears from washing down her face when she opened her arms wide to pull her mother in against her chest. Her father completed their family unit by engulfing them both in his big, strong arms. They were all crying. Harsh, racking sobs tore through Kelly's body. There was no quiet or easy way to do this.

Eternity might've passed by the time she finally pulled back. She sniffled and wiped her face with her hands. "I'm so sorry, really sorry. I have so much to apologise for."

Her mother, clearly reluctant to let her go, pulled out a tissue and handed it over, all the while combing hair back from Kelly's face. "Shh, there's nothing to be sorry about."

"There, there is," she hiccupped, "I sh-should've phoned you by now."

"We didn't know why you left." Her mother's face was streaked with tears. "We thought you were okay with your decision, but you weren't and we should've seen that. It's our fault, my darling girl. We're doctors, but we couldn't tell when our own daughter wasn't well."

"No, no, no." She buried her face against her mother's chest again as the tears continued to run down her cheeks. "I sh-should've stayed and explained."

Warmth covered her back when her father enveloped her again, giving her the kind of hug she needed, and confirmation and comfort that there was a way forward after she'd crushed everything they must've once believed in.

For now words were no longer necessary. All she needed was the touch and feel of her parents around her, knowing they still had her back. They remained tightly knit, rocking gently for a few moments as they gave their tears time to slow.

Why hadn't she phoned weeks ago? Why had she wasted so many months of valuable time? Because of anger and fear, at first, and then it had just been plain stupidity. Now she had more to regret in a life barely started.

She was about to apologise again, when the wail of a small child pierced the air. Kelly jerked her head up. It had come from close by. Really close.

Her father disentangled himself and trotted to the car that was only metres away. Her mother, Kelly noticed, never once let her gaze leave her face. Something didn't make sense. Why would her parents have a small child with them?

But through the partially wound down tinted rear window she could just make out a child's car seat. And the clear wail of 'Nanna ... Poppy' was unmistakable.

Kelly froze when those words finally formed some meaning in her head. Her heart rate slowed to such a degree that she almost self-diagnosed herself as deceased. Nothing was making sense. Why was her mother holding her again and rubbing her arm ferociously? She must be dead. That could be the only reason, except somehow, she was still standing.

A small girl—and Kelly didn't have to guess that she was about eighteen months old—was nestled against her father's chest, her thumb tucked comfortingly in her mouth. She had the darkest of black hair and the greenest of green eyes. Changed from the newborn blue they once were, now they matched her own.

The little girl's arms stretched out as a small tear dribbled down her chubby cheek. "Nanna." She hiccupped once. "Nanna."

Kelly's mother took the girl in her arms and tucked her face under her chin, then turned to Kelly. "This is your daughter, Gemma."

Kelly swayed and tipped backwards.

Patrick caught her just in time.

Chapter 17

P atrick wound his arms around Kelly's slack limbs as the shock of the news took over. It had stunned Patrick, too. He couldn't imagine the effect it must be having on Kelly.

Gemma squirmed in her grandmother's arms. "Down, Nanna, down."

Kelly's mother knelt and secured Gemma on her feet before letting her stand alone.

Patrick gently prised his arms away from Kelly and steadied her too. His gaze was drawn to the little girl who was a miniature version of her.

Crouching to her eye level, he asked, "Hey, Gemma, would you like to see some little birdies in a nest?"

For his efforts he was rewarded with a huge smile. When he reached for her hand, she happily placed her chubby little fingers in his and prattled to her grandparents. "Birdie, birdie, birdie."

The tender and soft curl of her little fingers in his roughened hand melted something inside of him. He couldn't remember ever holding the hand of a tiny infant.

He didn't want to leave Kelly alone, but she had to talk through this with her parents. As he rose, he eyed the tradesman, who was busy digging holes in the far corner of the property, and knew he wasn't needed there either. Taking Gemma away from the discussion was more important and this was his cue to do so.

He turned to Kelly's father, William. "I'll take Gemma to see a nest I discovered yesterday. Go inside and have a cup of tea. We won't be long."

"Thanks, Patrick."

When they'd arrived and Patrick had introduced himself, he hadn't gone into any detail as to why he was at the property. No doubt they were curious, but his presence would be the last thing on their minds at the moment.

With one hand clutching Gemma's tiny fingers, Patrick placed the other around Kelly's waist. He didn't say anything except to look deep into her still shocked eyes. He smiled, hoping to pass back the strength she'd selflessly passed on to him when he'd needed it. He placed a soft kiss on her cheek before turning to Kelly's mother, Margaret.

"We'll be back in a few minutes."

"Bye, bye, Nanna. Birdie, birdie."

Patrick chuckled. Was it normal for a toddler to so easily befriend a stranger?

Before they left, William crouched beside Gemma. "Now you be a good girl. Nanna and I are going to have a cup of tea with Mummy. When you come back you can tell your mummy all about the birdie."

"Mummy, mummy," she chattered, a wide grin spreading across her face before she looked up with adoring eyes to remind Patrick of his promise. "Birdie, birdie."

He laughed and patted her head, noting she barely made it past his knees. Though she was small, she sounded bright and confident, as if her experiences with family had taught her that the world was a safe place. He tightened his fingers around her little hand and made a silent wish that Gemma would never lose that sense of love and security.

He'd spotted the small sunbird nest dangling from a branch only yesterday. He'd inspected it with awe, taking in the intricate workmanship the parent birds had mastered to build a home for their babies.

With each slow step he took, he aligned it with Gemma's clumsy steps and reflected on how he wanted the chance to provide love and security for his own children one day. The invisible strings connecting his heart and emotions suddenly contracted together, and a fissure of excitement whizzed through his chest. He smiled openly. *Yes, damn it.* His destiny lay in his hands. No longer did he have to answer to his father. Why should he? The example his father had provided was not the one he wanted to follow.

At the edge of the rainforest, Patrick swung Gemma onto his shoulders. "Now you have to be really quiet." He pointed to the little nest where two eager beaks showed through the small opening.

She squealed when they opened their beaks wide. Apparently, asking her to remain quiet was like asking the gods to drop snow from the skies above Moona Creek. It just wasn't possible. He laughed and hoped the new hatchlings weren't too frightened.

⁂

Kelly's stiff legs somehow managed to carry her to the kitchen. Nothing was functioning, especially her head. She wanted to whoop for joy, jump high enough to touch the sky and twirl around in ecstasy. Her baby girl was here! She wasn't with an adopted family, after all.

Hey, everyone, my baby girl is here with me, she wanted to shout out.

But pain had found a comfortable home inside of her and wasn't leaving any time soon. She collapsed onto the closest chair and dropped her face in her hands. Why had she let herself miss eighteen months of her baby girl's life? How many more regrets would she have to add to her already long list? If she hadn't run away, if she'd phoned her parents sooner, if, if, if. How could she ever reclaim the lost time?

Tears found their way out again. She had no control over anything anymore, so how the heck would she manage as a mother? Uncertainty and fear consumed her and her muscles stiffened in protest. If she'd started from day one things would've been different, but to take on the role of motherhood this much later? She had no idea how to do it. Or how to halt the way her heart pumped inside her chest—hurting, hurting, always hurting.

"Hey, baby, don't cry." Her father knelt by her chair and held her in his arms.

She took the tissues her mother offered and made every attempt to stop the flow of tears and clean herself up. "Wh-what happened? Wh-what happened with the adoption?"

Her mum, sitting close, reached for her hands and held them tight. "Remember they told us you had six weeks after the birth to decide if you wanted to give your baby away?"

"They did?" How did she not recall that? Oh, good Lord, it could've saved them from all this heartache.

"The counsellor only mentioned it once and I don't think we ever discussed it again, but when you disappeared and we couldn't find you … well—" Her mother's voice cracked. She swallowed, her hands shaking around Kelly's.

"There was no way we were giving Gemma away," her father said. "As the weeks disappeared and we still couldn't find you, we couldn't let anything tear that baby away from us. If we'd lost you, we sure as hell weren't losing her."

"Is … is she legally my baby?"

"Yes," they both chorused.

"We fostered her until we could reunite her with you. We never gave up hope."

"Oh, Mum, you must think I'm the most idiotic person under the sun."

"Never. Hormones during and after pregnancy can really mess with you. You might have had postnatal depression without us even realising. Like we said, we should've been more attentive to you."

Kelly dropped her head, twisting her fingers in knots. "What do I do now?" Afraid fear would be streaked across her face, she wailed, "Oh, Mum, I don't know what to do!"

"Shh, that's why we're not going anywhere. We sold our house in Sydney and bought one in Innisfail and—"

"What?"

Her father chuckled. "That's right. We got out of the rat-race to be closer to you and Gemma. We know it will take time for Gemma to adjust, but we haven't stopped telling her about you and she's young enough to adapt. When this property sells, we can all decide what to do next."

Relief poured its way into every vein and artery. She absorbed the shock of discovering her parents had kept her beautiful baby girl and listened to everything they said. She let their words swirl around her and dared to understand the options now available to her.

She took one of each of their hands and squeezed them hard. "By the end of my pregnancy I really wanted my baby. Every time she moved inside of me, I believed it was her telling me not to give her away, but I didn't think I had any rights after I made the decision. When they let me hold her, my heart shattered. She was a part of me and I couldn't believe I'd agreed to give her away. I couldn't bear it and that's why I took off. I suppose I thought that if I left and went far away, the pain couldn't hurt me as much."

Tears again tumbled down her cheeks and she accepted another handful of tissues. "In-instead, it's tormented me ever since, the thought of someone else taking care of her. I couldn't handle it. I worried they wouldn't love her like I would, wouldn't give her all the opportunities I was given. It hurt so, so much. I'm so sorry."

She fell towards her hands again and her shoulders shook with sobs. The heavy and secure weight of her father's arms around her made the pain almost bearable. The pain she now felt was in realising how many months she'd lost. How would she ever regain them? All those precious moments were gone forever. She'd never forgive herself.

Determination, though, had a mind of its own. It shoved its way up, desperate to sprout branches and grow leaves. She'd seen the forest do it; so would she. From this day forth she would be everything to her daughter and would spend every waking moment absorbing, appreciating and loving her child.

There was no other way for her to move on if she didn't. How else would she allow forgiveness to come her way? If no space was left for anyone else in her life, then so be it. She had eighteen months to make up for and she had a feeling it would take a lifetime to achieve.

"Nanna, Poppy, Mummy ..."

The kitchen door swung open and that one word, 'Mummy', was all Kelly needed to hear to spring into action.

She swiped her face with her sleeve, leaped off the chair, crouched and opened her arms to catch Gemma as she pelted towards them. A few steps from her, though, Gemma halted, unsure. Kelly's mother knelt beside her, giving Gemma confidence to take the last few unsteady steps closer. When she reached them, Kelly and her mother hugged her together, and Kelly took the first step in bonding with her child. Gemma's gibberish attempt to tell them about her adventure—'Birdie, birdie, Nanna, Mummy'—was a balm to Kelly's soul.

Chapter 18

Patrick wasn't sure when it had happened. He couldn't pinpoint the exact day, definitely not the precise second, but in the three weeks since Gemma entered Kelly's world, Kelly had slowly, almost subconsciously, cut him off. He didn't blame her. He still worked a full day and received free board and bed, but he knew his days were numbered.

He'd spent those weeks cleaning and tidying the area near the falls. The recent heavy rains had strewn debris, leaving it wrapped around trees and saplings. The picnic tables had carried thick coats of lichen, each one requiring scraping and sanding before he'd been able to paint them. The cylindrical concrete bollards that led from the steps to the tables had taken an entire week to clean. He'd just finished painting the last one now.

Gingerly he straightened his back and stretched his sore muscles. Turning to the soothing flow of water over the falls, he glimpsed the black rocks. It was hard not to be reminded of the many times he and Kelly had kissed behind its silver screen. His vision blurred the harder he stared, but it wasn't the flowing water he saw.

He swore she was ready to apologise every time he tried to connect with her, but she would quickly switch her attention to Gemma. Things had changed. There were only a few useful working days left for him at the castle.

Kelly's life was filled with mother's groups, swimming lessons, feeding, nappies, sleeping patterns and toilet training. It was a whole new vocabulary for Kelly and a foreign language to him.

She no longer required the services of his dented, orange Camira, as her parents had arrived in their brand new Landcruiser. The three of them already spoke of their future together, without him, when the castle sold.

'What about me? What about your dreams?' he wanted to yell. Had she so easily forgotten them?

'What dreams?' she'd yell back. She didn't need them anymore, or him or his money. Not that she knew he had it.

He guessed it helped that she only viewed him as a recovering drug addict. Knowledge that he was one of Boston's richest would have complicated matters.

Most nights he slept alone at the castle. Kelly rarely made it back. Sometimes she did, only to dash back to Innisfail to be by Gemma's side when she woke.

He managed to get his driver's licence the day before. William had offered to drive him into Innisfail and he'd confidently passed the required test. So now he had no reason to stay. He could drive away any time, and he would. Because he got it. Kelly had a life and a new role as a mother and he didn't want to be the one to hold her back.

He pulled his shirt off and made his way to the pool's deeper edge before diving in. Screw his foolish heart. He'd find someone else. Hell, he'd gone to Samdarra to gain control of his drug addiction and he could proudly say he'd achieved that. He'd left Boston to learn to fend for himself, without the shadow of his father always towering over him, and in doing so, he'd matured a shitload. Another tick in the box. He'd learned the value of hard, physical work. Combine that with being off the grid in the most beautiful place he'd ever seen and it proved to be the best therapy for a recovering drug addict.

Go on, give yourself another big tick.

He just hadn't found his exact place in the world. Whether it was in Boston or Australia, he had no clue. He decided to stop by Samdarra for a while before he headed to Brisbane to see his sisters.

After that, who knew where life would take him.

Patrick held his breath and swam under the water towards the falls. He had a lot to thank Kelly for. He was proud of her and understood her predicament. A small part of him, though, wished she'd wanted him to share it, too. But what did it matter? He didn't belong here. He never had. He only wished he did.

Coming back up for air, he turned onto his back and floated. He wasn't going anywhere near the black rocks behind the falls today. As the current moved and eddied around him, he planned the next two days of work and another matter of unfinished business. After that, it would be time to go. Quietly, alone, with no fuss.

Shit, it was going to hurt.

⌘

"Big arms now, come on, Gemma, swim to Mummy." Kelly's heart swelled as the morning sun shone on their sunscreened skin.

Proud of her achievements, Gemma squealed with delight when she reached Kelly. William and Margaret hovered near the edge of the pool and laughed when Gemma babbled, "Nanna, Poppy, look me swim."

They all laughed. Other toddlers splashed nearby as parents and babies connected in the water, all eagerly listening to the instructor.

Kelly leaned against the side of the pool and waited for their turn.

"Patrick did a good job of the bollards and tables," William said. "The castle is looking so good. Let's keep our fingers crossed that a buyer surfaces soon."

Kelly nodded, but something tripped inside of her at the mention of Patrick's name. He *had* done a terrific job and she couldn't thank him enough. She'd barely seen him the past few weeks and tried to convince herself she was missing the time they spent together. But she'd be lying. Gemma consumed her every waking moment and she wouldn't change a thing, but still, guilt gnawed at her. She didn't know how to deal with the situation. She was aware of the way Patrick looked at her, always hopeful and always prepared to help her achieve her dream. When the property sold, how would she say goodbye to him?

It was hard to look away from him, so she stayed away instead. She couldn't stand the hurt and the big question in his eyes. Besides, Gemma was her everything. Her baby girl got first dibs and every minute of every day was spent making up for lost time. No apologies allowed, or she would break down and want Gemma and Patrick.

Margaret slid into the pool to enjoy some of the water games with Gemma. Kelly hoisted herself out and reached for a towel. When she realised she was yet to answer her father, she said, "He did, Dad. He's been terrific."

"Is he more than the hired help?" he asked with his eyebrows arched.

They'd broached a lot of subjects since her parents had arrived, but discussions involving Patrick were yet to surface.

She shook her head and water droplets landed on her arms. "I can't, Dad. I can't make him any promises. Not anymore. I can't share myself between him and Gemma."

He squeezed her shoulder and smiled. "I understand, honey. One thing at a time."

As she rubbed her towel over her torso and legs, her father's phone rang and he walked away to take the call while she pulled on a shirt and shorts over her swimwear. She'd return to the castle with Gemma so they could both shower and Gemma could have a sleep. A swimming session was a dead certainty to tire her out and an early afternoon nap was the only cure.

She hugged the towel, loving how in only three short weeks she had connected strongly with her daughter. Gemma called her Mummy and allowed her privileges she hadn't dreamed of ever receiving. Hugs, kisses, holding hands and special requests that her mummy read to her at bedtime. Kelly cherished every single moment, and although her heart had started to gradually repair, the old regret still hurt for now. She had a long road to travel.

"Kelly, that was Mr Blundell. He tried your phone but it didn't answer." William pocketed his phone and smiled broadly. "Looks like we could have a buyer. He's coming out to the property this afternoon to go over a few details."

"Really? Already?" Joy swirled around her at the news, but it was dimmed by the recollection of the visions and plans she'd once dreamed of with Patrick.

"Well, it's not sold until the monies are in the bank, but it's a positive start."

Still, she couldn't help the disappointment that lodged itself deep inside. Selling the property meant the end of a special time in her life, one she'd shared with Patrick. On the other hand, it signalled the start of something so much better. How her heart ached over the lost eighteen months. This reprieve was a golden handshake worth billions. She'd never trade her daughter for a life at the castle, where insufficient funds would eventually wear her down.

Then she remembered her grandmother's diaries. What were the chances the new owners would be interested in preserving history?

"Dad?"

Her father settled beside her once again. "Yeah?"

"Why did I never know about the castle growing up? I mean, you must've had an amazing childhood. How come you never spoke about it?"

He ran a hand through his greying hair and nodded, appearing to take a few moments to organise his thoughts. He was looking out into the distance, past the pool, into the nearby athletics park.

"You were only two when your grandfather remarried," he said. "She was a witch. No amount of trying was ever going to win her around. She despised me and your mother, and barely tolerated your grandfather. I couldn't understand the union. What the hell was his problem? Why did he marry her? Was he that desperate for a companion? I couldn't imagine she was anything else to him."

He grimaced and turned to face her. "We had an almighty row. It left me very bitter and hurt. I asked the witch if I could have some of Mum's things, but she refused to part with anything. I didn't fare any better by asking Dad. I never went back. She was quite a few years younger than your grandfather and I assumed she ended up with everything when he died. We didn't even know he was in a home until a couple of years after he'd been admitted. She must've missed her opportunity to get him to change his will though, because, thank God, the castle was still bequeathed to you."

"I was hoping to find his second wife and learn some more."

"I wouldn't. She'd probably end up putting a curse on you."

Kelly chuckled. "Okay, so I won't rush to look for her."

"Definitely no rush required."

His phone rang again and he hoisted himself up and walked away from the rowdiness of the pool. Kelly thought of her grandfather and the reasons he might've married someone so horrible. Maybe after his first perfect marriage nothing would ever be able to match it, so he'd settled for the first woman that came along? Maybe she'd presented herself at the right opportunity or she was simply an alternative to loneliness. Who knew? Except it was hard to dismiss how perfectly her grandparents had operated the property. Kelly's dream was still there. It would always be there, but if she shared it with the new owners, who knew what could happen.

Images of Patrick filtered through her mind. He'd championed her ideas, added his own and was forever positive about it. Lack of money had never entered their discussions. So easily, he'd managed to build up a storm of excitement and hope from nothing.

She smiled wryly when her mind travelled back to the days when they'd first met. He'd gone from irritating her to being able to ignite so much feeling with a single touch. Those feelings were still there, but she suppressed them, hid them for now. She didn't have the headspace and didn't think that would change any time soon.

Her biggest concern was having to say goodbye to Patrick. She may have been pushing him away and ignoring him for three weeks, but in the early hours of the morning, there was no escaping how her heart fuelled all her feelings and overrode her sensible head. Only in the darkened room, with her adorable baby in the cot beside her, did she quietly shed tears and bemoan the absence of Patrick beside her.

She hoped he could find it in himself to move on to a new and exciting life too.

Chapter 19

Kelly tore up the stairs to the top right-hand tower, swung the heavy door open and stared at ... nothing. No camping mattress. No clothes or towel hanging over the back of the chair that Patrick had moved up to the room.

Shit. Shit. Shit.

She'd registered the afternoon before that the Camira wasn't parked in its usual spot but hadn't questioned its absence. Patrick could have been anywhere. He could have been in Innisfail collecting hardware supplies or food. But she'd been in a hurry to have dinner with another single mother whose daughter was the same age as Gemma and hadn't given it another thought. Only when she'd returned to the castle this morning, alarm bells had started to ring, and now that it was afternoon and he still hadn't come back, she knew he no longer would.

She took tentative steps inside the room, but her stride faltered. The only piece of furniture was the lonesome stray chair.

The realisation that Patrick was gone hit home and speared her chest.

"Oh, my God," she moaned, "what have I done?"

Her legs buckled and she landed in a heap. For the first time since Gemma's arrival, she saw everything through his eyes—her detachment, her lack of interest, her distance, her abandonment of him. Just like his father had treated him.

She rapped her knuckles against her forehead and dropped her head to her knees. A part of her was no longer in the building. Gone. Vacated the premises. Hitched a ride with Yanko. Her Yanko. Her everything when she'd needed someone. Her rock.

She wrapped her arms around her chest. Bitterness threatened to erupt from her throat as she rocked to and fro. How had she missed all the signs?

"Hey, Kelly, want to go for a celebratory Moona Creek burger?" That was two days ago, after Mr Blundell had explained the possibility of a coming sale.

"Hey, Kelly, want to go for a swim at the falls?" Again, she'd refused the offer, claiming to be busy.

"Hey, Kelly, want me to cook dinner tonight?" No deal again. Her mother had already been cooking. She'd invited him to Innisfail, but he'd declined and declared an early night was in order.

Oh, you stupid, stupid girl. He was doing everything possible to say goodbye to you and you fobbed him off at every turn. No wonder he went quietly.

Oh, Patrick, come back. I'll do it right this time.

Tears burst past their barriers and she continued rocking. Faith in her ability to ever get anything right hit rock bottom. She missed him already. His support, his dependability, his friendship, his presence. Only now that he was gone could she appreciate what a wonderful gift he was. A friend like Patrick was a rare treasure and she'd tossed him aside.

She couldn't tell how long she sat with tears flowing down her cheeks as she relived every memory they shared. Only when she couldn't feel her legs anymore did she make an attempt to stretch them and wipe her face. Within seconds, pins and needles assailed her. She stretched along the cold concrete floor and waited for the pain to subside. The pain deep inside wasn't going anywhere.

When she raised her head, day was turning into dusk and she needed to get moving. She'd come back to the castle to organise some paperwork, a task not easily done with a toddler close by, and Mr Blundell would still be expecting it from her tomorrow.

She rose and walked to the window. Patrick's view was of the rainforested mountains and the meticulous lawns. The slowly setting sun was still partially visible through the treetops.

How did a person handle emotional setback after emotional setback? Was she always destined to take three steps forward only to be knocked back at every attempt?

She turned away from the pristine yet wild view and knew she'd never be able to look at a rainforest again without seeing Patrick. It was probably better that the property was selling faster than she'd hoped. She could move on without the constant reminder of failing yet again.

She swung the door closed a little harder than necessary. The reverberating vibrations resounded off the cement walls. Slowly descending the stairs, she touched the wall affectionately. Its coolness sent a shiver up her arm. She'd become so attached to the castle that her hazy future living arrangements rattled her. There was so much history here, so much to learn and so much she could give back.

She let her hand trail along the wall as the steps led her down. In the place where the two staircases met, she could've sworn she heard the echo of nattered conversation. A whispering breeze travelled up her arm and the hairs on the back of her neck rose. She came to an abrupt stop near the bottom of the stairs. Hell, she could live here even if it was full of ghosts. If they weren't friendly ones, she would shoo them away.

She chuckled, surprising herself. What would Patrick make of her idiotic thoughts? Remembering that there was no Patrick to bounce them off, she rested her hand over her heart, staring but not seeing.

Oh, Patrick, if only dreams did come true.

⁂

"Mummy, birdie wid Padwick."

Kelly smiled at Gemma. The cute way she spoke always touched a special spot within, but it surprised her that with Patrick having been gone for nearly two weeks and Gemma not having much to do with him, she still mentioned his name at least once a day. The daily visit to the birds' nest was the only thing Patrick had done with Gemma and in her toddler brain she always associated it with him.

"Mummy will take you. Do you want to go now?"

Gemma frowned, probably the first one she'd directed at Kelly.

Kelly crouched down. "What's wrong, honey?"

"Padwick here." She pointed to her shoulders and it clicked for Kelly.

She took Gemma's cute, chubby fingers in her own and kissed them. "Mummy is strong. I'll lift you up. Is that a good idea?"

Gemma showed Kelly the signs of a smile.

With relief, Kelly tugged her hand and they walked towards the edge of the forest. Gemma, happy again, prattled about all things important to an eighteen-month-old. It reminded Kelly again of how perfect it would be to raise her daughter here at the castle. She'd had further chats with her father and shared her grandmother's diaries. The stories flowed endlessly from her father, which only added to the happy and content images in Kelly's head of castle life in the sixties.

Still, the constant pull in her chest remained. If only she could keep the property and work her fingers to the bone. Her parents had money but nowhere near enough. They'd offered to help her renovate the castle if it didn't sell soon, but Kelly had refused their generous offer. They'd worked hard for their money over the years and it was time for them to enjoy it. Without a large injection of money, though, the castle would always be a sinking pit when it came to the amount needed to maintain it.

Reaching the edge of the forest, Kelly noticed with dismay that the birds had flown the coop. *Drat. Now how do I explain?*

"Mummy, up. Up, peese."

Reluctantly, she hoisted Gemma on her hips and stepped closer. *I better make this good.* "Look, Gemma, the birdies have gone away."

"Away?" She sucked on her thumb, not comprehending at all. "Where, Mummy?"

"They flew up into the sky." Kelly looked up and so did Gemma.

"Can't see, Mummy."

"That's because they have to practise how to fly lots and lots. Just like swimming. You have to practice lots and lots." Kelly reached in and placed a kiss on her button nose, hoping the explanation was enough. "How would you like something to eat? Are you hungry?"

Gemma nodded eagerly and Kelly turned for the castle before Gemma could ask more questions about the birds or mentioned Patrick again. That always hurt.

As she neared the kitchen door, she spotted Mr Blundell's car. Maybe he had news on the possible sale. She hadn't heard anything further since his last visit and a small part of her rejoiced that she could still call the castle home ... for now.

Gemma squirmed in her arms and Kelly let her toddle on her chubby legs to the kitchen door. She heard conversation inside and guessed her mother had put on a pot of tea. She let Gemma inside and followed after her.

"Nanna, Poppy, birdie gone. Birdie gone, fly in sky."

Kelly smiled at her daughter's exuberance. Thank God children had short term memories at this age. Reflecting on that thought, she realised she was quickly learning how to be a mother.

In the kitchen Mr Blundell stirred sugar in his tea.

Kelly smiled and said hello. "Have you come to give us good news?"

He took a sip first before placing the cup down. "Yes and no."

"Oh."

Her father made room for her. "We were just waiting for you to come in before John explained it all."

Kelly sat and accepted a cup of tea from her mum. "That sounds ominous. The place is either sold or it's not."

"Well …" Mr Blundell coughed to clear his throat. "It *is* sold but it's not."

She chuckled. "I don't think it's possible to be both."

"I'm confused," William added.

"Think again because you *will* have it both ways." Mr Blundell appeared to be enjoying himself and chuckled when he added, "Strap yourselves in. This is going to be one helluva ride and you don't want to miss it."

Kelly turned to her father. He clearly had no idea what Mr Blundell was going on about either. She shrugged and turned to her mother. With Gemma bouncing on her lap, she raised a hand to acknowledge she couldn't give an explanation either.

Kelly turned to Mr Blundell. "Is the property sold?"

"Yes," he replied unblinking.

"Does it have a new owner?"

"Sort of."

"Sort of? Well, can you tell us who the owner is?"

"Yes."

Kelly stalled for a fraction of a second, frustrated. "So, who is it?"

"It's you."

What?

Chapter 20

"It's who?" Kelly twisted in her chair to check if someone stood behind her, but when she saw that no one lurked around the corner, she turned back.

Mr Blundell lifted his briefcase onto his lap. "Confused?" he asked as he shuffled papers.

"Damn straight, we are," William spluttered. "What the heck's going on?"

Mr Blundell removed official paperwork and placed it on the table. "Here's a copy of the contract. The sale price was one point nine million and—"

"What?" Kelly stumbled to her feet. "That's nearly double what we asked for."

William snatched up the top few pages and quickly scanned them. "Do you recognise the company name, *Boston Breakaway Pty Ltd*?" he asked her.

Kelly shook her head. The name meant nothing to her.

"Well, the monies have come from that company with strict instructions that the property remain in your name, Kelly." He looked up from reading and eyed Mr Blundell. "John, are you going to tell us what's going on?"

Kelly had never heard her father address Mr Blundell by his first name before today. Perhaps that was the reason Mr Blundell couldn't wipe the smile from his face, but Kelly doubted it.

"It will be my pleasure. Are you all ready?"

When they nodded in unison, he continued. "It goes like this. A Mr Patrick Van Der Meeliko called into my office nearly three weeks ago and instigated the transaction. He said to give Kelly this letter when I told you the news."

He forced the envelope between Kelly's fingers, but she'd frozen.

Patrick? Her Patrick?

Once-dreadlocked-and-barely-able-to-afford-shoes, Patrick? The same Patrick who drove an orange car so dented it was embarrassing to be seen in it? Patrick? Her Yanko?

Her brain couldn't syphon the news. Not yet.

"Patrick was also the one who arranged for the washing machine and communications tower. And any day now I should have those old film reels back. He organised to have them transferred to new media."

Kelly looked up. "But I thought it was Mum and Dad who did those things." As for the film reels, she hadn't noticed their absence from the shed.

"Not us, honey," her mother said between feeding Gemma cake. "We would've if we'd known what you needed, but we had no idea what state this place was in."

"That tower's going to come in mighty handy," Mr Blundell added. "Get online and type in Patrick's surname and Boston. None of us had any idea who he really was."

"What do you mean?" William asked.

"He's a member of one of Boston's wealthiest families. Payment for this property was probably made with loose change."

"But Kelly hasn't signed anything," her father stated.

"Patrick assured me she would once she read his letter." Mr Blundell confirmed.

Kelly stumbled out of the kitchen, clutching the envelope Patrick had left her, and made her way to the steps that led to the falls.

Her hands trembled as she tried to absorb everything Mr Blundell had said. There must be a mistake. He wasn't talking about her Patrick. No bloody way, not possible. She tore at the envelope without understanding why she was angry. He'd never told her his surname, but it wouldn't have made any difference. She'd had no reason to cyberstalk him. One look at Patrick and no one would consider doing so.

She dropped down onto the top step. The warm sun burned her skin, droplets of perspiration forming quickly. There were a couple of pages in the envelope and she gasped when they fell on her lap. The top page showed a sketch of all the dream planning they'd done. He hadn't missed a thing when he'd duplicated the original sketch he'd done the day they were forced to stay indoors because of the heavy rain.

The second page slipped away from the first and she pulled it out.

Dear Kelly,

Now your dreams can come true.

You will always be the best of my memories.

Love Yanko (The best nickname ever)

She chuckled at the last line just as a sob burst from her chest. Her vision became increasingly blurry. She couldn't believe she hadn't said goodbye to him properly. Hadn't said goodbye *at all*.

She managed to put the pages, badly creased, back inside the envelope and tucked it underneath her shirt before giving her tears free rein. She allowed them to fall off her chin and onto her lap. She let them drip onto the concrete where the hot midday sun sucked them up faster than she could produce them. She let it all out.

Oh, Yanko, come back. I need you.

As hot tears rushed down her face, she half chuckled again. *The best nickname ever.* Only Patrick would see it that way. Her crying got louder.

With her head hanging and her shoulders shaking she knew she couldn't accept his money. Not now, not ever, and Mr Blundell needed to know it. She had to refuse the offer immediately, before the paperwork was completed.

With haste, she got to her feet. Clutching the letter, she wiped her face as best she could and quickly returned to the kitchen. Mr Blundell had risen and was preparing to leave when she hurried inside.

"I can't accept the offer, Mr Blundell," she blurted, trying to shield her face from Gemma because she knew she looked a mess.

Her mother came to her side, wrapped an arm around her shoulder and gave it a hard squeeze.

Mr Blundell's infernal smile still wouldn't leave his face. "Patrick knew you'd argue. The money is already in your bank account, the documents are all prepared for stamping by the duties office, and except for your signature, the transaction is complete. He gave explicit instructions that I wasn't to tell you the news until everything was officially done. His parting comment was 'tell her to get on with the job'."

⁕

Patrick took a couple of weeks to make his way to Samdarra. He stopped first in Townsville, where he returned the dented orange Camira to Adam and told him to sell it and keep the proceeds. Then he hitched his way, in a roundabout fashion, to Winton and finally Samdarra. He'd spoken to Mr Blundell this morning and knew Kelly had heard the news by now. How he wished he could've seen her reaction. What would it have been? Tears? Relief? Refusal? Had she shed tears over him? Had anyone ever shed tears over him?

He shrugged as he made his way to the clinic. Now he was just feeling sorry for himself. He'd shed a few tears himself over the past few weeks and had almost turned back a couple of times, too, when it had hurt the most.

Usually when he was alone, in his swag, unable to fall asleep. With an image of Kelly always there when he shut his eyes.

He smiled fleetingly and played with the word 'swag'. He liked the Aussie language. It was so bloody casual and the words easily rolled off his tongue. He loved a lot about Australia, but could he stay without the one thing he really wanted?

Stop it. Thinking that way wouldn't help anyone.

He spotted Janice waving from her donga. She signalled that he should make his way to the demountable building and not the clinic, so he changed his direction.

Unexpectedly, she wrapped her arms around his waist and gave him a huge hug. When she stepped back, she put her hands on her hips and took a good look at him.

"Oh my God, Patrick, you look good enough to eat."

He chuckled. The out-of-the-blue compliment was the last thing he expected. "Good to see you too, Janice."

"Come inside." She opened the door and waved him through. "Officially, I'm on leave for the wedding. I closed the clinic yesterday for a couple of weeks."

Of course, she was getting married next weekend. He envied the happiness radiating from her.

"Tell me all. Kelly mentioned a few things but, as usual, not enough. What would you like to drink, by the way? Hot drink, cold drink, an anything-in-between drink?"

He laughed, trying to keep up as she rattled off options. "A cold Milo would be great if you have it."

"Sure do. Look at you, one hundred percent Aussie already. You'll have to start importing Milo when you go back to the States."

A reminder of his future sobered him up quick smart. He flopped down onto a beanbag and, letting his head fall back, closed his eyes for a moment. He didn't doubt Janice was taking another good, long therapist's look at him. He opened his eyes when he heard her sit on the beanbag beside his.

She placed his drink on the small coffee table that sat between them and continued to assess him.

"How did you and Kelly get on?"

He smiled wryly and reached for the drink. "Fabulously." He used a spoon to scoop out the lumps of Milo in the milk and added, "She's everything I knew she'd be. Thanks for sending me there."

"What's the property like?"

He didn't know how to answer that question.

It's a castle. A bit ramshackle but magical.

It was impossible to express in a few words how the place had affected him. The setting, the forest, the turrets had all cast a spell over him. So he kept it simple.

"It required a lot of work to get the yard in order. We worked full-time for weeks. Kelly's managed to sell it, which I'm sure she'll tell you about when she comes to the wedding."

"And you and Kelly?"

Jeez, she wasn't holding back on the questions. Where did he begin to describe his and Kelly's fairytale time together? Again, he didn't know how to answer, so he kept it simple.

"We were doing great until her parents turned up with her baby girl, Gemma."

"What!" Janice sprang up from the beanbag. "Are you serious? Holy shoot! Oh my God, how did Kelly take it? What's Gemma like? Is she good with Kelly?"

"Whoa! Sit down. Please." He waved her down, trying to instil some calm.

Janice, clearly recognising her own reactions a moment too late, grimaced. "Bloody Kelly! I certainly wasn't expecting *that* news. I'm going to strangle her when I see her. Trust her to keep it from me." She raked a hand through her short blond hair and huffed. "You know what? I sensed something wasn't quite right. I don't mean I thought she was in trouble or anything like that, just that she wasn't telling me everything. Christ, I only spoke to her a couple of days ago. She didn't say one damn thing about you leaving, and she sure as hell didn't say anything about a baby." She stopped abruptly and shook her index finger in the air. "The only news she mentioned was that her parents had arrived and everything was fine between them."

Patrick smiled sadly. "Gemma's an amazing kid. Kelly's devoted to her and is such a great mum. She was overwhelmed to start with, but her parents are helping her adjust. With so much support she didn't need me anymore."

Janice's shoulders wilted. "Oh, Patrick, I'm sorry. I know your feelings for her are real." She pushed her beanbag closer, dropped onto it and squeezed his shoulder. "I wish things had turned out differently for you."

He shrugged. "She has to make up for a lot of lost time. I don't want to be the one holding her back."

He finished his drink, letting Janice contemplate all he'd told her. When it was time to leave, he said, "I'm staying a week, then I'll pack up my room. I should've done it before I left for Moona Creek, but I didn't expect to be away so long."

"Are you sure? There's no hurry to go. I love having you around the homestead and I know I'm not the only one who feels that way. What will you do?"

"I'll head down to Brisbane and spend a couple of weeks with my sisters and then return to the States." He tried to inject some enthusiasm into his voice when he added, "Boston is waiting for me. There's plenty of work I can do."

Except he didn't want the work that waited for him in Boston. Indoors all day, dressed in a suit. It wouldn't last, but he'd give it a go for a while. Get it out of his system and his father's. At least he understood the kind of work he wanted to do now. He'd find his way one day.

"I could use your help this week," Janice told him, "but I'm leaving in three hours. How fast can you pack?"

He raised an eyebrow. "What did you have in mind?"

"I was relying on my brother until he was silly enough to break his arm. We have to set up nearly fifty tents."

"Fifty? Where did you get them all from?"

"The army. They have a training base the other side of Winton where they hold annual camps. I was able to hire them for the wedding guests."

Patrick knew the wedding was being held on Janice's family property, about a two-hour drive from Samdarra, north of Winton.

"I'd like you to come to the wedding, too."

"But—"

His face fell. Kelly would be there. Could he handle leaving her for a second time? What if Gemma came with her? Would she ask him to show her the birdies? He smiled. Something always caught in his throat whenever he pictured her tiny face looking up at him adoringly.

"I know Kelly will be there." Obviously, Janice could read minds. "But don't worry about her. By the time I'm finished talking to her, she may as well be dead."

He laughed out loud. What the heck. He felt bad about walking away. This could be his chance to say goodbye. One last kiss. One last hug. The muscles around his heart constricted. One last opportunity to look into a pair of willow-green eyes belonging to a person who knew him better than he knew himself.

"So, what do you say?"

Snapping out of his trance, he looked across at Janice. "Do I have to wear a tux?"

She laughed. "Not out here, mate. I'll be hard-pressed getting the groom to wear one."

He chuckled. "Okay, then. Deal."

Chapter 21

Patrick didn't need three hours to pack up his meagre belongings and find his best pair of jeans for the wedding. He opened the door to his donga and scouted around for his backpack, knowing he needed to clean out receipts, bits of paper, his sketchpad and pencils, a mobile phone that hadn't been charged since he'd left Moona Creek, and rocks. Yes, rocks. They'd rattled often enough on his return trip to Samdarra, always taking him back to that first walk from the Moona Creek Roadhouse to the castle. The day he'd had no idea what would happen.

He pulled the backpack from under the bed where he'd flung it the day before and spoke aloud. "That's right, no bloody idea at all."

He unzipped every zipper and tipped it upside down. It was easier that way.

After he put aside his phone and charger, sketchpad and pencils, all that was left in the pile were scrunched up bits of paper and food wrappers, which he tossed in the bin, and the rocks. He gathered them in his shirt and took them outside.

At the house pets' water trough, he filled an old metal saucepan, placed the rocks in it and began washing off the pungent rainforest dirt still clinging to them. He'd take a quick look at them and decide whether they were worth keeping.

The water muddied quickly. He emptied it onto a nearby shrub and scooped another saucepan full of water. His gaze was drawn to a green rock. Reaching in, he took hold of it and turned it over in his palm.

Letting out a hiss, he dropped the saucepan, and water and the remaining rocks spilled over his boots. He peered closely at the rock still in his hand.

"Holy shoot!"

Grabbing the saucepan, he scooped more water and scrubbed at the heart-shaped rock. He had to verify whether it was what he thought it was, and until he did, he didn't want to get his hopes up.

Satisfied it was clean enough, he dried it on the lower half of his shirt, then held it up and turned it, squinting as he inspected it from every angle. His hand began to shake when he saw that the inscription, 'All my love, P', was still clearly etched on it.

His chest filled with wonder. Of all the rocks he might've collected that day, this unimaginable find was one of them.

He had no idea how long he stood in the midmorning blaze, the sun's rays biting into his skin. The jade stone shone on his palm and he was only vaguely aware of the dry wind swirling around him. It whipped up brown leaves and dirt, causing dust to fill his nostrils. He sneezed, but his brain was on freeze-frame.

Holy flipping heck, he had the pendant Kelly's grandfather had once gifted to his wife. *Oh my God*. He had the real thing in his hand, had unsuspectingly picked it up thinking it was a rock. He vaguely remembered a cloth or leather-type material around it but had dismissed it at the time leaving it behind. Maybe it had been wrapped around it for protection. How was he to know?

Now what?

The tension in his shoulders eased. There was nothing to debate. The pendant belonged to Kelly and he'd get it back to her. It'd be his parting gift; he owed it to her. She could put it on display when the castle opened to the public.

His fingers tightened around it. He couldn't believe it. He wanted to whoop and dance and maybe skip. *Shit.* Had he ever skipped?

He continued turning the pendant over and over in his hand, thinking about everything that'd happened since he'd arrived in Australia. If a clairvoyant had told his fortune a year ago, he would've laughed at any suggestions she made. In fact, he would've demanded his money back and told her to get a real job, because he never would have believed that Ella's reappearance in Boston would set in motion so many tumultuous changes in his life. Not that his drug-addled brain would have allowed him to think much about it at the time.

He gazed around the homestead and the vastness of the isolated property. His conflicting feelings jarred with each other. Moona Creek, a world away, had a lot of magical qualities, but there was something about the Australian outback that he'd really missed. While he didn't have the headspace right now to think about how it would feel to leave Samdarra, he considered that one day he might return to Australia and buy his own outback property. Ella had once made the suggestion and he was beginning to think it wasn't such a far-fetched idea after all. Except … what about Moona Creek? With his boots squelching in the muddied dust around his feet, he was hard-pressed to decide which climate he'd choose over the other.

"Good morning, Patrick."

He turned to find the mistress of the homestead eyeing him with concern, her voice breaking the spell he was under.

"Linda, hello."

"Is everything okay?" While not a trained psychologist, she was always one to ask questions with good intentions.

He squeezed the jade pendant and smiled. Really smiled. He was more than okay and grateful to have one last surprise to bestow on Kelly.

"Despite the fact I'll soon be leaving your lovely hospitality behind, yes, I am more than okay."

Relief took over her features.

"This isn't the last you'll see of me," he said. "I promise I'll be back again one day."

"We're happy to have you back any time. When are you leaving?"

"This afternoon with Janice. I'm going to give her a hand with the wedding preparations."

"Well, come and have one last cuppa. Hubby's due back any minute and the kids would love the chance to say goodbye. They adore you. You're so good with them."

She beckoned and he followed gladly. His discovery had laid a thick coat of disbelief over everything and a cup of tea was a great way to celebrate.

On the gravel path to the homestead, Linda threw back over her shoulder, "You'd make a good father one day."

He looked up, but she'd already turned for the homestead.

A father?

He did have good rapport with kids. Even the short stint with Gemma was enough for her to worm her way into his heart. As for having his own ... hell, that sounded like something he'd leave for the very distant future. The idea of having a family was so disconnected to the memory of the life he was returning to that it wasn't worth thinking about.

It was time to change the subject. "What's hot out of the oven?"

Linda laughed. Her cooking was legendary and this wouldn't be the first time he'd scoffed her scones and cakes.

He tucked the jade pendant into his jeans pocket. So much hinged on it. Its importance, to Kelly and the castle life she was going to recreate, was crucial in his mind.

Linda held the door open for him, but he stopped short.

All my love, P. P for Paden. His eyes widened at the realisation that only struck him that very second. P for Patrick. Could history be repeating itself? But ... he was returning to Boston.

He wanted to yell 'shut the fuck up' at the side of his brain that always questioned everything. He took a moment to channel good vibes before he ruined the day.

Stop it, dude, he told himself. The initial on the inscription was pure coincidence and a lot of bad luck on his part.

"Come in, Patrick, don't be shy."

Linda's words jerked him back to reality. He'd have to be careful otherwise she would order another round of psychological help for him.

"Sorry, I just want to wipe my boots clean," he said, grappling for any excuse to hide his delay at the door.

His mother had often spoken of fate and colour, the reasons why life took you in a certain direction and the people you met on the way, but it had all sounded like hogwash at the time. As he wiped his boots on the rough doormat, he glanced up at the ceiling just in case she was watching him from wherever she was and he might see her before she disappeared again.

He shook his head and chuckled. *Idiot.* Nothing like overthinking things to work up an appetite. If he didn't get inside and make a chocolate cake vanish soon, he'd instigate another round of sessions with Janice himself.

With mostly clean boots, and a definite bounce in his steps, he made his way into the homestead's large and friendly kitchen.

"Patrick! Patrick!"

Excited voices travelled from down the hallway before two young children barrelled into his legs. He pushed the pendant to the back of his mind for now and concentrated on mock fighting the two terrors who could never get enough rough and tumble play whenever Patrick had a few minutes to spare.

Chapter 22

Patrick threw his two bags in the back of Janice's utility and his backpack on the front passenger seat. "Do you need me to load anything for you?"

"Actually, yes. There are a few boxes and things in my donga. They're stacked near the door. Thanks, Patrick."

"No worries." Patrick was about to turn when he asked, "Is anything breakable?"

"Nah," she said, heading in the opposite direction. "I just need to get a couple of things from the clinic. Won't be a sec."

He nodded, made his way to her donga and took stock of the small pile of boxes. He picked up the top two. On his third trip to the utility, he spotted Janice returning with a visitor. The afternoon sun was slanting across the paddock, casting them in shadow, but a sudden unease gripped him. He knew that silhouette.

I don't need his shit today.

The last time he'd dealt with his father, Kelly had been there to pick up the pieces and put him back together.

He swallowed nervously, with his feet frozen to the ground. It didn't take long for Janice and his father to emerge into the sunlight and for them to appear whole and human right in front of him.

"Look who I found at the homestead asking for you."

"Patrick." Thomas greeted with a nod.

"Did you get everything?" Janice asked.

Her words galvanised Patrick. He nodded and forced his feet to make the few necessary steps to the back of the utility, where he neatly stacked the last of the boxes.

"Why don't you take your dad out of the sun? Make yourselves a cup of tea in my donga, the kettle is on the bench. I'm going to say a quick goodbye to Linda and will be back in half an hour."

Janice gave him a meaningful look before she left and Patrick read everything she wasn't saying. She knew the whole story and understood this wouldn't be easy for him. It was probably an act of kindness on her part that his father was even allowed thirty minutes because he swore her sort-of-friendly smile was really a scowl in disguise. He also didn't doubt she'd be back with half a minute to spare.

He led his father inside, went straight for the kettle and found a couple of mugs. Thomas drank coffee, so he didn't bother asking what he wanted, and he made himself another shot of Milo.

His father pulled up a chair and sat down. "I wasn't sure if I'd find you here. I tried calling your phone."

Patrick shrugged.

"Janice tells me you're leaving this afternoon."

Patrick turned with the full mugs and took the only other chair in the confined room. "Yeah. I'll make my way to Brisbane before I head back to Boston."

"Oh. What happened to the girl?"

His gaze flicked to his father's. "Nothing. Why?"

Thomas gave a noncommittal shrug. "I liked her."

Again, Patrick couldn't help thinking this man wasn't his father. Thomas rarely took any interest in his friends, male or female, and had never approved of them when he *had* taken a fleeting interest.

They eyed each other warily until Patrick gave in. "What do you want? Why now after all these years?"

Thomas held his gaze for a few moments. His voice came out scratchy. "I wanted to share your mother's birthday with someone."

Patrick's hand jerked, causing some Milo to spill from the mug.

Mum's birthday? Shit, the date had completely bypassed him. Did he even know what day of the week it was?

He mopped up the mess on the table with his sleeve before winding his fingers around the mug again.

"I did love her, Patrick, despite the bad days I'm sure you remember better than the others."

Patrick froze, his mind incapable of taking in his father's words with any great speed. Then something snapped inside of him and the mug clattered on the tabletop when it slipped from his fingers. Did his father really expect him to believe this bullshit?

He scraped his chair back as a sudden rage gurgled dangerously below the surface. It was getting the better of him. He didn't usually succumb to bouts of anger, but this time it forced its way out and burst angrily into the open.

"What the hell do I care about how much you loved her? It's too late now. It's not like you can bring her back." He savagely raked his hand through his hair and rose on unsteady legs. His noisy and laboured breathing filled his head.

Thomas shuffled in his chair. "I feel responsible for her death. It's taken me a long time to reconcile with it, but it's something that will never leave me."

"*You? Responsible?*" Patrick screeched.

He couldn't believe it. No way. He couldn't do this anymore. It was now or never.

His agitation caused his heart to pump faster. Lightheaded, he swayed and grabbed the back of the chair to keep himself upright. He had to say it. It was time to tell the truth. He would never talk about it again if he didn't unburden himself right now. As much as he hated this man, *he'd* been the one to force his mother's hand that day. He couldn't let anyone else take the blame. He had to be man enough to admit it or he'd never be able to live the life he wanted.

His angry words burst from his lips. "*I* killed her."

Thomas's chair scraped back and almost hit the wall behind him. "What are you talking about?"

"You don't get it do you?" Big, salty tears spilled down his face. His legs buckled and he collapsed onto the floor, cradling his face in his hands.

His father crouched beside him, but his sudden concern for Patrick's welfare couldn't override the anxiety and hurt that never left him.

"Tell me, son. Did something happen that day?"

A huge moan escaped Patrick's throat. "Yes!"

His shoulders shook and he vented big gulping sobs as tears soaked his shirt. He wanted to shove his father's arm away, but he couldn't seem to find the strength to do it.

All his life he'd waited for any sort of attention from this man, and in a screwed-up way this was what he needed. Regardless of how much of a bastard he'd been to his mother, getting the love he'd never received from him was what Patrick wanted right now. If it meant crying until he could cry no more, then so be it. So he did—and it wasn't long until the front of his shirt was soaked.

With time he managed to calm down, and Thomas continued to sit beside him. A ripple passed through his shoulders, as though the shackles of the guilt he'd held all these years finally loosened.

His words spilled easily.

"On the day she took her life, I told her I hated her. I called her weak for not being able to stand up for herself." He shook his head and tears sprayed onto his jeans. "I should've blamed and accused you. I couldn't understand why she didn't leave you. I always blamed you, but I never told her that." Wretchedly, he hung his head, then pulled his shirt out and mopped his face. "When we found her, it was too late to tell her anything."

Thomas was frozen beside him, but Patrick didn't look at him. He'd just bared everything to the man he hated most. Strangely, he felt better for it. It wouldn't bring his mother back, but somewhere, in the dark recesses of his mind, he was reconciled with that. It was as if he'd made peace with his mother and she understood he never meant what he'd said. He knew that wherever she was, she still loved him.

In the past, when he'd confessed to Janice and Kelly, he'd experienced relief and a lessening of the burden. Today, though, it was liberating.

His father rose to his feet.

Patrick didn't want to say any more on the topic. He was drained and needed to clean himself up before Janice returned. "Are you leaving the country soon?"

"Yes," Thomas whispered.

"I better wash these mugs so Janice and I can get on the road." He tidied the kitchen and ignored his father. He didn't want to see the expression his face held.

"Son."

Patrick stilled, then turned around slowly. It was hard to dismiss the misery that shadowed his father.

"I don't know what I did to deserve you, but I'm grateful. You've taught me a lot and I know your mother would be very proud."

Patrick stared at his father. Surely it wasn't him talking.

He tried to make light of the compliment, which meant more to him now than the last time his father had said it. "So I'll see you in Boston, whenever you get back."

"You don't have to work for the company. I've already told you that."

"I'll give it a go. You're right, it's not for me, but I'll find my place one day."

Thomas nodded. "Okay, I better let you go. I'll see myself out."

Patrick scrambled for words. "Hey, Dad."

Thomas stopped and turned back.

"Thanks for coming. I'll keep in touch."

A glimmer of a smile wavered at the corners of his father's mouth. For Patrick, that was smile enough, and a surge of adrenalin shot through him. Now it was time to move on.

Chapter 23

Kelly walked around the cluster of tents trying to get a stronger signal on her phone. When it didn't look like it would get any better, she punched in her mum's number but it failed to connect. She groaned and sent a message instead, hoping it might eventually get through. She'd wanted to say goodnight to Gemma before the wedding.

It wasn't her fault she was used to having excellent communication facilities now the tower had been installed. Going back to having only a measly two bars was frustrating and beneath her, and yeah, there was a touch of smugness in there somewhere.

Don't forget you still have to thank Patrick. She threw in the reminder because a quick phone call or message would've done.

She'd been angry after the shock of the property settlement had subsided. Patrick must have known he'd leave some day. Meanwhile, he'd made her plan the castle's restoration, with the 'money thing' lurking in the background the entire time. He would have chuckled plenty over the way she'd skimped over every cent. Loose change, Mr Blundell had said. But worst of all, why had he left without giving her the chance to say goodbye?

Earlier, wedding stewards had directed her to a tent and when she'd ducked into the tiny space, loneliness had struck her. Sure, she was excited about seeing Janice and everyone from Samdarra who treated her like one of their own, but she really missed Gemma. She'd almost insisted her parents come to the wedding venue instead of staying the night in

Winton. Though she was only away for one night, it didn't lessen the pain of being separated. It prompted memories of holding Gemma for first time and then giving her up. It was the same type of hurt and she hated being reminded of it.

With still an hour to go before the ceremony she entered her tent again, deciding she wasn't in the mood for socialising. She flopped onto her swag and lay on her stomach. Her hair would be a mess, but this wedding was a lot more casual than the last one she'd attended. Of course, *that* wedding brought its own memories. She remembered the magical night she and Patrick had spent on the beach at Port Douglas, and the even better times they'd shared at Moona Creek. Where was he? Was he still in the country? She couldn't bring herself to phone or send a message. And the few times she'd clicked onto his Facebook page she hadn't been game enough to request a friendship. Having learned who he really was, she assumed he was embarrassed about their friendship, that leaving quietly was how the wealthy did it.

Make the break clean and quick.

Still, she carried Melita's number in her contacts. Maybe one day she would ask her of his whereabouts. For now, loneliness attached itself to her heart and she allowed herself to wallow. It wasn't like she'd change anything. Now that Gemma was back in her life, nothing else mattered. Except losing Patrick meant a small part of her heart would be forever broken. And all the what-ifs in the world would never repair it.

❦

She smiled and oohed and aahed like everyone else when the bride and groom kissed for the first time as husband and wife. The couple glowed with radiance in the garden of the family's homestead. Janice's mother would've prepared for months to have the lawn looking as green and the flowers as colourful as they did. The recent rains had no doubt made the job a lot easier to accomplish.

The afternoon was starting to slip away. Kelly rose and made her way over to congratulate the couple. She wore low-heeled shoes and a knee-length hyacinth dress that clung to her curves. Her bare legs appreciated the afternoon breeze that had drifted in to suppress the midday heat. Thankfully it had lingered for the entire ceremony.

She glanced at the guests she passed. About two hundred people had sat on the plastic chairs surrounding the flower-covered arch. Others had risen too, now that the official ceremony was over. They stretched their legs, greeted neighbours and friends, and made their way to the drinks and nibbles table. A crowd this size wasn't unusual—any social occasion in the outback was always well attended.

As Kelly neared the bridal couple, Janice spotted her and met her halfway.

Kelly kissed her cheek. "Congratulations, girl! You look sensational."

Clearly not too worried about her dress, Janice gave her a big hug. "Thanks for coming, Kel. I can't wait to catch up with you, but it'll have to wait until breakfast. Make sure you're still here. I have a bone to pick with you."

"About what?"

Before Janice had a chance to explain, other guests closed ranks around her. She gave an apologetic little wave and blew Kelly a kiss before being tugged over to the photographer.

What the hell did she mean by that? Kelly hoped to be on her way back to Winton before breakfast. Now she'd never be able to sneak away without Janice picking that bone with her.

Groaning inwardly, she turned and glanced around, hoping to spot Linda and her family. There was a long night to get through and she didn't want to be sitting alone for all of it. She was even eager to see Samdarra's two little rascals and recognised one of them darting in and around guests when a hand tapped her on the shoulder.

She spun around.

"Patrick!"

"Kelly."

His blinding good looks took her breath away. She couldn't help but gape. His long-sleeved white shirt had the top button undone and showed the hollow of his throat. No tie for Patrick in the outback. How he'd be relishing the casual air of this wedding in his jeans and cleaned-up riding boots.

Somehow, she found her hand in his. Her heart thumped inside her chest as her gaze gradually connected with his. She delved into the incredible blue of his eyes and became hopelessly trapped. There was so much to read in them, to take in, regret and apologise for. Her tongue refused to work. Where had her anger gone?

"Where is that beautiful little girl of yours?" he asked quietly.

The tension in her shoulders gave way and a sob sounded from her lips. *Oh, Patrick, you never once blamed my little girl for what happened to us.*

Now Patrick held both her hands, which was probably for the best. Her legs didn't feel secure enough to hold her up, and her hands squeezed his, as if proving she needed his support.

"She's with Mum and Dad in Winton. I miss her so much."

"Oh, Kel. It's okay to miss her." He leaned in and gently kissed her cheek, then whispered in her ear. "I've missed you, too."

She blinked rapidly, needing to hold her emotions in. Having Gemma in her life was still too new. She couldn't have it both ways. Didn't think there was enough of her to go around.

But she couldn't say it back, couldn't tell him she'd missed him. She didn't want to give him hope when there was none. "You didn't let me say goodbye."

He drew her closer. "It was for the best."

He was right. Make the break clean and swift. She couldn't promise him anything anyway.

She rested her cheek against his and a hint of stubble rubbed against her skin. "I wondered whether you were still in the country. I never expected to see you here."

He drew circles over her hand with his thumb; her pulse came alive under his touch. "I'll spend a week or so in Brisbane and then head back to Boston."

She pulled back and looked at him. "To work for the family business?"

He nodded.

"But you'll hate it."

"I will, but not as much as being here without you."

"Oh, Patrick. I'm so sorry."

She dropped her gaze, but he reached out and cradled her jaw. She turned into his palm and he gently angled her face until she had no choice but to connect again and look at him.

"Don't be. Things happen. Circumstances change. You never saw it coming, did you?"

She bit her bottom lip and shook her head. The tears in her eyes were dangerously close to spilling over. "She's so amazing. I still can't believe how lucky I am."

He brought her closer still, his arms tightening around her back. "I would've done the same thing."

When he pressed his mouth to her forehead, she inhaled everything about him, wanting never to forget. Closing her eyes, she vowed to remember this moment forever.

The band started up and wedding guests laughed and chatted as they mingled. The aroma of cooked meat, doing its final turns on the spit roast, filled the air as caterers geared up to feed the crowd. The sky was slowly turning a dusky lavender as the bright orange orb of the sun started its descent behind the mountain range. For once the dry and dusty outback had a touch of moisture in it after the recent rains.

Patrick rested his hands on either side of her neck and gently rubbed. "Do you have time to talk later? I'm sorry I didn't say goodbye and I'd like the chance to do so." He quirked an eyebrow and added, "There might also be a thing or two you want to discuss with me?"

She groaned and chuckled at the same time. "Yanko, you're damn straight there are a few things to discuss."

His face exploded into a smile, making her heart beat double-time, and his laughter surrounded her like a favourite blanket. "Phew, I didn't think I'd ever hear my nickname again. No one in Boston will have a clue about it."

Caught in the sun's rays slanting across the lawn, his expression sparkled. Verging on sun-bronzed, he looked healthy and masculine. If she were living another life, he was everything she wanted. Tonight, she had one last chance to show her appreciation for all he'd done for her. One final gift she could give in return for him changing her life around.

Lightheartedly, she asked, "Can I kiss you later?"

His expression changed. He stared at her hard and the dynamics between them transformed in an instant. Her body understood and was doing its own thing. Moisture built and pooled; a throb quickly spread.

His gaze never left hers. "I think I can manage that."

She nodded, before he closed his eyes and sought her mouth. The kiss reminded her of rain-soaked kisses, a diamond waterfall and a fairytale castle.

Yep, her heart might be damaged for good after tonight.

Chapter 24

The band played from a makeshift stage a metre high. Pale, ghostly eucalypts surrounded the dancing space. Branches overhead swayed with the circulating breeze while dry leaves crackled underfoot. The dirt floor was packed hard with sawdust and broken up bales of hay. Nobody cared about the lack of flashing lights and smoke haze. Who needed a nightclub or a regal function room? Patrick would never forget how the breeze, now with a slight chill, whispered around the crowd. The music had changed from lively modern dance numbers to the slower songs meant for couples holding onto each other and making promises in the night.

Lighting hung from any suitable fixture, most of it directed at the bar and food tables. Though they'd managed a filling meal and a couple of drinks, Patrick had rarely let Kelly sit while the music played. She'd discarded her shoes hours ago, and he'd rolled his sleeves up even earlier. Patrick felt the electricity between them in every touch and movement.

He looked over Kelly's shoulder at the bridal couple dancing in each other's arms. They were great together, the envy of everyone. He'd met them both during his first week at Samdarra and nothing changed the good vibes they exuded every time Patrick had been in their presence.

He wanted to believe he and Kelly were good together too. Too bad life had a way of shitting all over his plans. Would his feelings change when he returned to Boston's concrete jungle? Would he look up his old mates and past girlfriends? Was he even the same person?

His sigh must've been audible over the slower music because Kelly stopped swaying and pulled back.

"You okay?" She rested her hands on his shoulders and they burned through to his skin like they had all night.

"When do the bride and groom leave?" he asked.

"They'll be the last to leave. You wait and see."

She took him in tow and led him away from the dance area. Under a tree that fringed the garden, away from most of the guests and in semi-darkness, they found a couple of plastic chairs.

Patrick gestured for her to sit on his lap and wrapped his arms around her. "Do we have to wait that long?"

When she twisted to face him, there was enough moonlight to read an invitation of sorts. "What did you have in mind?" she whispered.

"I promised you a kiss."

She smiled. "We've been doing nothing but, all night."

"I mean real kissing. With you lying in my arms. Like Four Mile Beach. Remember?"

She nodded, then dropped her forehead against his. "How could I forget?"

"Is it too early to leave the party and see them at breakfast?"

She chuckled. "Breakfast will be lunch. There'll be too many sore heads to rouse people earlier."

"Then get changed into something comfortable and come to my tent. Janice let me set it up near the river. It's a short walk but worth it."

Her warm breath brushed against his skin and her lips touched his fleetingly. He tightened his arms around her waist, but pushing up her dress she readjusted her legs to sit astride him. He took control of her mouth, committing everything to memory, and when her tongue darted inside, he groaned and his groin hardened in the confines of his jeans.

The party was a distant melody, a growing memory bank of songs that would one day jolt him back to this moment. Every so often, the rowdiness of some of the guests intruded, but he'd even store those sounds away and review them again and again when his nights became lonely and unbearable.

She pulled back. "I'm ready to go now."

His stomach folded in half, folded again and then collapsed. "Are you sure?"

She bit her bottom lip and nodded.

⟨◦⟩

Keep it together. Give her the chance to change her mind.

Changed out of their wedding finery, they left the sounds of music and partying behind and walked hand in hand down the track that led to the river nearly two hundred metres away. Patrick had been told that homesteads weren't built close to rivers in case of flooding. He'd flinched when the stockmen had joked there were no crocodiles down this way because the thought had never crossed his mind. Apparently, while the Flinders River was Queensland's longest, the saltwater crocs were found closer to its mouth, and that, thank God, was not anywhere close. Torch in hand, he mulled over the fact there was a lot to learn about this country. But learn he would. He had a feeling he would be back one day.

Taking his mind off crocodiles, he scrambled instead to think whether he carried a packet of condoms in his bag. It'd been a while since he'd gone looking for any, but he was pretty confident that if they were needed he was prepared.

He'd set up camp at the end of this very well-worn track, which led to a popular fishing spot used by the ringers and stockmen. There was also a shanty-cum-cabin near the water's edge, which he'd used as a shelter for his tent. Built on a raised concrete foundation, the open-sided cabin overlooked the river. He'd been lucky enough to witness a number of sunsets over the past week, and it had dawned on him that Mother Nature was spectacular. It made any problems and insecurities he had look trivial. His whole perspective on life was changing, and it had only taken a few inspiring sunsets for it to happen. If he'd grown up surrounded by all this natural beauty, his life might've turned out differently.

Kelly walked quietly by his side. Only their footsteps and the nocturnal animals in the thick scrub around them made any noise. He squeezed her hand to remind her he was there. No other reason.

She gave his hand a squeeze back. "After I read the letter you left with Mr Blundell and the shock wore off, I was angry with you."

Patrick stopped abruptly and turned to face her. The trees swaying in the breeze cast dark shadows across her face. He couldn't quite read her expression but was certain it was no longer anger.

"Come on, we're nearly there. Just around the next curve. Then you can dig your nails into me." He tugged on her hand and chuckled, leading her forward. "And, just for your info, I knew you would be."

"Yanko, I'm going to do more than sink my nails into you."

"I'm banking on it."

She groaned at his lame joke, but he kept the torch trained on the ground.

⁂

On the front step of the cabin, Patrick held Kelly against his chest as they sat in quiet contemplation. He moved her hair aside and set his mouth to the delicate skin of her neck.

"So, how rich are you, Yanko?"

He chuckled, briefly lifting his head. "Filthy rich."

He found he *could* laugh about it with Kelly. In Boston, he'd never allowed himself to relax about how much money he had. In his mind it was only money, and in outback Queensland it was only money, but in Boston, it was anything but 'only money'.

"Mr Blundell claims you used loose change to buy the castle."

Facing away from him, Kelly didn't see his sudden grimace. He'd liked Mr Blundell from the first day he'd arrived at Moona Creek. Compassionate and kind-hearted, he was also switched on.

"He's one smart cookie," Patrick said. "I'd say he nailed it."

"Shoot."

"What?" Patrick tightened his arms around her and let his face drop against her soft hair.

"Isn't it every girl's dream to marry a rich man? Damn it, I gave you the flick instead."

She chuckled and he joined her. It was funny. She was funny. She had a way with words and their laughter carried into the quiet night and spread across the slow-moving river.

Until her words sobered him up. "You did give me the flick."

It took her a few moments to catch his meaning, but when she did, she stilled in his arms. Then she rose and turned to face him. "I never meant to hurt you."

When she looked down at him, he could see the truth in her eyes and expression, so he didn't badger her.

"I want to give you something," she said. "I know it's the wrong thing to do and I don't want to repeat my past mistakes but—"

"I'll make sure it doesn't happen."

"I don't know how else to thank you," she whispered. "It feels like the right thing to do, but I'm being selfish because *I* want it, too."

He reached for her hands, but she resisted. Instead, she raised her shirt and took it off. He sat transfixed, memories of dancing in the rain intruding. Next came her bra, and in quick succession, her denim shorts and underwear. She reached for his hand and tugged on it, and when he rose from the step, she made quick work on the few items of clothing he wore.

He led her inside the tent, dimmed the lantern and they lay on their sides, just looking and appreciating. Until his hand trailed from her shoulder to her stomach and a dance as old as time began in the slowest of waltzes.

He moved to capture her mouth in a sensual kiss. The occasional moan from Kelly reminded him this wasn't a dream. Then she reached down to touch him and everything spiked—his body, his temperature and the sheer intensity between them. It ended in a frenzy of passion so strong it shifted the axis of the world as he knew it.

He couldn't move after they both fell against each other, the sound of her heavy breathing ringing in his ears. He tucked her against his chest and wound his arms around her. He could manage that much.

Fear, real fear, crept its way in. What if he never experienced something that good again? He held on to the moment, never wanting to let it go. He inhaled her womanly scent; it mingled with the strong eucalyptus fragrance drifting in. It didn't take her long to fall asleep, and soon, her even breathing managed to calm him.

With the breeze gently flapping the sides of the tent, he listened to the river make its way past. His eyelids slowly relaxed, but he couldn't say when he tuned out for the night because Kelly waited for him in his dreams. And, man, they were good.

Chapter 25

There was little chance of sleeping through the early morning call of a laughing kookaburra, but if she admitted it, Kelly didn't want to. Patrick's heavy arm across her waist brought her memory back to speed and she languished closer to his side with no inkling of the time. She twisted her head carefully and watched as the sun made an early show through the creamy-brown paperbarks outside the tent.

Patrick slept. She was amazed he managed it with so much noise around. The Australian bush was anything but peaceful and quiet.

She watched him in the early morning shadows and smiled—at the wonder of nature and the unexpected journey her life was taking. After the night she'd just shared with Patrick, her body pulsed. Regretfully, she didn't have one good memory of the night Gemma had been conceived. Something stirred inside her chest; she was sorry there would be no conception of a beautiful baby to forever remind her of this night.

She had no idea how two people could get it so right together. Should she change her mind and beg Patrick to stay? Indecision swirled around her head until an image of Gemma overtook it and she pushed the uncertainty away. She'd made her choice and was reluctant to change it. Gemma was too important and she *needed* to be a mother—one who could give her baby one hundred and ten percent to make up for the lost eighteen months.

You don't deserve anything else, girl.

Patrick stirred beside her and she placed her mouth over his. She might not deserve this sort of happiness, but she was greedy enough to take more. Patrick sprang to life immediately and she felt him go hard when he gathered her in his arms.

"Good morning, beautiful."

"Oh, Patrick." All of a sudden, she started tearing up. Not her style at all, but leaving this beautiful man was too much to bear.

"Shh. Just enjoy it. You're amazing."

She raised a hand in the pre-dawn light and gently traced his mouth. "How can you be so casual about it?"

His gaze bored into hers and she froze, sensing there were words he wanted to shout, things he wanted to say. Instead, he groaned and dropped his mouth to hers.

"Trust me, there's nothing casual with what I'm about to do with you."

She helped him with another condom and when he entered her, fully erect, she moaned against his chest. He was home, where he belonged. Where he was meant to be. For now. When they shattered together, ironically, the laughing Kookaburra returned.

Oh, life was hilarious, in a horrible sort of way. She wanted this and she wanted Gemma. Except one lousy Kookaburra was reminding her that having it all wasn't an option. She entwined her legs with Patrick's and rested her face in the crook of his neck.

"I'll never forget you, Kelly."

"You will, Patrick. One day you'll look back on this as an adventure. You'll meet an amazing girl, one without baggage, and you'll make an incredible husband and father."

It hurt like hell to say it. She should be begging him to stay.

In response he tightened his hold and kissed her. She could sense he wasn't game enough to say anything. She understood those moments. When you couldn't be certain of what or how you would say something, it was better to say nothing.

She closed her eyes and let him kiss her, too forlorn to move.

She must've fallen asleep again because Patrick's voice broke into her dreams. "Come on, sleepyhead. It's eleven o'clock and I could do with a feed."

With her eyes still closed, she smiled and stretched her legs. She couldn't stay unhappy forever and wanted to make their final moments count—until thoughts of Gemma waiting for her return intruded and a small twinge looped around her heart. She'd been intent on leaving early until she saw Patrick. She understood now how letting Patrick into her life could take her off course.

She'd wrap this night close and let it warm her for years. After the wedding brunch, it would be time to say goodbye. She'd sidestep Janice's bone-picking with a promise to ring her soon. No doubt Patrick had told Janice all her news.

"I have something for you." Patrick whispered.

She flicked her eyes open to find Patrick leaning over her. Sadness surrounded his aura.

"You've given me more than I deserve."

"I have to. It belongs to you."

He reached into the side zipper of his bag, removed a small cloth-covered item and placed it in her hand.

"What is it?" she asked.

"Take a look."

Still naked, she sat up. As she took the gift, Patrick leaned towards her breasts. She gasped when he wrapped his mouth around her nipple and began to suck gently. As she wound her arms around his neck, she dropped the gift but promised to look at it as soon as they'd satisfied this new wave of desire.

She was desperate to have him inside her again. Moisture pooled between her legs as they fumbled with a new condom, wasting precious seconds. Finally, he slammed into her, but it wasn't enough for Kelly. She wanted him to reach her inner core, reach the part of her that would never forget him or this experience.

Patrick began a rhythmic pull and thrust; his mouth brutal over hers. There was nothing calm or slow about their lovemaking this time, so it was no surprise when their climaxes shattered around them too quickly. She welcomed his weight when he flopped onto her chest—until she struggled to get air into her lungs.

"I can't breathe, Yanko."

He chuckled and rolled onto his back but took her with him.

"Thanks. I was close to death."

They giggled, comfortable with each other and deliciously satisfied again.

She spied the gift, lying near his right shoulder with the cloth around it unravelled. Her laughter stopped abruptly and she frowned, trying to make sense of what she saw.

'All my love, P' looked back at her.

Her vision blurred as she reached for it. "What's this?" She sensed Patrick's gaze on her.

"What does it look like?"

She turned the heart-shaped jade stone over, confused as to why Patrick would duplicate the gift her grandfather had given her grandmother. Then she remembered how rich Patrick was and realised he could've organised this with one phone call. Did he love her that much? How much harder would their goodbye be now?

Tears welled in her eyes until she remembered his words. *"It belongs to you."*

She looked up. "What do you mean, it belongs to me?"

"I found it."

"You did?" She struggled to sit up but couldn't help the resentment that crept into her voice. "Why didn't you tell me?"

Patrick spoke quickly. "I didn't know I had it until last week." He calmed her by cradling her in his arms.

With her naked breasts once again resting on his chest, she clutched the pendant. Then Patrick rolled them to their sides and her legs rubbed comfortably against his. She was too shocked to process how she felt, but she knew she held the pendant that had once belonged to her grandmother. Aside from the diaries, it was all she had to prove her grandparents' great love.

Patrick recounted how he'd found the pendant on his first day at Moona Creek but how he hadn't discovered what it was until he'd cleaned out his backpack. Kelly tried to absorb every word he said, but her vision blurred again and she thought she might be starting to hyperventilate. This was too much for her to take in.

To receive this unexpected gift ... well, it floored her.

"I had to return it to you. This weekend was the perfect opportunity."

Patrick found her mouth again, sending shock waves of a different kind around her body and defogging her head. There was little chance they'd make brunch. It was more likely that breakfast would turn into dinner at the rate they were preparing to leave. Or worse, some poor, unsuspecting fishing enthusiast would discover them naked. That at least would force them to get ready.

Either way, Kelly wasn't moving while Patrick was kissing her. When his hand moved down and delved inside her, sparks flew again. She didn't want him to miss out either, so she took the opportunity to make his body shudder against hers one last time.

Slick with moisture and delicious sweat, she made a herculean effort to sit up and find her clothes, still gripping the pendant in her hand.

Patrick noticed. "If I were you, I'd put it in a glass display cabinet near the visitors' book. You could have a short history inscribed on a plaque hanging nearby so visitors can read about it and further immerse themselves in the magic of the castle."

"Oh, Patrick, you have it all planned, don't you?"

He rose and walked to the tent's entrance. "I'm hoping when you look at it, you might read it as 'All my love, Patrick.'"

She gasped and relaxed her grip on the pendant before taking another look at it. When she looked up, her eyes were drawn to the perfect shape of Patrick's bottom as he ducked under the tent flap and retrieved their clothes. Meanwhile, she couldn't move.

'All my love, Patrick' had a perfect ring to it.

Was the pendant's discovery weaving some sort of magic? Was it enough to make her change her mind?

"Hey, I didn't mean to make a big deal of it," he said as he handed back her clothes, jolting her back to the present. "I just thought it was a coincidence it should suit us, too."

He stretched his shirt over his head but not before Kelly caught a glimpse of wretchedness streak across his face. He was all smiles, though, as soon as his shirt was on.

"Thanks for an unforgettable night, Kel. Now, you have a baby girl to get back to, and if I remember correctly, she'll be harassing her grandparents with questions like, 'when will Mummy be back?'"

A sob found its way past her throat. At the mere mention of Gemma, a shaft of pain so sharp speared across her chest. The urgency to get back to her baby was once again at the forefront of her mind. Only spending a night with Patrick had been strong enough to shadow it temporarily.

"Thank you," she said as a lone tear trickled down her face and mounting emotion ran amok in her body.

By now, Patrick had his shoes on too. "If you get stuck for ideas with the castle, ask me. I'm only a quick message away."

She clenched her jaw tight, fighting a wave of sadness as she dressed. "Patrick, it's your castle. I can't even claim ownership of it."

He was frowning when he reached for her hands and hoisted her up. In the confined tent, she didn't miss the way his mouth straightened.

"Let me remind you about how you own it. That castle belongs to you and only you. Everything we spoke about came from here." He pressed a hand against her heart. "I want the full story. Photos, details of your progress, everything. Got it?"

She tried to smile, but it came out lopsided, and gave a hopeless, sad half-chuckle. With the pendant still clasped in her hand, she threw her arms around his neck ferociously. "I promise."

"Good," he muffled into her hair. "Now, let's make this our goodbye. I don't think I can do it twice."

His hold tightened as tears fell silently down her face. This moment would go down as one of the hardest of her life—and she already had a few. She hoped to God she was making the right decision and wouldn't regret it after Patrick was gone.

Chapter 26

S ix Months Later

Rising from her chair, Kelly bent over the wide expanse of the solid timber desk her father had gifted her and sorted through a pile of papers, looking for the sketch she'd received only last week. In her periphery, she kept an eye on Gemma, who was building a tower with the wooden offcuts she'd sneakily collected from the room next door—either the tradesmen no longer required the pieces of wood or indulged Gemma and let her collect whatever she wanted. As a result, her small office had started resembling a scrap heap.

Work on the castle had only begun in earnest of late. It'd taken months to get through the consultation and planning stages, and the same again to get the required approval from local council. But now, finally, the sounds of saws, hammers, drills and tradesmen hummed constantly in the background each day. Every cent she spent was accounted for and each section of the castle had an assigned team, including the small, private cottage being built in the rainforest. But despite her busy days, Kelly always made time for Gemma. Who cared if the castle renovations took longer to complete?

She stopped her search now to smile at her clever daughter and watched her being industrious with her blocks of timber. As usual her heart skipped a beat every time she looked at her precious baby girl. Having her made all the pain and heartache of leaving Patrick that little bit easier to accept.

Last week they'd celebrated Gemma's second birthday with her grandparents and newly made friends. The moments leading up to it, the joy of baking the cake and putting two candles on it, and the thousand photos Kelly had taken were more precious than this castle would ever be.

But the castle was important too, and when the Moona Creek community had become aware of her plans, pressure had mounted to recreate the past for the benefit of future generations and the burgeoning tourism industry. As she gradually brought the castle back to life as the older locals remembered it, she was constantly reminded of the gratitude she owed Patrick.

Thoughts of him had her returning her attention to her desk and she spotted the slip of paper she was looking for. True to his word, whenever she asked for advice or ideas, he replied. Not in writing but in sketch. And he put in the corner of each sketch a drawing of a man sitting at a desk with his back to the observer. He was always depicted wearing an ill-fitting suit, and with each sketch that crossed cyberspace, the dreadlocks on the man grew longer.

Like a hopeless addict, Kelly often made up questions purely for the joy of receiving another of Patrick's sketches. She kept them all safe and secure in a closed binder, except for the one she was working on. One day, they would go on display too.

She never asked the question, but she wanted to believe that Patrick had dreadlocks again. Poor Patrick. He despised wearing a suit every day. If it wasn't his father's business, he would've been cast out months ago. Dreadlocks and all.

She selfishly hoped he'd get sick of working in the family business and return to Australia. But her better side wanted him to achieve and overcome his doubts. She wanted him to forge ahead and build a life based on hard work and sincerity.

"Mummy, can we go for swim?" Still busy with her blocks, Gemma didn't look up.

Kelly dragged her thoughts away from Patrick and flopped onto her office chair. "Yes, we can, honey. Give Mummy a few minutes and then we'll go."

Gemma seemed satisfied with this answer, meaning Kelly had some extra time to choose the cornice designs for the main room where the two staircases met. She'd photographed the options the builder had given her and emailed them to Patrick. He'd replied with a sketch showing the room with both cornice options. Kelly shook her head. She'd originally planned to put decorative cornice around the room's entire border, but Patrick's sketch highlighted how overdone it would look.

She leaned against her chair and its soft cushioning hugged her back. Holding the sketch aloft, she took a good look at the drawing of the man in the corner. He was sitting at a desk piled high with files on either side and they looked ready to tumble. She had a feeling Patrick was telling her something. Was he really busy, or not coping with the kind of work he had to do in his family's business?

Oh, Patrick. He loved hard physical work—she'd seen evidence of that both at Samdarra and Moona Creek. Would he ever be able to live the life he preferred, not the life he was expected to?

"Excuse me, Kelly."

She turned to the voice. One of the tradesmen stood at the door.

"There's a visitor wanting to see you." He pointed towards the kitchen. "I told him to wait at the door."

The tradesman left as Kelly rose and dropped the sketch on the desk. Visitors weren't common here. Sometimes Mr Blundell called through and occasionally brought members of the historical society with him. Anyone else who happened along was usually expected. The castle was a long way from being ready for the public.

"Gemma, come to Mummy."

When Gemma did as she was told, Kelly reached down and hoisted her onto her hip.

"Swim, Mummy?"

"I'm not sure, darling. We have a visitor."

Gemma wound her tiny arms around Kelly's neck and bobbed up and down as Kelly made her way to the kitchen. On the other side of the screen door, a man waited. He looked to be in his fifties. His hair was jet black with the occasional grey strand.

Kelly greeted him with a smile. "Can I help you?"

"Are you Kelly Sheppard?"

"I am. What can I do for you?"

"It's what I can do for you."

"Oh." Her feel-good senses plummeted. She didn't need some travelling salesman pushing cheap products onto her just because rumour was spreading about her renovation project.

He thrust his hand in her direction. "Michael Tampalavo."

Reluctantly, she shook his hand.

"I know I'm the last person you expected to see, but my mother heard you were at this property and sent me here on an errand." His tight black curls shimmered in the early afternoon sun, bringing out the light brown tone to his skin. "She suffered a stroke recently, so she doesn't get around like she used to, but she once lived here. She was married to your grandfather."

"Oh." Kelly shuffled Gemma on her hip. "You're right. I never expected to meet your mother or any of her family. I never knew my grandfather and I heard things didn't go well between my father and your mother."

He looked embarrassed for a moment. "I don't know the full story, but you'd be surprised how a stroke can change a person. She suddenly has regrets and wants to right them."

Kelly nodded slowly. "I see."

"Mummy, Mummy, swim, swim." Gemma bobbed up and down.

Kelly put her down, on her chubby little legs, and held her hand. "Just wait, honey." She turned to Michael and asked, "What sort of regrets does she have?"

He looked away briefly. "I have three boxes in the car, full of memorabilia she took when she left. She asked me to return it to you. Thought you might be able to use it in your restoration project."

Really? This felt like winning lotto! Besides the pendant, the diaries and the old film reels, she didn't have a single other relic from her grandparents' days.

He hesitated before asking, "Would you, ah, like them?"

She took a step forward, dying to know what treasures he carried. "Yes, please."

It was easier now to plaster a smile on her face and her heart began to hammer excitedly; she couldn't believe the good fortune that had come calling. Gemma was tugging at her hand, so Kelly swung her onto her hip again.

"You bring the boxes in," she said, "and I'll get a cup of tea ready." Turning towards the kitchen door, she stopped short. "I'll phone my parents. They'd be delighted to meet you. Can you stay?"

Relaxed now, he rolled back on his heels, put his hands in the pockets of his knee-length shorts and returned her sunny smile. "Yes, I'd love to."

Chapter 27

Patrick undid his top two buttons, loosened his tie and pressed the ground floor button. It was Fall in Boston and he couldn't seem to warm up. The weather here was nothing like the searing heat of Samdarra, which could fry the outer layer of your skin. He smiled at the memory of a stockman cooking an egg, one blistering summer's day, in a small frying pan placed on a rock. On that day sweat had oozed—no, poured from his skin. Temperatures had soared to record-breaking numbers. He'd never felt so alive.

As he left the high-rise his father owned, he tucked his laptop under his arm and headed for the small grove of trees he often escaped to during his lunch break.

As usual, others occupied the small park. He resented the invasion of what he wanted to believe was his space. He knew it was selfish, but after living in the wide-open spaces of Samdarra and the isolated castle and its surrounding forest, nothing could loosen the claustrophobic feeling. Still, he managed to find a vacant seat and, not wanting to share, spread himself along its length.

Lying his laptop on his stomach, he crossed his arms behind his head and looked up. Pale, sickly light seeped through the grey clouds; rain was likely to drop at any moment. Summer had been okay in Boston, but Fall was turning out to be the pits.

He had no idea what the few small trees growing in the grove were called. Each one looked like the next. But place eucalyptus trees in front of him and he would recognise them in an instant. He'd often marvelled at the way a gum tree would shed its bark, and the papery feel of it in his work-roughened hands. There'd be a trail of green ants scurrying down the trunk to their nest, and the tree would be craning its branches towards the life-sustaining water of the nearby creek. Rarely was there a riverbed not populated by the ordinary gum tree. It was so commonplace, so outback Queensland. It was everything he missed and yearned for.

He groaned and promised himself only a few minutes. The tent, the riverbed. Kelly. Eight months was a long time, but his memories still ignited so easily. Often, a few minutes would turn into hours. Immersed in his memories, a night could disappear in a blink.

He changed his mind and clamped his jaw tight. Better to stop before he got carried away. Remembering would only leave him maudlin and he had a meeting to prepare for that afternoon. His father had returned from his overseas volunteering a few weeks ago and already you could feel the vibe and tension in the office increase tenfold. His father had that effect on people.

Still, Patrick saw his father differently these days. He had a knack for bringing the best out of the people who wanted to work hard in their industry, and Patrick respected that. It just wasn't what *he* wanted to do. Someday he hoped to escape this funk, this half-life that felt like a washed-out version of his time in Australia.

Feeling like a weary old man, he sat up and opened his laptop. His fingers moved deftly over the keys, his hands pale. Once upon a time they'd been golden brown, with the tendons visible on the backs of his hands whenever he moved his fingers. He clearly remembered the way they'd looked. Kelly had stroked his skin and remarked on it.

He let his eyes close for a moment. A cool breeze lapped against his skin and furled its way around his neck and dreadlocks. His father had frowned when he'd spotted Patrick's dreadlocks.

Then there was Lisa. She didn't mind his hair, his quiet moodiness or his avoidance of social events. Probably not his money, either. *No, stop.* He shouldn't be so crass. She was a nice girl and meant well. She'd been the first to try to rope him back into the social circle he'd left all those months ago. She was great to look at and worked her arse off for the company. But after a night of sex he'd realised it was all wrong. He'd left her place immediately, had curled up in his bed and bawled like a kid. Nothing measured up to the one night he'd spent with Kelly. Her words that he would find someone else and look back on their time together as an adventure was bullshit. She'd ruined him for life, and some days he resented her for it.

Slowly rolling his neck to ease the tension, he opened his eyes and looked down at the laptop. He flicked through the many emails from Kelly. For months, she'd kept him busy sketching solutions to where all the memorabilia should be placed. He swiped through photo after photo of all the goodies returned by Kelly's step-grandmother; receiving it all must've been like unearthing a hidden treasure chest. The haul included framed photos of historic events—some featuring famous people—photo albums, perpetual trophies, newspaper clippings and signed visitors' books dating back to the castle's earliest days. It was a treasure-trove and Kelly wanted to display it all.

She'd sent recent photos, too, of the cute little cottage hidden in the trees on the right-hand side of the driveway. And lots, always, of little Gemma and her magical smile. Had the sunbirds returned to the nest?

Shot by shot, the castle slowly transformed in front of his eyes, and the restoration was exactly how they'd planned it. From a photo Kelly had taken of the entrance, he could see the new awnings, the outdoor table settings and the kitchen in the background—the new perfectly complementing the old.

The fountains, resurrected from their lichen-encrusted state, spouted water in well-coordinated arches into the lily-covered ponds. No doubt Kelly was a step closer to serving locally produced food and drinks.

Patrick closed his eyes again and raised his face. He tried to imagine it was the humid heat of the tropics touching his skin instead of the limp, cool breeze that was clamouring over it. He wanted to be there. Moona Creek was where all the excitement was happening.

Unexpectedly, he let out a chuckle and opened his eyes. Was he out of his mind? Had he changed that much that an isolated castle perched on a high bank with a waterfall cascading alongside it was his definition of exciting? No wonder his friends thought he was crazy, or hugely damaged by his earlier drug-taking. No doubt they'd been talking quietly among themselves, telling each other how lucky they were to have escaped any real side-effects of their careless days. How thankful they were to have made it to the other side sane and in one piece.

They had no idea.

He clicked on the most recent email received only yesterday. There were no photos attached and it contained just one sentence.

I'd like to call it Kelrick Kastle. What do you think?

He'd spotted the combined use of their first names and had been rendered speechless. In fact, after reading the email, he'd slammed his laptop shut and had stalked off. It wasn't like him to show anger so quickly. Nevertheless, he'd stormed out of the high-rise and walked the streets of Boston. Only when the light had begun to fade and the chill of having left the building without his jacket had seeped into his bones had he forced his way back to the office. He'd then worked until midnight to catch up.

Eight goddamned fucking months and she still had the capacity to floor him with a single sentence. It was her castle. Couldn't she leave him out of it?

Now, he closed the lid of the laptop and considered sending a sketch to show he hated the name. He could draw something that hinted she should get on with her own life and leave him alone.

Except he thought Kelrick Kastle had the perfect ring to it. He smiled fleetingly at his earlier attempts to name it. Karradmas Castle had become a firm joke between them. But his smile slipped and disappeared. He knew she was waiting for a response. She had a massive advertising campaign to set in motion. But he couldn't commit to it. The name implied he was part of it—and he wasn't.

What if he stopped sending sketches? Refused to reply? Cut off access to his email address. Let her flounder on her own for a change. Forced her to live without constant contact from him. His shoulders dropped at the misery that drew forth. He may as well give up now.

A shroud of sadness enveloped him as he rose and headed back to the office. Lunch? What was that? He rarely ate these days; his body was a far cry from the strong one he'd left Australia with all those months ago.

<hr />

A week later he jerked upright in bed. A quick glance at this bedside clock showed it was 2.14 am. He got up and floundered in the dark, scrambling for the sketchpad he'd flung aside days ago.

Put the bloody light on.

It was stupid, he knew, but talking to himself had become the norm. Shunning a huge chunk of social activities left him mostly with his own company.

He stumbled towards the switch and squinted when light flooded the room. He looked around the untidy space and remembered how different he'd been with his meagre belongings at the castle. There'd been purpose and a reason to rise each day. His room had always been kept in order.

As he focused on his surroundings, he saw it for what it was. A bloody mess. He hunched his shoulders, feeling downright miserable, and couldn't for the life of him shift his feet. His brain ticked over.

He thought of how his father continued to try his hardest to mend the broken bridge between them, but old habits were hard to kill. Maybe if he was in a situation he liked, he might've made it easier for his father. Maybe if he was working in thick bulldust, at a hot-as-hell outback station, he might've made it easier for his father. Maybe if he was stranded in some derelict castle, trying hard to ignore the calming flow of water over the falls, he might've made it easier for his father.

But he wasn't in any of those circumstances.

He trudged to work, day in and day out, wearing a suit that was uncomfortable as hell and resenting every moment of his life that slipped away. His feelings for his father were a by-product of everything going wrong with his life. A small part of him felt guilty because his father was trying so hard despite being rebuffed. Patrick was the bastard this time.

As he came out of his trance, he roughly kicked aside yesterday's dirty clothes and spotted the sketchpad. He knew what message to send Kelly. It was what had woken him. He'd cursed and sworn all week. Deliberated over how to sketch his views and feelings about the name Kelly had suggested for the castle. In fact, at this ungodly hour of the morning, he couldn't believe what the big stink was all about. *I mean, really?* All she'd asked for was a simple 'yes, I like it' or 'no, I don't'. She didn't want a synopsis of 'how to totally screw up your life worrying about the name of a castle'.

Had he even eaten this week? He frowned. Where had that thought come from?

A pencil lay close to the pad. He picked them both up and settled back in bed, resting against the headboard. His dream had shown a party of people, balloons everywhere and guests holding champagne flutes. The name Kelrick Kastle had been clearly displayed in the background.

He clenched the pencil tighter than normal. Ready to begin, his fingers suddenly froze. He couldn't draw the scene. It should've come naturally for him. Hell, every other sketch had. But the weird thing was, his fingers had a mind of their own and haltingly took control; he couldn't stop what they did. He began drawing the man in the corner first, and an hour later, he photographed the sketch, pressed send and then collapsed back in shock.

Shit. What did I just do?

He'd killed any chance of getting more sleep tonight.

Chapter 28

"The tickle monster's coming to get you." Kelly tickled Gemma, making her squeal. "Tickle monster! Big, big tickle monster."

It was their first week of officially living in the cottage. Gemma often came into Kelly's room once she woke and Kelly welcomed her with open arms, hugging her, holding her too close and branding her with kiss after kiss on her cherub face—until the tickle monster made an appearance and her baby girl filled the room with the childish squeals Kelly could never get enough of.

Kelly halted her tickling and Gemma quietened down and snuggled up against her. Her little heart pulsed against Kelly's cotton nightie. Reluctantly, Kelly pulled Gemma's tiny finger from her mouth.

"No sucking, darling."

Not fazed by the reprimand, Gemma grabbed a fist full of nightie and settled in for more sleep. As the early morning light dappled through the trees into her room, Kelly smoothed down Gemma's soft, black hair and tucked it behind her ear.

When this little bundle of joy was in exactly this spot, Kelly had it all. Anything but a handful, Gemma was always ready to please and, between her doting grandparents and Kelly, Gemma knew she was loved. Everything Kelly had dreamed of for her, when she'd thought Gemma was lost to her forever, had eventually happened. Gemma would get the same blessed childhood she'd been given. And her happy personality made every sacrifice worth it.

Except for one small glitch.

Gemma's even breathing signalled sleep again and Kelly turned her thoughts to the meeting happening later today—with Gemma's father. Though she'd made every effort for a very long time to block that night out, she had a vivid recollection of who the father was. It had just been a matter of making contact and suggesting a DNA test. No doubt the news had come as a shock for him, but Kelly was over making excuses. Gemma would one day want to know who her father was and it would only cause problems down the track if Kelly delayed their meeting. If he chose to become a part of Gemma's life now, Kelly hoped it wouldn't impact her too much. Her parents agreed.

She slipped out of bed and left Gemma sleeping. The cottage was only a two-bedroom dwelling with a small office. She'd moved all her equipment and paperwork from her temporary room at the castle only a week ago, leaving the tradesmen to finalise the last of the renovations. They were only weeks away from their first function and advertising had begun in earnest.

She should be thrilled with how everything was turning out. Television, radio stations, local and state newspapers carried her story of the castle's restoration. Interest from tour groups wanting to include the castle as an attraction on their itinerary was rapidly growing. Patrick had always said it was perfectly positioned, being only one kilometre from the main highway, and damn it, he'd been right. So, why had he cut her off?

She flopped onto her office chair. Hunched over her desk, she scrunched a handful of hair and pushed it away from her face. Patrick's last sketch sat in the middle of her desk. She'd printed it out weeks ago and it got shuffled around whenever she needed to work, but for some reason, it was always somewhere in the middle, reminding her this was the only downer in her otherwise perfect life. The sketch hadn't made sense when she'd received it and it still didn't. She'd asked for an explanation that never came. Eventually, she'd stopped asking.

It didn't feel right to officially open the castle without him. She'd been only a few clicks away from inviting him a dozen times. Why the silence? Why would he stop communicating?

Kelly picked up the sketch and stared at it. Her mind whirred, but she was reluctant to admit she already knew what the sketch meant. Its meaning lodged itself inside her memory and would remain there forever.

You told him to get on with his life.

He was just doing what she'd asked.

She leaned back and the wheels of her office chair squeaked on the tiled floor. She held up the sketch and tried to find answers—again.

The page was blank, except for the man in the top right corner. His back was to her, like normal, and his dreadlocks were that little bit longer. His elbows rested on the desk and his fingers were hidden in his dreadlocks. If she looked long enough, she believed she could see his agitated fingers moving beneath the thick hair.

The man's shoulders were hunched over the desk, as though in defeat. The piles of files and books on either side of the desk had toppled to the floor and sat in a mess around the man's feet. His tie was loosened and flung over his shoulder. The sketch clearly depicted a distressed man, and as much as she didn't want to admit it, it really explained everything.

───※───

"Hello, Aidan."

"Hi, Kelly." Aidan kissed her cheek.

He'd clearly moved past adolescence and was well on the way to manhood. At twenty-two years old, he was supremely fit and healthy and was ready to live life. She was almost sorry to have thrown a spanner in his works by telling him he was a father. Almost.

Despite the awkward situation, Aidan and his parents had arrived as agreed. Sydney was a universe away from Moona Creek, so she understood their shock at having to venture past Sydney into regional Australia. She remembered the feeling well, but whether they came to appreciate the natural wonder of this place and the attachment she'd formed to it, she didn't care. In fact, she doubted they would. Some people found it hard to adapt to change, and she suspected Aidan and his family were of that ilk. They'd taken their annual holidays overseas, visiting some amazing city. The idea of going to a place where rainforest grew or dust billowed had probably never hit their radar.

Margaret set out afternoon tea on the small patio that overlooked the rainforest for his parents, while Aidan and Kelly sat in the lounge room, watching Gemma play with blocks. It never ceased to amaze Kelly how intricate her block building was for someone so small.

"She's engineered that perfectly. She must be my girl."

Kelly looked up at Aidan. She'd expected denial, refusal to accept Gemma as his own, all of the above. Instead, he'd shown openness from his first remark.

With a lopsided smile, he added, "I'm doing civil engineering at Sydney Uni. I might have to come to *her* for advice one day."

Kelly chuckled. So, it wasn't only in her biased imagination that Gemma was clever.

She sobered up and looked away for a fleeting second. Could things work out between them one day? She zeroed in on his face again and could've sworn from his expression that he was wondering the same thing. Then an image of Patrick bloomed in front of her and she squashed the stupid thought.

"Thanks, Aidan. For accepting it. I want Gemma to know she has a father and that she can communicate with you whenever she wants. You're welcome here any time."

Aidan's face fell and his fingers knotted. "Do you need anything? Help, money, assistance of any sort. I wish you'd told me ..."

Kelly raised her hand. "I've already explained what happened. I can't change anything, but I'm sorry it turned out this way."

He nodded. "You're right. I wasn't in a good place back then and I don't think I would've handled it."

"Thanks. The only thing I ask is that you accept things as they are. I don't need money, I just want you to visit whenever you can and remember she's yours too."

"I won't forget. She's beautiful like you."

Kelly felt the light beginnings of a flush. She remembered those heady adolescent days—until drugs had dulled a lot of it.

"I never did forget you," he admitted. "Honestly. I wondered where you'd disappeared to but was never game enough to ask your friends."

"They didn't know. I broke contact with everyone, including Mum and Dad."

"Oh, Kelly. I wish you hadn't done it alone."

She grimaced. "I have a lot of regrets, but thanks for your concern. I'm in a happier place now."

For a few moments they continued watching Gemma. Soon she'd invite him to the patio so his parents could have time with Gemma.

Eventually, Aidan looked up from Gemma and walked to the window to study the view. "This place looks amazing, especially the waterfall. How did you end up here?"

Thoughts of Patrick filled her head. "My grandfather owned it. He built the castle for my grandmother and left it to me in his will."

Aidan nodded, still looking outside. "I've heard about it. Had no idea where it was, and even less idea that you were connected with it." He turned and tucked his hands in his pockets. "You've obviously done a lot of advertising."

"We're a couple of weeks from our first function. I'll show you around later."

"Have your parents permanently left Sydney?"

When she nodded, his eyebrows rose. It'd be difficult for Aidan to imagine anyone choosing to leave Sydney for this.

"Would you like to go for a swim?" she asked. "The wet season hasn't quite started, but it's hot enough and you'll feel better afterwards. Gemma can show you what a good swimmer she is."

At the mention of her name, Gemma looked up and asked, "Mummy, swim? Swim, Mummy?"

Kelly opened her arms and Gemma ran on her chubby legs towards her. "Yes, we can. How would you like to go for a swim with Daddy?"

Aidan flinched, which didn't surprise her. The shock that he was someone's daddy would hardly have worn off. In time, he would come to accept it.

Suddenly shy, Gemma put her thumb in her mouth and, turning away from Aidan, tucked her face in Kelly's breasts. The word 'Daddy' didn't mean too much to her yet, but Kelly had every intention of introducing her to it and would be sure to keep photos of Aidan handy.

"When is her birthday?"

Kelly turned Gemma around and gently pulled her finger away from her face. "How old are you, Gemma?"

Gemma climbed onto Kelly's lap and shyly held up her little hand. It wasn't obvious that she was trying to stick up two stubby fingers, so Kelly folded away the other three to make it more obvious.

"Her birthday is the second of July."

Talking to Gemma for the first time, Aidan asked, "How would you like Daddy to come and visit you on your next birthday?"

Gemma, who no doubt remembered the fuss of her recent birthday, nodded.

Tears formed beneath Kelly's eyelids. Maybe she was mistaken about Aidan. He seemed willing to take on the role of Gemma's father, calling himself 'Daddy' with no hesitation. Surely that was a good sign?

"Would you like some cake, Gemma?" Kelly asked.

"Yessy, yessy." Gemma wiggled her way off Kelly's lap and darted out to the patio, where she could hear the grandparents talking.

Left alone with Aidan, Kelly discreetly wiped a finger under her eyes.

"Hey, Kelly?"

She looked up.

"You're a great mother. Thank you."

Now *that* was the very last thing she'd expected Aidan to say.

She burst into tears, knowing exactly what caused them. It was the build-up of everything happening around her—the renovation on the castle, meeting with Aidan, worrying about how he and his parents would react. Gemma was their first grandchild and fear had laced through her every day. What if they tried to take Gemma from her?

Aidan didn't hesitate to cross the small room and take her in his arms.

That was what else was making her emotional. She missed having Patrick in her life. She wanted his arms around her and his bright smile in front of her. She wanted to laugh with him at his dismal jokes. Yes, she was happy and exactly where she wanted to be, but oh, something great was still missing from her life and it wasn't Aidan.

She knew that with certainty.

Chapter 29

Patrick looked around the cubicle he called his office and couldn't believe he'd stuck it out in such a small space for nearly twelve months. There wasn't too much to pack; he reached down for some personal stuff and started filling the box he'd brought in. Who knew? He might even come back one day. No longer did he hate the work, it just bored him stupid. He couldn't help but resent the way money was accumulated by the wealthy, himself included.

He looked up at the sudden commotion at the door.

"For he's a jolly good fellow, for he's a jolly good fellow, for he's ..."

Lisa stood at the helm of co-workers, holding a cake and singing. She'd become a good friend over recent months; he'd told her a lot of things he hadn't been able to tell anyone else.

He smiled at the fuss they were all making. For the first time in his life, he didn't feel like the boss's kid. He'd been treated that way for most of his life, so the time spent anonymously in Australia had suited him for that reason. Somehow, in this very building, he'd shed the layer trapping him to his exclusivity and had become part of the team. It was probably the only reason he'd stayed so long.

When the singing ended, Lisa made a speech. "Patrick, we all want to wish you the very best of luck. We've enjoyed your friendship and working with you and you'll be missed."

Patrick couldn't brush away the thought that, in leaving, he was also breaking her heart. Oh, she kept her feelings hidden and didn't flash them in his face, but the signs were there. Her behaviour reminded him of his own during the many months he'd tried to impress Kelly.

Patrick cleared his throat and made room for the cake on the corner of his desk. He waved everyone into his tiny office.

"Thanks, everyone, for making me feel at home." He chuckled, making light of the decision that had harboured at the edge of his mind for months. "You never know, I may return sooner than you think."

He wanted to believe he wouldn't be back any time soon. His ultimate dream was to buy his own Samdarra and while away a life in the heat and dust of outback Australia.

"But it's time for me to leave and ... and ..."

Do some searching? Find my tribe? Find where I'm supposed to be?

He shrugged, not knowing how to continue, and instead asked, "Anyone for cake?"

Laughter and chuckles erupted from the group. Conversations were picked up again and someone shouted from the door, "Hey Patrick, what'll it be? The usual latte?"

He nodded and his colleague left for the coffee machine down the hall.

He tried to swallow the lump in his throat. This was another closure for him, and God how he hated them. He clearly remembered the last one. In fact, he could still smell the scent of eucalyptus, two slick bodies and her womanly fragrance. Heady, strong ...

Shit. Stop it!

A slight shake of his head and he was back in the room again. He ran a hand over his face and took a moment to look at everyone. Among this crowd were people he'd genuinely come to respect and like. Eventually, his gaze fell on Lisa. She was busy organising plates and napkins and her eyes were shadowed with sadness. He understood but was helpless to change things.

Lisa knew of his plans to backpack across Asia. She'd been the one to force his hand and make him take the plunge, having sensed the need in him. That lost and 'I'm drifting' feeling that would only fester and become uncontrollable if he didn't give it some oxygen. Eventually, he'd admitted to her he would be rounding out his travels with a stop in Australia to visit his sisters and check Kelrick Kastle. If what he read on the internet was anything to go by, the castle had become a tourist hotspot in the four months since it had officially reopened.

Lisa didn't know how the name Kelrick had come to be. He'd never referred to Kelly by name—she was only ever 'that Aussie girl'. But being very intelligent, Lisa had put two and two together.

When she looked in his direction, he forced his mouth into a lopsided smile, hoping to convey how sorry he was that things hadn't worked out between them.

"Post some shots on Facebook so we know what you're up to," someone suggested from the crowd.

"How about a piece of cake? My coffee's getting cold," an intern shouted over the noise.

Lisa elbowed him and said, "Patience, you big oaf."

Everyone laughed and relaxed. He was a tall string bean of a boy straight out of college.

"You finished talking, yet, Patrick?" another smart arse called out. "We've got cake to eat and your dad will be on our case if we don't get back to work soon."

As people laughed, Lisa attacked the cake with a little more fervour than necessary.

"Thanks, everyone. I've enjoyed working with this team. I'll keep in touch and let you know where I end up." He pointed to the cake and added, "Now eat up."

Noise erupted around them again as Lisa approached with his piece. "Here you go."

Others helped themselves and conversation faded into the background when Lisa offered him the plate. Her chocolate-brown eyes shimmered under the fluorescent lights and his chest constricted knowing he was the cause of her pain.

"Will you keep in touch?" she asked.

His heart plummeted. It was too much to ask. He couldn't make that promise.

When he didn't answer, she attempted a smile, but it came out lopsided.

She tried to inject some cheeriness into her voice. "Patrick, until you find that Aussie girl you're heartbroken over, the rest of us will never stand a chance." She took a tissue from her jacket pocket and wiped the corners of her eyes. "Go find her and make things right, otherwise you'll never be happy. You're stuck and can't move forward. Sort it out, make it okay, clear your head and then come back and find me. If you're lucky, I might still be waiting."

He released a noisy breath. She had no idea how impossible a suggestion that was, even though she'd summed up his situation perfectly. Christ, if he thought he'd had half a chance with Kelly, he would've never left in the first place. He took the offered plate and with his free hand caressed her cheek, hoping like hell he didn't do anything stupid like end up in tears.

He forced his lips into a wobbly smile. "Thanks, Lisa."

He couldn't say anything else for a few moments. Emotion swelled inside his chest and he damned the day he'd ever met Kelly. Christ, he wasn't supposed to feel things for her after all this time and there was no plausible reason for not being able to move on. He'd cut her off so he could try to forget and move forward. Instead, she'd grabbed him at the jugular, come close to choking him to death and had damn near taken him to hell.

When his hand fell away, Lisa's expression was pitiful. She was a mind-reader, a bloody good one too, and he had no one else to blame for his inability to move on. It was definitely time to leave. That way he might be able to reactivate his brain cells and give them something new to think about. Maybe deal with someone else's problems. His were boring him.

"Excuse me, excuse me. Is Patrick hiding in here?"

Patrick spotted the receptionist peering over everyone's heads, trying to push past the crush at the door.

When she saw him, she raised her hand and waved. "Patrick, there's an urgent phone call for you."

He sucked in a breath. Was something wrong with his dad? His sisters?

"Go to the office next door and I'll send it through. You won't hear a thing in here."

Urgent implied bad news; he should know. Melita had phoned him using those words on the worst day of his life. His body froze whenever he heard them.

Patrick forged his way past everyone, escaped to the empty office and shut the door. The phone beeped and a red light flashed, signalling a waiting call. His stomach churned as he reached for the handpiece.

With his heart running a marathon, he picked it up and said, "Hello, Patrick here."

"Patrick, thank God I managed to get you. It's William here, Kelly's father."

⚜

"*Nooo!*"

Patrick's heart-wrenching wail pierced the air. It echoed off the walls and bounced back, hitting him. Hurting, hurting and still hurting.

His legs buckled and the handpiece dropped against his chest long after the call had ended. He caught his hands in his hair and wrenched at his dreadlocks, twisting them into angry shapes. He pulled hard, oblivious to the pain. He pulled harder again, doing all he could to block out the pain.

He refused to believe the news William had just delivered, but still, his howls grew louder.

"No, no, no."

They echoed back. Taunted him. Burned his throat. This hadn't happened. No fucking way. It wasn't fair, and if he'd once believed in God, he certainly wanted nothing to do with him now.

Pissed off, that's what he was. He slammed the handpiece against his chest, over and over. He was past caring if he inflicted bruises. Physical pain was a welcome relief to the searing emotional pain settling around his heart.

His cries forced their way through his barely open lips, his jaw clamped tight and teeth clenched together. Shock set in and his head wanted to deny the news, pretend it was a bad dream.

The door flung open. Lisa stood in the doorway with concern washed over her face. "Patrick! What's wrong?" She rushed to his side.

Tears dripped down his cheeks. He had no idea when he'd started to cry and used his sleeve to clear his vision. He looked past Lisa and in that split second he knew exactly what to do.

Chapter 30

*T*wo Days Earlier

"Mum, the busload is due any minute." Kelly clipped her mobile phone onto her belt and rushed through to the kitchen. "Guys, get ready for forty-odd hungry tourists."

"Got it covered, Kel," the young kitchen hand called back.

And they did, thank goodness. Most days. Except today when two staff members called in sick. Kelly and Margaret had done their best to fill the empty spots at the last minute.

"Gemma, come to Mummy."

Gemma toddled on her tiny legs and wrapped her arms around Kelly. "Mummy play?"

"Not now, darling."

Kelly would've loved a break, but visitors kept driving in. Who could blame them? The day was glorious, the sky a reflection of the ocean, and the water spilling over the falls sparkled. These were the days she loved. The weather was predictable, even though it was still humid. The summer storms that could wreak havoc were still months away.

She picked Gemma up and gave her a tight hug. "Mummy loves you and really wants to play, but I can't just now. When Poppy gets back from town, he'll play with you."

Gemma bobbed her head up and down. "Yessy, yessy, Poppy play, play, play."

Kelly planted a big kiss on her cheek and put her down in a small alcove they'd converted into a play area for her. It was hidden from the crowds but close enough that Kelly could keep a close eye on her.

"Darling, you play with your toys and blocks and Mummy will put a movie on. What would you like to watch?"

She chuckled when Gemma produced a DVD from the small pile of her favourites.

She hated using the television as a babysitting tool, but some days it couldn't be helped. Additional flights were landing at Cairns International Airport, from China especially, and it seemed everyone had put Kelrick Kastle on their itinerary. It wasn't something she could complain about.

Today, with the help of an interpreter, Kelly was playing tour guide. Her usual staff member was down with the flu, but she knew the story by heart. The only twinge would come when she talked about the jade pendant. Usually, she managed to hold her emotions in, at least until she was alone.

"They're here," Margaret called out as she passed by the secluded alcove.

"Okay, coming."

The bus company always appreciated the visitors being met and welcomed, and today wouldn't be any different.

"I'll be back to see how the movie is going as soon as I'm finished."

"Okay, Mummy."

"I love you."

"Love, Mummy," Gemma garbled, already biting into a biscuit from her snack container.

Kelly rose, smoothed her blouse and skirt and hoped her hair was still neat. Not that it mattered. The visitors came to view the magnificent property and experience the tropical rainforest. The forest walk was always a crowd-pleaser; phones and cameras always clicked nonstop. If they were lucky, visitors would be treated to lorikeets, sunbirds, curlews, kingfishers and brush-turkeys. If they were very lucky, a cassowary might pass closely by. If they were very, *very* lucky, a tree kangaroo would be perched on a branch near the path. That's when the phones really went crazy.

Very few of the Chinese visitors ever felt inclined to take a swim. Occasionally a brave soul would walk down to the picnic facilities to take better photos, but those who swam were usually European or American backpackers, or locals, of course. Kelly doubted she would need to go near the falls this afternoon.

She rarely ventured there with a crowd present. Her special time of day was early in the morning when Gemma slept. She'd slip down to the water and make her way to the black rocks. Sometimes tears would trickle down her face and mix with the water from the fall's spray. It still hurt that Patrick had cut her off so completely.

Margaret chatted to the young bus driver. He was a familiar face; this tourist company made the trek here at least four times a week. Kelly watched the group of middle-aged tourists disembark and stretch their legs. They'd come directly from Cairns, an hour's drive away.

Kelly waved and smiled as the visitors meandered towards their interpreter and listened to his words. Leaflets, designed and prepared by William, were handed out. They took away the stress of having to repeat the story over and over and meant the Chinese visitors would have an immediate sense of the place before the tour began.

As always, the tour would end at the café and souvenir shop, where her father struggled to keep up with the demand for trinkets and holiday mementos. Again, William had arranged a whole array of items carrying the image of Kelrick Kastle. Shirts, caps, tea towels, pens and key rings. The range had astounded Kelly at first, but she was more than happy for her father to take control.

As Kelly directed some of the tourists to the toilets, she estimated it'd be another fifteen minutes before everyone was ready to take the forest walk. Reminded of the many hours she worked, Kelly looked up at the opal-blue sky and gave a quick thanks. She would've never managed here without her parents by her side. They'd taken to the daily workings of the castle like a baby did to a dummy. They thrived on the energy and buzz around the place when its lawns were filled with visitors.

Weekends could be bedlam when locals joined the fray. They'd picnic and swim at the falls, coming in a constant stream and rarely leaving without an ice-cream for the kids and buckets of deep-fried chips. The place had a family vibe, and as alcohol was contained to the licenced spots near the castle, they rarely had any problems.

"Is Dad back yet?" Kelly asked her mother.

"I haven't seen him, but he had a few errands to do. We could use his help when he returns."

William had taken on marketing and advertising for the castle with relish. He loved every bit of it, reminding Kelly of how he'd been when they'd lived in Sydney. If he appeared in the social pages of the newspaper, he was a happy man. This project allowed him the same sort of exposure but on a whole different scale.

"They'll only be a few minutes now, Kel. I'll check the kitchen and make sure everything's on display. If I don't, Sophie will hear about it." Margaret chuckled. "Here's praying she gets over her diarrhoea soon."

Along with their tour guide, Sophie, one of their valued chefs, had called in sick this morning. Kelly chewed on her bottom lip. It was a balancing act, juggling the right number of staff with the high cost of wages. Surprisingly, there was still money in the bank after Patrick had paid for the property, and that's what hurt. She had so much to thank him for and wanted to tell him personally. She thought of getting a message to him via Melita but didn't have the heart to do so. If he'd wanted to stay in contact, he would've.

Forty-five minutes later, Kelly had finally finished pouring her heart out to the visitors via the interpreter. While she'd taken a step back from this role, on the occasions she did it, she was always buoyed by it. She loved this castle, its history and the fact it was a part of her family's heritage.

After she directed the tourists to the café, she made her way to the side door with every intention of checking on Gemma. The movie would be close to finished and there was a good chance Gemma might've nodded off—though she didn't always need an afternoon sleep these days. Kelly smiled. She didn't mind. If Gemma didn't have a nap, it usually meant she'd have an early night and would sleep right through until morning.

She spotted William in the staff area having a cup of coffee. "Hi, Dad."

"Hi, Kel. All good out there?"

"Perfect. I'm just checking on Gemma."

"Gemma? I heard a movie playing, but she wasn't there. I assumed you'd taken her with you."

Ice trickled down Kelly's back, but she tried to curb it. She knew it was a mother's instinct to feel things, but she over-worried all the time.

"No," she said, "I left her to watch the movie."

William frowned, scraping his chair back, and that was when real fear barged past every defence Kelly had in place. She ran towards the alcove to check Gemma hadn't returned. Ignoring the visitors looking at the memorabilia on display, she sped around the last corner but found no Gemma. Her heart plummeted when she spotted the childproof gate ajar.

William came up behind her. "Is she there?"

She shook her head, said, "I'll check with Mum," and ran to the kitchen. Panic would set in if she didn't find Gemma with her mother.

The kitchen staff were frantically filling food and drink orders. Dread rushed up Kelly's throat when she didn't see Gemma anywhere near Margaret.

"Mum," she yelled over the din, "have you seen Gemma?"

Margaret looked up, her eyes widening with alarm. "No, not at all."

She was removing her apron and pressing it into the hands of someone close by when William raced into the kitchen on his way to the gardens.

"Check the rooms, Kelly," he called as he raced past. "All of them. There aren't too many places she can hide, but do it just in case she went upstairs."

Kelly turned on her heel and did as she was told. Her father was in control, so it was easier to follow his orders. If she didn't, she'd fall apart and not be any help at all. Checking both the left and right turrets she came up empty. She checked the downstairs rooms and the café, in case she fell asleep under a table, and then the laundry and amenities area.

Still no sign of Gemma.

Kelly clamped down on her teeth, doing everything possible to convince herself that Gemma was somewhere close by. She wasn't going to break down. God help her.

Get outside and look for her!

She ran through the laundry door, out into the grounds—and froze when she heard a piercing yell. It was William, she knew it.

She couldn't tell exactly where it'd come from, but it echoed in the rainforest surrounding the castle. Round and round went the sound of her father's scream, like a vortex. Or was it just in her head?

When her vision cleared, she noticed her mother stood at the steps to the falls, her phone attached to her ear. William burst from the concrete stairs—with Kelly's little girl limp in his arms.

Then it was her screams echoing and circling the castle. They went on and on and on until she processed that William was giving her baby mouth-to-mouth and pumping frantically at her little chest. Kelly found herself on her knees beside him, doing whatever he yelled at her to do.

A paramedic appeared and took over. In a fuzzy state, Kelly viewed everything as an outsider, and her gut instinct told her the blue tinge to her baby's skin would never change back to its rosy pink. Never, never, never.

When they drove away with her baby, Kelly screamed and screamed at the unfairness of it all.

Her cherub wasn't coming home.

⁘

Kelly combed her wet hair back from her pale face and secured it in a ponytail. Today was the day they were cremating her baby girl. A week ago, the notion had been unfathomable. Saying goodbye to her little girl for the second time in her short life was the hardest thing Kelly had ever had to do.

She looked up again at her reflection in the mirror. Who cared how she looked? Her parents didn't look any better. She bet they hadn't slept much in the past week either.

They'd closed the castle for the week. But doing so had given her too much time to think, too many reasons to blame herself for Gemma's death.

She searched for her sunglasses to hide her red-rimmed eyes. She'd rehashed that day and asked herself a million questions about what she should've done differently. The stupid questions circled her overtired head. Day, night, day and night. As if sleep mattered. It was too late now. How many days could a person go without sleep until they collapsed from sheer exhaustion? Another stupid question she couldn't answer.

Then there were those she now asked the mirror in front of her. What if she'd been more attentive of the gate? Had she clicked it into place properly? What if she'd taken Gemma on the tour with her? Tourists always took to her cheerful and bubbly personality and she normally ended up being the bigger attraction.

The only answer Kelly could come up with was that she'd given Gemma up once—she hadn't deserved a second chance.

With that thought, the pain really hit. Tears flowed down her face again. She would have to face the truth for the rest of her life. It would never go away.

William came into the room and put his arms around her. "Hey, baby."

He was a wreck. Her parents each blamed themselves, but that was a pointless exercise. Sharing the burden of guilt wouldn't change anything.

Tears dripped down William's cheeks and he took a well-used tissue from his pocket. "Ready?"

She nodded. What else could they do? Somehow, they'd pick up the pieces and move on, one day at a time.

Ironically, the only peace she'd felt since that day was when she watched the water cascade over the falls. She swore Gemma's spirit touched her each time she sat at the water's edge.

But that was crazy. Why didn't the falls trigger memories of her baby being pulled out? She should hate the falls, the swimming hole and the entire castle. She should despise the whole place and blame it for taking away her baby girl.

Except she couldn't drum up enough energy to hate it. And when spray from the falls touched her cheeks, she desperately wanted to believe it was Gemma kissing her.

Her father wound his arm around her shoulder and together they walked outside to the waiting car. Staff, friends, Aidan and his parents, Mr Blundell, and so many from the community, no doubt genuinely devastated by the news, would congregate with them. Kelly appreciated their well wishes, even if she didn't have the strength to thank them yet. Getting that strength back meant moving past the denial of what happened, but she was still waking up each morning expecting to see Gemma stumble into her bed. Anger would then attack, and again, she'd ask the same questions. Why hadn't she checked the childproof gate? Why hadn't she taken Gemma with her?

She couldn't see any road past the blame game in her mind. It was there for life.

◦───◦

The service must have been poignant and sweet, but the many photos of Gemma playing on the screen tore at Kelly. They captured the best of the times they'd shared with Gemma. The best and worst year of Kelly's life.

When they left the church, the pallbearers carried the tiny white coffin outside. Kelly clutched her mother's hand tightly as she struggled to make her legs function. She wanted to collapse on the ground and wail like a mad woman. She wanted to raise her face and scream at the god who'd taken her little girl from her and demand to know why the hell he'd done it. Gemma was the perfect daughter.

Was it because she hadn't been the perfect mother? *You gave her up once, you didn't deserve her.*

Everyone's well wishes washed over her; it was too much to process all at once. She hoped one day she could look back and not hate the words: 'I'm so sorry.'

As she looked around, she could barely make out the faces she saw—if she ever stopped crying it'd be a miracle—until the outline of one person stood out from all the rest. Blinking away her tears, she tugged her hand away from her mother's and reached for her supply of tissues.

"Patrick?" she whispered.

Was she hallucinating from lack of sleep?

He stood taller than the rest of the crowd. He appeared bigger, stronger and not from this world. Certainly not from the world she'd been thrust into this past week.

The image kept coming closer, even with the crowd of well-wishers in the way. When he was close enough for her to look into his blue eyes, he opened his arms wide.

She'd wished for death many times during the last week. Maybe God had finally granted her wish.

But then she heard Patrick say, "I'm here now, Kel. I'm not going anywhere." His arms wound around her tightly until she could barely breathe.

For the first time since that horrific day, a pinprick of light became visible. Even with her eyes shut, as she sobbed against Patrick's chest, she could make out the tiniest thread of light. Until something slipped and slammed shut inside her heart.

Unwilling to accept the smallest speck of hope, she pushed back and made a promise.

Never again would she give her heart to anyone. It hurt too damn much when it broke.

Chapter 31

Patrick broke through the earth with another whack of the mattock. He'd taken his shirt off and was savouring the hot sun searing his skin. To prevent it from burning, he'd lathered on sunscreen, enjoying the heat for a change. Unsure of which road he'd travel next, he took every chance to physically exert himself. Working his muscles calmed and cleared his head.

When he'd fled Boston, he abandoned his plans to travel to Asia with the sole intention of getting to Kelly. What really hurt was that he'd been so sure of his reasons for coming. Had been damn near certain Kelly would need him and heal with his help.

He shook his head, spraying sweat across his shoulders. Life had a way of screwing things up until they were so twisted there was little chance of untangling them. He'd known that the instant Kelly stepped back from his embrace. He had no idea how to thaw the ice-cold wall she'd erected around herself, so he was giving her time—time to get over the pain of losing Gemma.

"Want a hand?"

Patrick looked up briefly. William approached looking in no better condition than Kelly. The funeral had been held only five days ago and the castle was open again and a hive of activity. Not enough time, in Patrick's opinion, for either Margaret or William to recover. But the tourists had other ideas, and in a way, keeping busy was a good thing.

He spent a few more minutes finishing the corner section he was working on.

Thwack. Thwack. Thwack.

He hadn't expected Kelly to be okay but thought she would at least want to talk. The few words she'd spoken to him had been terse; she'd told him to go back home and get on with his life. It wasn't the first time she'd told him that. And just like before, each word was a blow that caught him in his middle, hurting with the same intensity of a knife stabbing him. But this wasn't about him. It was about a beautiful baby girl and the tragic end to her short life. So, Patrick pushed all the pain he was feeling to the far corner of his mind where it belonged.

"I suppose you want to know what I'm up to."

William stepped back and crouched in the shade of the forest. "I've never questioned your actions, Patrick. You always seem to know what you're doing."

Really? That was news to him. He never knew what he was doing with his life. One step had led to another and he certainly didn't feel as if he had any control over the direction.

Patrick kept attacking the rectangular patch of dirt he'd outlined with line-marking paint. He hadn't done anything so physical in a long time; it was a balm to his excess energy and frustration.

Goddamn it.

He tightened his grip on the wooden handle. Determination drove the dirt out faster than he would've without the mental challenge William had thrown at him. He was going to have the foundations dug and his life sorted—all by the end of the afternoon.

These were his options, he reasoned. He could either cower, forget about Kelly and return to his plan of trekking through Asia. Or—and he handled more dirt before he let his mind go down this path—he could follow his heart and try to convince Kelly that she had a choice. But first he needed to find his true place and now was the time to start. How many more years was he going to waste? His father might have a point.

He liked William and Margaret and, on the flight over, had envisioned a life at the castle—sharing the workload with Kelly. He could easily live the rest of his days here and there was evidence of plenty of work needing to be done.

He stopped what he was doing and straightened. "She won't talk to me. Says I should leave."

"I know. She said as much to me."

Patrick dropped the mattock and picked up his discarded shirt. He mopped the sweat from his face and gave himself one last shot. "Why won't she talk?"

William shook his head. "This has been tough on all of us, Patrick. You included. She said it would be wrong to let you back into her life after she chose Gemma over you in the first place. Says she would be on the rebound. And some other rot about never giving her heart to anyone again."

Patrick's chest constricted at those words. She hadn't said any of that to him.

He picked up the mattock again and continued to hack at the earth. His suffering muscles were screaming at him to take it easy. He'd be aching the next day, but then again, he'd been hurting for a long time.

"I'd like to build a shrine in memory of Gemma, if that's okay with you."

When William didn't respond, Patrick stopped and rested on the handle, a little out of breath. Tears trickled down Williams's cheeks, his hurt too strong to be forgotten so soon.

Rising, William swiped them away and came out of the shadows. "You're a good soul, Patrick. You don't need to convince me."

He patted Patrick on the shoulder, as though he was planning to leave him to it, but when a sob escaped his throat, Patrick wound an arm around his shoulder and let him cry. Man to man, away from the women and tourists. This man had raised that little girl from birth. Her sudden death had upset Patrick, but how much worse was it for him and Margaret?

Taking a well-used tissue from his pocket, William apologised. "Sorry, mate. Didn't mean to land that on you." He turned to go but halted. "Thanks for doing this. She may not appreciate the importance of it straight away, but she'll come around. Give her time."

"I was hoping to build a small seat so she can come and sit and enjoy the view of the waterfall."

William nodded. "Strange, I know. I thought she'd hate the falls and the swimming hole, but she spends the afternoon watching the water flow, and when she comes inside, I always sense she's a little calmer." William paused a moment and looked towards the falls. "Time, Patrick. It's what we all need."

When William walked back to the castle, Patrick almost gave up. He was moments away from pushing the dirt back to its original place and driving away with the utility he'd purchased the day before in Innisfail. Time was a nasty word. He'd dealt with it plenty of times over the years. But he hadn't just lost a child, and had no idea how much time it took to recover from something like that. So what if he hurt and suffered some more?

He'd watched Kelly the past couple of days. Every afternoon she would make her way to the top of the concrete steps and sit. Once the tourists were gone and the gate had been shut, she had a couple of hours to herself. He'd approached her on the first day, but she'd turned away, saying, "I'm sorry, Patrick. I can't do this."

He'd left her to her grief. Because he understood the blackness that descended. No matter who tried to break through, you only wanted to thrash at them to leave you alone. Oh boy, did he remember. So he'd pushed back his own grief at losing Kelly and had walked away.

He sighed at the tangle of emotions pushing against his chest. He squared his shoulders and picked up the mattock again. He had a job to do, and if it was the only legacy he left them, he would have to be satisfied with that.

It took Patrick an entire week to complete the shrine. Each morning he parked his utility in the public car park and carried his tools and materials to the edge of the trees in full view of the falls. He'd formed the framework, mixed cement by hand in a wheelbarrow he'd found in the shed, then poured the cement into the frame. The hard physical work was therapeutic in a lot of ways.

The shrine was a square seat with a high back but no sides. Constructed on a rectangular base, it could've been designed for royalty. Patrick was proud of his work and was now only waiting for a brass plaque to arrive. He'd screw it onto the backrest so that when Kelly leaned against it, she would touch the memory dedicated to her daughter. Finally, he'd ask William to create a small garden of flowering natives around the base to ensure the spot was kept special.

With each day that Kelly avoided him, his sense of purpose strengthened. He'd taken to looking at the real estate shopfronts and knew where he was headed next; he just wasn't sure how long the drive would take. He could buy any property, anywhere he wanted, but had only one desire—Samdarra had ingrained it into his psyche. He'd come to love the rich red of the Australian outback, the intense heat that drove all other thoughts from your head, and the sparse landscape where humans numbered in small pockets. He'd healed there once. It was where he'd heal again.

Patrick had his meagre belongings packed in his utility and was ready to hit the road. He could head in a few different directions, depending on which property he wanted to inspect first.

William walked around the vehicle, checking the tyres. It was a fatherly thing to do and a gesture for making goodbye easier. It was going to hurt like blazes to drive away but Patrick hardened to it. He was only waiting for Kelly to come out of her cottage, now that the working day was over. If she didn't come to say goodbye, he would go to her.

"I've packed you some snacks to tide you through a couple of days," Margaret said.

She managed a smile these days. Patrick could see it hurt, but at least she was trying.

"Thanks." Patrick swooped in for a hug and she trembled within his embrace.

"If you come across any problems, give us a call, mate," William said. "We're always here for you." He came to stand beside Margaret and put his arm around her.

That was the thing about Kelly's parents. They weren't saying it in passing only. They really *would* be there for him if he needed help. Knowing it made leaving even harder and the pain inside intensified.

When there was no sign of Kelly, all three of them looked towards the cottage.

Patrick took a deep breath and held it in for a moment before releasing it. "I'll go and say goodbye."

"Sure." William shook Patrick's hand again. "We're going to head off now too, so we'll leave you to it. Take care on the roads and watch for the roos at dusk."

Patrick nodded and turned for the cottage.

He didn't bother knocking. Didn't want to stand at a door she was never going to open. He didn't immediately find her when he walked in, so he made his way to her bedroom and called her name softly.

She put on a brave face each day for the staff and tourists, but when he found her curled up on her bed with one of Gemma's stuffed toys pressed against her chest, he wasn't surprised. Her cheeks glistened with tears and her midnight black hair was a tangled mess spread over her bright orange quilt. Her eyes were shut and she wore a pained look.

He called her name again, gently. She didn't react at first but then slowly opened her eyes and moved her head a fraction until she caught sight of him.

With only a few seconds to debate his next actions, he lay behind her and curled his body around hers, cooing soothingly, close to her face. At first, she stiffened, but he refused to let go.

"I'm leaving, Kelly. It's what you asked me to do."

She began to whimper.

He rose on his knees and perched over her. His heart broke in two when he looked into her eyes—two bottomless pools of misery.

"I'll come back, Kelly. I promise."

She shook her head as fresh tears coursed down her face.

He'd been so strong since coming back to Kelrick Kastle, but her tears were his undoing. A sob slashed at his throat and the tears he should've cried with Kelly were finally released. When she rolled to her side, he dropped his face against her shoulder and let it all out. Her hand went to his cheek and rested against it. He'd never forget her touch for as long as he lived.

When it was time to leave, he rose from the bed and wiped his face with his shirt. Kelly lay motionless on the bed, her gaze pinned to his. He doubted she would rouse to eat dinner; she was already starting to look like a collection of skin and bones and it tortured him to see her that way.

"I'm so sorry, Patrick. Please forgive me."

He spotted a box of tissues and plucked a couple out. "I already have."

She gave the slightest nod.

"Will you promise me one thing, Kel?"

This time, she didn't nod. But neither did she shake her head, so Patrick took his chances.

"If I send you a message or anything, will you promise to answer it?"

He waited, sure she'd stay frozen forever. Then he saw the slightest of nods and his spirits soared. One day at a time.

Suddenly buoyed and cheered by the first sign she was still planning to live, he managed a lopsided smile. "I promise I won't spam you. It'll be nice to check you're doing okay, if I can find reception wherever I end up."

With feigned confidence, he leaned down to kiss her cheek. He couldn't gather enough sunlight from that one kiss alone, but he would relive the many they'd shared in the past. Each one had warmed him plenty, as though he'd been kissing the sun itself. His memories had helped him through many sleepless nights over the past year and he would draw on them again if he had to.

He latched onto her watery gaze one last time. "I love you, Kel. Don't ever forget."

Then, taking determined steps, he left the cottage and the castle in the forest.

It was time to find the real Patrick Van Der Meeliko.

Chapter 32

When she heard the soft click of the front door closing, Kelly knew Patrick was gone. She squeezed her eyes shut, hoping she wouldn't hear the sound of his departing utility. If she had the strength, she'd cover her ears.

She'd done everything to avoid witnessing his departure. Had even denied herself the time she usually spent at the falls, the only place where she felt Gemma's spirit. Watching the water flow helped her feel less depressed, but she'd shied away from leaving her cottage, hoping to miss the intense hurt in Patrick's eyes when he left.

She should've known he would never leave without saying goodbye. As predicted, she'd seen his pain etched on his face when she'd found the strength to look at him for the final time. She was good at hurting Patrick and she would pay for it one day. Maybe she was now. Hadn't she hurt him once before? She had to believe she'd done the right thing when he'd turned up out of the blue. There was no space for him left inside her. Grieving for Gemma took everything she had.

I'm so sorry, Patrick. So, so, sorry.

She hugged Gemma's favourite teddy tighter and muffled more tears against it as the quiet of the cottage and the surrounding forest weighed down on her.

Her parents had spent weeks camped in the lounge room as they'd grieved together, but lately, they'd been returning a few nights a week to their home in Innisfail. It was a long shot to say they were over the worst. Margaret still burst into tears without any provocation and Kelly had seen William wiping at his eyes on a daily basis. Gemma had been their world and Kelly didn't want to be in this one without her. She'd needed to send Patrick away. Didn't want to drag him down too. Pushing him away was for his own good, whether he believed it or not. Gemma had taken her heart with her.

The need to join Gemma had been Kelly's constant companion these past weeks. It wasn't the first time she'd considered suicide, contemplating the how and where. For the second time in her life, dark thoughts emerged—but her parents' heartbreak after Gemma's death caused her to flinch from them. She'd pushed her way through darkness before and would do it again. Time was all she needed. Yet some days dragged with alarming slowness and stretched the pain into eternity.

Sleep was another issue. She would snatch a few hours here and there when all she wanted was to sleep day and night. In her dreams Gemma was alive and whole, healthy and cherubic, but sleep was elusive.

Kelly's stomach growled loudly in the quiet cottage and she pulled the teddy away. Food hadn't interested her for a long time. The cook had left her a meal, but since she'd lost all inclination to eat, she'd put the vegetable lasagne in the fridge. Except now, lying on her back and looking unseeing at the ceiling, she was tempted to take a few bites. What had changed? Was being so alone alarming her body into action?

She slid to the edge of the bed and rose on unsteady legs. Her knees wobbled as she made her way to the kitchen. She was surprised she wanted to eat. Maybe this was what she needed—to be truly alone, so she could kickstart her inner strength and get through this.

She put the ready-made meal in the microwave and set the timer for a minute. When it pinged, the noise startled her. Shocked at how fragile she felt, she rummaged in a drawer for her headlamp and strapped it to her forehead.

With food and fork in hand, she wanted out—she didn't know where she wanted to go, only that she wanted to get out of the cottage for starters. Claustrophobic claws threatened to suffocate her if she didn't get outside and breathe. Was she having a panic attack?

Breathe, girl, breathe. Come on, you can do it.

Without knowing where she was headed, she walked alongside the castle and the outdoor table settings. Past the pretty awning that kept the sun off the tourists while they drank and snacked. Past the fountains that shot water gracefully into the air when William switched the pumps on in the morning. Finally, she caught sight of the memorial she'd watched Patrick build from her periphery. Never once had she asked what he was doing or offered to help, but when William had told her what he was building, a spurt of anger had crossed her chest. How would a shrine help? It couldn't bring Gemma back.

Determined to see it up close, she ignored her food until she reached the shrine. The moon, clearly visible above, shone brightly, so she switched off the headlamp.

Tentatively, she sat cross-legged on the seat and felt something cool touch the back of her neck. She twisted around to see what it was and, switching her headlamp back on, stared at the brass plaque. Her jaw dropped as she read its message.

In Memory of Gemma Sheppard.
You brought the stars to your mother's eyes
And laughter to her heart.
You made her sing with happiness.
You were the centre of your grandparents' world
And you taught them how to live again.
Take care of the birdies in heaven, little girl.
Your family will all hold hands together again one day.
Tragically taken from their embrace on …

By the time she reached Gemma's date of death, Kelly couldn't read any more; her vision was too blurred. She couldn't believe Patrick had engraved such a beautiful message for her baby girl. It embodied everything they'd shared as mother and daughter in the short time allotted to them. She turned back to face the waterfall, switched off the headlamp and rested against the cool brass plate.

Tears flowed down her face until she had no more to give. She stared unseeing into the darkness, letting the sound of flowing water mesmerise her. In time, it managed to calm her.

She noticed, on the ground beside the shrine, a couple of boxes filled with potted natives. The conversation she'd overhead her parents have, about Patrick wanting William to plant flowering natives, now made sense.

She smiled fleetingly, surprised her body allowed it. It was still too early to be able to smile, surely? But in the perfectly balmy night, she ignored her doubts and invited peace to surround her. Patrick had contributed so much to her castle, but this native garden, perhaps his smallest gesture, would flourish for years to come.

Remembering the forgotten lasagne, she forced the meal down, bite by bite. Her brain told her she needed nourishment, so she ate. Surprisingly, a faint shimmer of energy returned to her body and she felt better for it.

Then an idea came to her. She switched on her headlamp and made her way to the small shed where she stored garden tools. She would plant the natives and tend them daily. Patrick had intended for the shrine and the garden to give her peace and solace and she could see that it might work.

She worked late into the night, planting the natives until they formed a neat border around the rectangular base of the shrine. When she returned to the cottage with no inkling of the hour, she showered and went to bed, falling asleep soundly for the first time since Gemma's tragic death.

And her last thoughts were of Patrick.

Patrick's utility rattled over the rough corrugated road, causing a cloud of dust to billow behind his vehicle. In the days since leaving Kelrick Kastle he'd inspected three properties, spending three or four days at each. He'd really liked one but was holding off on making a decision until he inspected the fourth property on his list.

He squinted into the late afternoon sun, not sure if he should camp on the side of the road and start afresh the next day. This next property was the furthest from the coast and he'd been driving all day. The others were each about a two-hour drive from Kelrick Kastle but in three different directions. None of them were as isolated as Samdarra; Patrick liked the idea of being relatively close to the coast.

As he came around a bend, he braked suddenly when he spotted a dark utility parked on the side of the rough-edged road. A man was shuffling gear around the tray.

Patrick slowed and sidled up beside the vehicle. "Everything okay?"

The tired and haggard-looking fifty-something stockman stopped what he was doing and, arching his back, rested a hand on his hip. "I think I left me jack in the shed. Shit. Should've put it back when I finished with it. I gotta flattie and won't be goin' nowhere until I change it."

"How far's home?" Patrick asked.

The man pointed down the road. "The entrance to the property's only a coupla k's down thata way. So bloody close."

"I'll give you a hand," Patrick offered. "We can use my jack."

They worked quietly as the gentle afternoon breeze rustled the leaves on the tall eucalyptus trees lining the road. Spindly dry grass hugged each tree and the exposed earth surrounding them was cracked. If Patrick had picked up anything in the past two weeks, it was that the long seven-year drought hadn't broken yet. While he knew weather predictions were good for the coming wet season, no one he'd met was getting their hopes up.

"Where you headed, mate?" The stockman asked.

"To a property four hours away on this road, if my directions are right."

"Where you staying tonight?"

"I was going to camp in my swag on the back of my utility."

The stockman scratched his stubbled cheek and leaned on the side of his vehicle. "You're not from around these parts, are you?"

Patrick nodded as he packed up his jack and stored it in its place.

"How about staying the night with us? The missus can give you a feed. It's the least we can do to thank you."

Patrick loved how friendly people were in remote areas. "It won't put your wife out?"

"Nah. She'll enjoy some new company. Gets tiring talking to the same old bugger every day." He managed a tired smile, removed his Akubra and raked a hand through his greying hair. Putting his hat back on his head, he offered his hand. "Darcy's the name."

Patrick took Darcy's hand and gave it a good shake. "Patrick, and I'd love a nice meal and a hot cup of tea."

"Deal," Darcy said. "It's about a five-k drive to the homestead from the entrance gate."

"Sure, lead the way."

Patrick kept some distance between them to avoid having to suck in the billowing dust from Darcy's vehicle. He eyed the gate up ahead and slowed even further. He wouldn't get lost from this point, but if he could keep the dust from filling every possible cavity under the bonnet of the utility, it'd save him a lot of work later when he attempted to clean it.

As he indicated to turn into the property's entrance, he spotted a real estate agency's sign and stopped to read it. The property was being auctioned in two weeks. Why hadn't Patrick been given the details? If Darcy's place was up for auction, it meant it was up for sale. *Hmm.*

Patrick looked up at the archway, supported by two semi-rusted posts, above the entrance to the property. He squinted into the sun's glare, trying to make out the wrought-iron lettering. *G, E, N, S, P, P, I, N, G, S.*

Gensppings? Gensprings? Gemsprings?

"Holy shoot. Gem Springs."

A simple name but one that instantly reminded him of Kelly's little girl.

A shudder rippled across his shoulders. He wound the window down and gulped in mouthfuls of air now that Darcy's path of dust had settled. A premonition wavered. There was a reason he'd been on this road. A reason he'd stumbled upon this auction sign. Under any other circumstances he would've driven past without ever glimpsing it.

He tucked a wayward dreadlock behind his ear and fought the ludicrous idea that fate had brought him here.

If you don't believe in fate, turn around and drive away.

But although he had no idea what he would find five kilometres down the road, he believed he wouldn't be at this junction unless it was meant to be. Put him in this same situation two years ago and he would've laughed it off as a bad joke. A wrong turn in the road. A mistake. But he was a different man these days and could confidently say it was his destiny to be in this exact spot at this very moment. He caught a fleeting glimpse of a dust spiral a couple of kilometres ahead and put the utility into gear.

He headed for the homestead, daring the non-believers to stop him.

Chapter 33

Patrick took in his surroundings as he drove slowly down the drive. He wasn't prepared to miss a thing, but he smiled guiltily. If he didn't gas it soon, Darcy would send out a search party.

Still, there was plenty to see and he wanted to absorb it all and get a lay of the land. The paddocks were dry and barren, but patches of forest provided decent shade for the few cattle dotted around. The fencing looked in awful need of repair; there wasn't a thirty-metre stretch that wasn't broken. In the distance, a blue mountain range ran parallel with the bumpy road, and the orange glow of the late afternoon sun falling behind the peaks had his jaw hanging at the natural beauty. The rutted road, though, was potholed and corrugated, and was deteriorating with each kilometre he drove, so he slowed even further. If he wasn't careful, he'd damage his vehicle, which would delay his inspection of the final property.

From the tumbledown entrance sign, the sad state of the fencing and the dreadful condition of the road, it was clear the property was in dire straits. Samdarra had an entirely different vibe, and the three properties Patrick had already inspected had displayed a veneer of pride, despite the long years of drought.

His arrival at the homestead didn't dispel his initial opinion. Could these good-hearted people afford to feed him? Reluctant to impose on their hospitality, Patrick parked the utility and stepped out hesitantly. Darcy waited on the porch, where a timber step had snapped in half.

Patrick attempted a genuine smile as he approached Darcy and the woman who'd come to stand beside him. The odds looked stacked against this pair, but Darcy reached an arm around the woman's back to lend support. That one small gesture did something to Patrick, as if restoring his faith in human strength. That anyone could go through such hardship but keep a relationship intact was a lesson he would take from this, if nothing else.

Darcy helped his wife over the broken step and they met Patrick in the yard. "Patrick, meet my wife, Evelyn."

Evelyn's hair looked prematurely greyed and she carried the same tired lines around her eyes as Darcy.

Patrick took her work-worn hand in his and gave it a light shake. "It's my pleasure, Evelyn. I hope I'm not imposing."

She gave him a weary smile. "A visitor is always welcome. Thanks for helping Darcy out. He would've had to walk back if you hadn't driven by."

The gloomy aura surrounding them hit Patrick in his middle. "I'm not in any hurry to reach my next destination. I could spend a couple of days giving you a hand. I don't expect a roof over my head for nothing."

Patrick didn't miss the pained look that fleetingly crossed their faces as they turned to each other. Darcy reached for his wife's hand and he swallowed a couple of times. "There isn't much left for us to do, but you're welcome to stay for as long as you need." He waved Patrick forward, adding, "Anyway, come inside and join us for dinner. Evelyn says it's ready and we have enough for three."

Patrick heard the noisy whirr of a generator as he climbed past the broken step and into the dimly lit homestead. Boxes lay strewn across the living area. Some were taped closed, others only partially packed.

So, they really are leaving their beloved home. Patrick sensed their reluctance and heartbreak to say goodbye to this place, and the depressing sight of the packing boxes cemented his decision—he wouldn't leave this property until he had all the facts.

He hoped he didn't come across rude, but he didn't want them to know he was on the hunt for a property. Keeping that from them meant he had a better chance of hearing the truth. If they weren't on their guard, he'd learn a lot more.

Evelyn dished out a simple stew that smelled delicious and they ate quietly for a few moments before Patrick put his fork down and asked, "Why is this property going to auction? Aren't places like this snapped up quickly?"

Darcy wiped his mouth with a serviette. "Everyone knows we've been struggling for a while. They're vultures waiting for the final blow to come. Why pay what the land is worth when the bank will auction it off for a tenth of its value, take what's owed to them and leave nothing for us?"

Bitterness laced his words and Patrick understood. Hadn't he seen with his own eyes how ruthless banks could be? Their only goal was to make a profit.

A single tear slid silently down Evelyn's cheek.

"How long have you been here?" Patrick asked gently, wanting to know why things hadn't worked out for them here. What would it take to make this place a success?

"Nearly thirty years, but that's not long enough. To make a go of it out here you have to have inherited land debt-free from your great-great-grandfather and hope to God you don't experience a bastard drought like this one. You need a bank that doesn't screw you over and for the cattle prices to stay okay. It's not bloody rocket science, but make a few bad decisions outside your control, and it's all downhill. The drought hasn't helped."

A sob escaped Evelyn's throat.

Darcy covered her hand with his. "I was the fourth son, so I was never gonna git the family property handed to me. But farming gets in your blood, Patrick, so instead you buy a place you probably shouldn't. You want to live on the land so bad you're willing to work your fingers to the bone to make a go of it."

Darcy dropped his head and Patrick swallowed, gutted by his pain.

"I failed you, luv," Darcy added, lifting his head a fraction and turning to Evelyn. Unshed tears shimmered in his eyes.

Patrick sat, awkwardly transfixed, his heart bleeding for these two hardworking people. He understood how the Australian outback got into your blood. He'd tried to shake the feeling off before, but he'd found he couldn't. Despite the harshness of the land, he understood.

Desperate to change the subject, he asked, "How did the name Gem Springs come about?"

"The entire property is bordered by a small tributary that usually flows all year round." Evelyn sniffled and answered for Darcy, probably knowing he'd struggle to speak. "It's the lifeblood of this property. When it rains again, the water will gush its way towards the main river, tumbling over whitewashed rocks and sparkling granite that resembles gemstones. I was a young mother to be when I fell in love with that creek. We named it Gem Springs soon after."

"I like it," Patrick said and was rewarded with Evelyn's first real smile, fleeting though it was. "I'd like to take a look at the creek. Would that be possible?"

"Darcy was going to have one last look around the property this week. You're welcome to join him. I'll stay here and keep packing."

Darcy seemed to have his emotions under better control and picked up his fork to keep eating. "I wouldn't mind a bit of company."

<hr />

"In our best years, we fed around three thousand head of cattle. You need a minimum of a thousand breeders to make this property work, but any more than three thousand and you'll run out of land."

"Can you droughtproof it at all?" Patrick asked. They sat under the shade of a eucalypt and the thin trickle of water from the creek beside them was barely audible.

"If you hadda bit of financial backin' you could organise silage, to lower the cost of extra feed. Possible but bloody hard work as long as you're not afraid of it."

Patrick mulled over Darcy's advice. This was one stockman with years of experience and a vast amount of knowledge who wasn't afraid of hard work. Patrick could do worse for a property manager.

"Why do you want to know, anyways? Sounds like you don't belong in these parts."

Patrick looked up, not perturbed by Darcy's curiosity. He'd only been stating the truth. Patrick *didn't* belong in these parts, so he would need someone like Darcy to guide him.

"It's all very interesting," he said. "What are your plans for after the auction?"

Darcy shrugged. "Try to find somewhere cheap to live in Mount Garnet. Me daughter wants us to go live with her in Townsville, but I wouldn't last long in the big smoke."

They'd spent the night in their swags, a fire between them, talking under the stars. Patrick learned of their two daughters, both settled on the coast with husbands and children. They'd begged their parents to sell years earlier, but Darcy had said he wouldn't budge until he absolutely had to. Things had been getting worse ever since.

After listening to Darcy's story, Patrick was fit to burst. He refrained from saying anything though. He wanted Evelyn to be there when he spilled his news. From the moment he'd managed to decipher the name Gem Springs, every action and conversation between himself and Darcy had been leading to the decision he'd now made. He just had to share it with them.

In a few minutes they'd pile their gear into the back of Patrick's utility and drive back to the homestead. He'd volunteered its use, not sure if

Darcy and Evelyn could afford the extra fuel, and together he and Darcy had driven kilometres across the vast expanse of the property, with Darcy believing it would be his last time.

Darcy sighed, as if he sensed his chance to reminisce had come to an end. "I reckon Evelyn will have dinner ready for us if we head back now."

Patrick rose and stretched his legs, looked westward at another spectacular sunburnt-orange sunset in the making, then bent to gather his gear and take another slug of water from his cooler.

"You married or somethin'?"

Patrick screwed the lid of his water cooler back on. "No. I wanted to make someone my wife, but life got in the way."

Wistfully, Darcy looked westward too. "The only thing that got me through these tough years was me wife. Find someone you love, and if she loves you back, nothin' else can kill you. Even though the world is bloody well trying."

He began laughing at his own joke, but his chortles quickly changed to almighty sobs, and for the second time in as many weeks, Patrick was confronted with a crying man. Unsure of what to do, he gave Darcy a few minutes of quiet while he piled their gear in the back of the utility and strapped it down. When he was finished, Darcy was using his sleeve to mop his face.

"Sorry, mate. Always better to avoid letting your wife see you cry. They feel too much and try to hide it from you."

"It's okay. You're both in a horrible situation. I'm glad you have each other."

Darcy gave him a lop-sided smile, though his heart clearly wasn't in it. Turning, he surveyed his land one last time before opening the passenger door and getting in.

"Thanks," he said through the open window. "I'm ready now."

Patrick rounded the vehicle and climbed in the driver's seat. It was time to get Darcy home and put him out of his misery.

Chapter 34

Dinner that night was a delicious roast with vegetables—simple fare but satisfying. Patrick could get used to Evelyn's cooking. Either that or he'd have to beg her to teach him how it was done.

While Darcy showered, Evelyn asked Patrick how Darcy had taken his last trek over his land.

"He's hurting as expected," Patrick told her. He didn't think it was necessary to give details.

"He doesn't like to show it, but he carries so much guilt, Patrick. He's always been such a hardworking and considerate man. I couldn't have asked for more. I just wish things had turned out better for us. Take him away from the land and he may as well be dead. I'm worried that leaving here will lead him to an early grave."

This was exactly the kind of opportunity Patrick had waited for most of his life. He always wanted to help people who deserved it, but he'd never known how to go about it. He had more money than he'd ever spend in a lifetime, which had scared him plenty over the years. Fear that he would be taken advantage of if he helped the wrong type had always held him back.

But he was getting stronger of mind and better at understanding when it was right or wrong to help. Call it growing up, but something told him he would never have reached this point had he continued living in Boston. There, he'd lived among people who didn't understand what money meant to people who didn't have enough. They wouldn't understand the Darcys and Evelyns of the world, who earned every cent with their blood, sweat and tears. If Patrick made a success of Gem Springs, he would help more people. Samdarra was stamped all over his heart—that place had received his tick of approval from the earliest of days—so he knew just how he'd go about it.

The beauty of staying incognito meant that Darcy and Evelyn had no idea who he was or what his plans involved. He'd listened to them unburden the details of their financial hardships with no restrictions or embellishments; they'd simply told the truth. With his mind made up on arrival, the knowledge he'd gained since proved that gut instinct wasn't something to be ignored.

Darcy and Evelyn believed Patrick planned to stay a couple of days before moving on. They knew he was travelling from the States, but telling them he was from Boston hadn't meant much. To these good country folks, America was America, so they'd lumped him into the same category as Yanks.

Patrick was okay with that.

All he had to do now was break the news—either tonight after a hearty meal or in the morning after a good night's sleep.

⁂

"How do you like your eggs, Patrick?"

Evelyn was making a special breakfast for his departure.

Patrick wound an elastic band around his shoulder-length dreadlocks and answered, "Well-cooked, thanks."

"It'll be a few minutes. Do you mind calling Darcy? I think he went out to the back shed."

Patrick went outside and headed towards the rear of the homestead, his booted feet kicking up dust with each step. Water was precious in these parts; unless you were licenced to extract it from underground, it wasn't worth wasting any on keeping the lawn around the house green. A bore positioned close to the home would ensure a fresh and inviting garden even in the toughest of times.

Once inside, they all sat for breakfast and talked about some recent news headlines—the possibility of an early election being called, the murder of an innocent foreign student and an earthquake in Indonesia.

When Patrick couldn't wait any longer, he asked, "Which town is business conducted in when you live in these parts?"

"Atherton's pretty much got everything you need. Banks and decent supermarkets for shopping. You can get there in two hours." Evelyn offered.

"Would you both like to come for a drive with me?"

When wariness crossed Evelyn's face, Patrick realised he was a stranger asking them to accompany him in his vehicle. His dreadlocks probably didn't help either.

Darcy picked up on Evelyn's unease and patted her shoulder. "We were heading that way soon. What do you need us for?"

Patrick's heart thumped inside his chest. Kelly was the last person he'd helped, but he hadn't needed to face her. He'd purchased the castle without her knowledge and with no idea of how she would react to the news.

"Is your property being auctioned by a bank in Atherton?" he asked.

As if resigning himself to their predicament, Darcy only managed a 'yeah.'

"Well ... um ... how would you like to make an appointment with your bank manager?"

Now Darcy's expression grew cautious. "No need to see that bastard any time soon. Where's this headin', young man?"

"What's Gem Springs worth?" Patrick hedged, trying to prevent Darcy and Evelyn from clamming up on him.

"Way more than those mongrels will sell it for. Whatsit to you, anyway?" Cagey all of a sudden, Darcy scraped his chair back and rose. "Are you one of them come to spy on us?"

Alarmed at how badly the conversation had turned, Patrick rose and waved for Darcy to take his seat again. "I promise I'm not here to spy on you. I want to buy Gem Springs, but only if you tell me what it's really worth."

Both Darcy's and Evelyn's jaws dropped. Their eyes stretched wide. They were clearly stunned, unable to speak. Patrick feigned a casual air and continued to eat his bacon and eggs on toast. He allowed himself a couple of mouthfuls, noting that although Darcy twitched on his seat, Evelyn sat frozen. No part of her moved. Had her heart stopped beating from shock at his announcement?

"I'd like you both to remain in the homestead and manage the property with me. There's a lot you can teach me."

Darcy spluttered. "You mean, you wanted this all along?"

Patrick put his fork down. "When I met you, I had no idea it was up for auction. I was on my way to Georgetown. If I hadn't stopped to help with your flat tyre, I never would've seen the auction sign. But, yes, I'm looking for a property and have already inspected three. I'd pretty much chosen one but wanted to inspect one more." He lifted his mug and took a sip of hot, sweetened tea. "Discovering Gem Springs changed everything. Meeting the pair of you has confirmed my choice."

He noticed a small twitch from Evelyn and gave her a sheepish smile.

She finally asked, "So you ... you want us to remain here? But where would you live?"

"I'll build a second homestead. And you can advise me of the best place to do so. I'll need you both to help me make a lot of the decisions." Patrick put his mug down and added, "I've fallen in love with the Australian outback. It's gotten into my blood too and there's no getting away from it."

"But ... you want to pay what it's worth?"

"I sure do."

"And you can afford that?"

"Yes, I can, so don't skimp on the numbers. I can get an independent assessor to come out if needed."

This was what Patrick had feared. They were too honest and 'fair dinkum'—an Australian expression made exactly for these sorts of people—but he wanted to make sure they were paid what was owed to them. It wasn't right to cash in on thirty years of hard work and then gloat at getting a bargain. Patrick wouldn't sleep at night if he took advantage of them.

"Where are you really from?" Darcy asked.

"Boston, America."

"What sort of folk do you come from?"

"I'll tell you what. The first thing I'll do is get satellite telecommunications set up here, then I'll show you articles about my family on the Internet. They're not bad people but I'd rather you kept quiet about my family for a few years. People tend to look at me differently when they know how much I have. No one needs to know, do they?"

Evelyn wiped away at her eyes when tears emerged. "Your secret is safe with us."

Patrick looked at Darcy's still-shocked face and into Evelyn's moisture-filled eyes. He saw gratitude so deep it brewed fresh tears in his own eyes. There were worse places he could end up, but he had a feeling Darcy and Evelyn would be helping him more than he'd be helping them. They would never see it that way, but he hoped to show them one day. In the meantime, he had a bank manager to meet with, Mr Blundell to make contact with (he may as well stick to the one lawyer he knew and trusted), telecommunications people to deal with (he almost groaned at the thought, recalling the time it'd taken to get a tower installed at Kelrick Kastle), and a homestead to build.

"Let me know what needs to be fixed with your home," he said. "We'll bring it back up to scratch."

Darcy rose and Patrick assumed he was about to stretch his arm across the table to shake on the deal. Patrick rose, prepared to shake back, but instead, Darcy rounded the table, pulled Patrick against his chest and wrapped him in a huge hug.

It was almost Patrick's undoing. He couldn't remember his father ever giving him such a hug—the kind he would've performed cartwheels for when he was a kid. It was a new experience, one filled with the human spirit he'd missed out on as a child. He'd experienced something similar with Kelly, but the emotions involved were different with a woman. He wanted to feel that again one day, but to stand beside this man and connect in this way was all the confirmation Patrick needed that his decision was the right one.

He'd never back down from it.

Chapter 35

K elly plucked at the weeds around the shrine. Crouching down, she winced when a stone dug into her knee. She rubbed at the spot with her gloved hand before flicking the small rock away and carrying on. The intense afternoon sun burned against her back; she'd be glad in a few minutes when it fell below the tree line. Only then she would have mosquitos to deal with when dusk brought them out in droves.

She smiled, content to have hardships to deal with, and prepared to head back to the cottage before she was eaten alive. Satisfied that she cleaned up enough weeds, she rose and pulled off her gloves. She found the afternoons, once the gates were closed, so peaceful. Sometimes her father would come and sit with her for a few minutes and check out the garden. Her mother usually made the trek early in the morning, coffee in hand. They each dealt with their grief the best way they could.

She wanted a few more minutes of closeness before heading off to tackle the castle's accounts that were a week overdue. She sat cross-legged on the shrine with the beautiful plaque cooling her neck. She knew every word, each one engraved on her heart.

Every time it touched her skin, she was also reminded of Patrick. She'd lost track of how much time had passed but guessed it had been close to seven months since he'd left. And not a word from him. She didn't blame him. Only lately was she starting to feel differently, like she might have some space for him in her heart. She wasn't ready to make any promises, but it was a sign of the progress she'd made. Most days were still hard, but the experts were right; time did heal wounds eventually. Little by little, day by day. Not completely and not forever, but the searing ache around her heart hurt a little less with each passing week. Sometimes there were setbacks, like when a vivid memory or child's song would reignite everything and drag her backwards. Then she would navigate her way through the thick mud to where she'd been before the disruption. Most days, though, she did okay.

Kelly stretched her legs and slipped off the seat. *Sleep tight, little princess.*

They were the same words she recited every night to her baby girl. Doing so gave her a sense of closure and allowed peace to settle around her as each day slipped into the next. It was almost like an insurance policy, assuring her of a good night's sleep. If she was lucky.

Before making her way to the cottage, she took a few moments to stand at the top of the stairs that led to the falls. The breeze brushed up against her skin and she smiled to herself, believing it to be Gemma's spirit talking to her—and to hell with anyone who dared her to think differently. She was smart enough to realise it was a mind game, one she played to keep herself sane. But some things she couldn't bear to change or think otherwise.

Having eaten and showered, Kelly ran a comb through her hair and switched on the computer. She had her monthly business activity statement to lodge, which wouldn't take all night, but the deadline was looming, as it did every month.

An icon flashed to let her know she had a new email.

She opened up her browser to check if it was important and her pulse sped up when she read the name of the sender. 'Patrick V.'

She nervously tapped the desk beside the keyboard, hesitant to open the email. Was he back in Boston? He'd promised to come back. He didn't know it, but she was almost ready to talk to him and share things again.

So why didn't you contact him first?

She kept using the same lame excuse, telling herself she was gathering the strength she needed to contact him, that she wanted to be as strong as possible, the person he knew her to be. But she'd convinced herself she wasn't quite ready and kept delaying it.

When she was alone during the evenings, though, she felt she needed someone to talk to or she'd go crazy. Her parents had gently encouraged her to meet up with the friends she'd made in her young mums' group, but she couldn't; her pain was still too raw to see their children healthy and alive.

During the daylight hours at the castle she was social enough. Each day she put on a brave face and dealt with staff and tourists alike in a chirpy and happy way. It cost her a lot of energy, leaving very little to spare.

Most evenings, though, were long and lonely.

No more, she decided and grimaced in the quiet cottage.

"Open the damn thing," she hissed.

She clicked on the unopened email and her heart pounded as she waited for it to open. Her jaw dropped when she read the first line.

Hi Kel, I've bought a station ...

"What the heck?" She settled into her chair to read the message.

It's just outside of Mt Garnet, about a two-hour drive from Kelrick Kastle ...

Kelly gnawed on her nail. *He's been this close all along?*

Sorry I didn't get in touch sooner. I hope you're keeping well.

I stumbled across this property a couple of weeks after I left. I remember how you loved Samdarra. You'll love this place, too ...

Kelly leaned back in her chair and gulped. She *did* love Samdarra. Strange as it was for a city chick from Sydney, living in the harsh Australian outback; but she'd come to love it more than the city. If someone had told her during her teenage years that one day she would prefer to live in the outback, she would have thought it ridiculous. But then a lot of things hadn't gone to plan when she'd run away from the pain and havoc she'd created.

She leaned forward again, eager to keep reading Patrick's message.

It was painfully slow to get proper communications equipment set up out here. This is my first message out ...

Kelly's chest clenched and a lungful of air whooshed out from between her lips. *He hasn't forgotten me.* Even after she'd ignored him when he returned from Boston. Tears crowded in her eyes and blurred her vision. She didn't deserve him. She certainly didn't deserve the attentions of such a good man. And he was good, regardless of everything life had thrown at him, including her.

I've kept the original owners on as property managers and they're teaching me a lot. Sometimes there aren't enough hours in the day ...

Sometimes her days would drag by painfully slowly.

She rested her hand upon her breast, unable to suppress the yearning to be with Patrick. To share those busy days with him.

I'll surprise you with the name of the station once I get a chance to repair the main entrance sign. I'll admit the place is a bit rundown, but it's nothing I can't sort out. My current project, though, until the drought breaks and allows us to increase the cattle numbers, is to make a start on the new homestead. Can you help me ...?

With her heart hammering, Kelly kicked back her chair and rose. She tangled one hand in her wet hair and pressed against her scalp. The other hand she clenched by her side. She paced her office. The day had gone from zero to a hundred in just the past few minutes. With every word Patrick had written, she read a whole heap of unsaid stuff. Their roles were now reversed. When she'd needed help planning the castle's renovation, she'd leaned on Patrick for nearly everything. Now he was asking the same thing of her.

Gingerly approaching her computer, she sat and rolled her chair closer, reluctant to touch another key in case it blew up in her face. She might have sat transfixed all night if the word 'idiot' had not rumbled around her head. She shook her head in dismay, then clicked on the attachment. A rough draft of the homestead's floor plan popped up with a hand-written note below it.

Kel, I'm not good at this sort of thing. Can you make any suggestions? You've seen more homesteads and have a better idea of where rooms should be placed. I'll take any advice you can give. Everything will run on solar-powered batteries, so there might be some limitations to what we can do, but then again, that's why a person chooses to live in these parts ...

She sighed with relief, knowing she could do this. Patrick was spot-on when he'd said she'd seen many homesteads in her time. She noted how the open verandah ran the entire length of the house, a dominant feature of many outback Queensland homes. On a hot and dusty day, a lot of living happened under the shade of the verandah.

She sent the attachment to the printer before reading the remainder of his message.

A beautiful creek borders one side of the property. It's very dry at the moment, but for most of the year it's usually a pristine spring that tumbles over granite boulders and falls into perfectly sized swimming holes. No waterfalls, so I'm told, but nothing could replace the one I miss ...

Afraid to read any more, Kelly quickly exited the email and a minute later the screensaver started up. Three-dimensional shapes changed maddeningly, getting larger and smaller, continuously on repeat. She sat staring at the screen until nothing penetrated her mind and she wasn't seeing anything.

She needed a break from Patrick's message; it was killing her hard-earned equilibrium, opening up chasms in her heart that she purposely kept closed. His message threatened to destabilize everything she'd worked towards since losing Gemma, but she owed this to him. He hadn't faulted her when she'd needed his help, so she would do the same for him.

Then she remembered her overdue bookwork.

Damn! Time to get that done and out of the way before deciding how to reply to Patrick. She would tuck away her yearnings and memories of the times they'd spent together and concentrate on one project at a time. The homestead's design was first on the agenda, but she secretly hoped there'd be other projects he'd need help with.

Don't get your hopes up.

She wouldn't. She had a castle to run and Patrick deserved so much better.

Chapter 36

Patrick mopped his brow with his sleeve and shoved his akubra back on. The heat was stifling, but he wouldn't have it any other way. *God, I love it out here.*

His days were long and busy, and all he had to do was hang up his hat, remove his boots and the night would end even better with a message or two from Kelly.

One more job to do before he could call it a day. He wanted to check on the young kelpies he'd recently purchased. The breed was highly recommended for outback cattle properties, and in a few weeks, an expert dog trainer would start on their training. There was so much to learn his mind boggled, but he'd never been so satisfied with a day's work. There was purpose in it and an end goal to achieve. Each day was so physically exhausting, he slept well at night.

He entered the shed that'd seen better days and the dogs yelped when they spotted him.

"Hey, Bluey, howya doing?" Patrick smiled. He made a point of talking Aussie slang to his dogs to get some practice in. "What about you, Jacko?"

The second little mate wasn't going to be ignored and jumped onto Patrick's Blundstone boots.

Steel purlins creaked above as the searing hot day started to cool. Patrick mentally pushed aside the list of repairs needing to be done on the shed roof; he would start on those after the homestead was finished.

Patrick laughed when the dogs ran riot around his boots. "Hey, you guys wanna take it easy?"

Most stockmen laughed when he mixed his Yankee accent with Aussie slang, but his dogs were immune to it and crawled all over him as he crouched down. Evelyn insisted on feeding them every day, and without fail, their water container was always full and a half-chewed bone was left lying around. These two little mites ate every morsel of food. Their dishes were always licked clean and their speed of growth surprised Patrick.

He'd never owned a pet and never would've believed the hypnotic effect these two little fellows would have on him. A couple of minutes in their company quickly turned into half an hour, and occasionally an hour, before his stomach rumbled to remind him it was dinnertime.

Bluey nipped his fingers and Patrick laughed—a good solid laugh that'd eluded him for many of his adolescent years. When Jacko tried to crawl over his face, Patrick lost it and fell backwards, chuckling with their antics. Tails swished and tiny claws pricked his sweaty and stubbly face. He gave them a few more minutes of his time, allowing his body to completely unwind as he enjoyed their capers.

"Okay, boys, that's enough." Patrick sat and picked up one pup in each hand. "Time for sleep."

Jacko whined.

Patrick chuckled and held him up. He looked into his mesmerizing puppy-dog eyes. "You didn't just whine, did you, Jacko?"

The dog continued to whine half-heartedly. Patrick was beginning to believe these mutts could understand every word he spoke, but rule number one was that they were working dogs and couldn't live in the house.

Not that he had a house yet. He'd watched the homestead being built over the past two months, the progress fuelling so much excitement that some nights it kept him awake in excited anticipation as to how it'd look once finished. Thanks to Kelly, things with the house were moving along just fine, but for now, he kept that little bubble of hope linked with Kelly locked away. He didn't want to build it up, fearing he'd come crashing down if he expected too much. He'd been there before—too many times already.

He switched his attention back to his dogs and rubbed noses with each one, wishing them a good night's sleep before tucking them into their baskets. Rising, he looked down at them, trying to ignore their magnetic appeal. He didn't doubt, if he'd been allowed a dog as a kid, he would've either slept in its kennel or snuck it into his bedroom.

He shook his head, recalling how terribly lonely his childhood had been. It was hard to swallow such sadness some days. On the bright side, owning this property had given him a permanent light on the horizon, helping to quell the depressing thoughts that would have him spiralling downwards if he dwelt on them too long.

"See you boys tomorrow, okay?"

Patrick left as Bluey gave one last bark. His dogs made him smile, hard work made him happy, and soon he would have his own home. It wasn't a mansion in Boston's most sought-after suburb, but it was paradise in his books.

Stranger still was that his father wanted to come for a visit. Patrick had asked him to wait for the wet season. They'd experienced a couple of short afternoon storms but nothing drought breaking. Not enough to dampen the dust. He'd promised his sisters and father that he'd throw a homestead-warming party and invite them all.

He hadn't issued any such invitation to Kelly. Not yet.

Patrick made his way to the small shearer's donga where his camp bed was set up and his dinner would usually be waiting for him. He'd only agreed to Evelyn cooking his meals if she allowed him to cook Sunday dinner under her direction. He wasn't sure who was enjoying the experience more. Again, he smiled. How quickly could he shower and eat? How long before he could check his email?

The homestead was close to lock-up stage, and soon Patrick would need to choose tiles for the bathroom, cooking appliances for the kitchen, etcetera—all the choices that made him shudder. Evelyn had offered to come shopping with him and he wanted to invite Kelly, too. It was no secret that he wanted it to be her home one day, but how could he invite her?

He sprawled in his makeshift office chair, its heavy cushion failing miserably to mask the rough and sharp edges—not comfortable at all after a hard day's work. He reached for his mug of coffee and took a moment to inhale its rich smell before taking a sip.

"Ouch." He burned the tip of his tongue and, swearing loudly, plonked the mug back on the desk, making it wobble on its uneven legs. Yup, a decent desk and chair were already on the list of things to buy when he fitted out the new office.

Once the computer was up and running, he didn't hesitate to check his email. As expected, Kelly's waited; she'd shared her opinion on paint colours for the interior and exterior of the homestead. Patrick didn't mind her choices; they aligned well with what he had in mind. He was going for a rustic look with a timber verandah and exposed interior beams, all of which would be oiled to enrich the natural colour of the penda timber they'd sourced.

"Tough as nails out here and the termites won't come near it," Darcy had advised.

Patrick clicked on the photos of the shrine that Kelly had attached to her email. The native flowering plants looked healthy and the colours vibrant against the green forest in the background. Kelly had made no previous mention of the shrine, and for all intents and purposes, he'd forgotten about it. Surprised it looked so well cared for, he read the last paragraph of her message.

This thank you is well overdue, Patrick. I took no interest in what you were doing at the time, and when Dad told me what you were up to, I initially resented the gesture. Please accept this apology and replace it with a very huge thank you. I sit on the seat almost every afternoon and I know the words on the plaque by heart. I didn't deserve it, but you gave it to me anyway. I've taken it upon myself to tend the garden as you wanted and I hope I've done you proud. Words will never be enough to express how special this spot has become to me. Spending time there has helped me make it through some very dark days. Thank you.

Patrick gulped more coffee, then released a long and drawn-out sigh. Once he'd placed his mug back on the desk, he tangled his fingers in the mess of his dreadlocks. While massaging his scalp, he tortured himself with thoughts of asking Kelly the one question he'd been stressing over.

He'd already taken photos of the new entrance sign and had been thinking over his plan for days. But how to invite her to Cairns the following week? He needed a few days to sort out the kitchen, bathroom and tiles, but once he was finished, he wanted to take her snorkelling off the Great Barrier Reef. Darcy and Evelyn had already agreed to join him—safety in numbers would prevent him from doing anything stupid if he and Kelly were left alone.

Before he lost his nerve and changed his mind, he took a deep breath and began to reply to her email, hoping he'd given her enough time to grieve. He attached the photos of the entrance sign and gave a small explanation, then added a few lines inviting her shopping and snorkelling. He pressed send before he could back out, inhaled deeply and finished his coffee. He switched off the computer and headed for the sink to rinse his cup and brush his teeth.

His chest ached. Really ached. He wanted to get this right. His life would hang in the balance until she replied. Typically, she responded once a day, so he only had to wait until tomorrow night—but man, were the hours going to drag until then!

Already wearing a loose singlet and boxers, he flopped onto the camp bed he'd substituted for his swag and picked up the James Patterson novel Evelyn had loaned him. But the words weren't penetrating at all. He managed a page and a half of mumbo jumbo before putting the book down in disgust. Instead, his traitorous mind took him back to a certain camp by the river.

He rolled over and groaned into his pillow. *Don't torture yourself.* But of course he would—as he did most nights.

Chapter 37

Lightning crackled outside the cottage. The storm was right on top of them, but Kelly managed to boil the kettle before she ran around unplugging appliances. It was easier to disconnect everything electrical now rather than replace it all tomorrow if lightning struck the cottage. And it sounded entirely possible—she only counted one or two seconds after each strike before booming thunder followed.

She handed William and Margaret their hot drinks as they waited out the storm. There was no point in them trying to drive home while strong winds and rain whipped hard against the cottage windows. It was pointless talking, too, since they couldn't hear each other. Instead, William read the local weekly newspaper while Margaret worked on a small cross-stitch piece that she carried in her handbag. Kelly, eager to know if Patrick liked her choice of colours, grabbed her mobile phone and decided to check her emails. She normally waited until she'd showered and eaten, but with everything unplugged, she wasn't preparing anything for dinner just yet.

His first words were: **Before you read any further, click on the attached photos.**

They often exchanged photos and she loved keeping up-to-date with how the homestead was coming along. It gave her the sense that she was there with him ... and she so badly wanted to be.

This need to be with Patrick had snuck up on her. Only recently did she realise what it meant.

She missed Patrick. Her yearning to be with him was a growing ache. At night, she fell asleep dreaming of Patrick instead of Gemma. At first it'd frightened her. She'd been worried that she'd forget her little girl. But with her sleep becoming more relaxed and restful, she'd let the worries dwindle away.

The three photos Patrick had attached to his email had been taken of a sign at different angles. The words 'Gem Springs' were easily legible, but she frowned, not understanding where they fit in with the homestead. She peered closer and registered the tall metal poles holding the sign and a road leading away from it. Something tumbled inside her chest. She quickly tapped back into the email and read his message.

Kel, when I stumbled across this property and learned it was called Gem Springs, I instantly thought of your beautiful little girl. I hope the name doesn't make you sad, because for me, it keeps her memory alive. It was one of the reasons I bought the property.

Over the noise of the storm, Kelly gave an almighty sob. She hadn't anticipated feeling anguished over the name of a property. It was only a name, but then it wasn't. And, of course, that made no sense. Not when Patrick was involved. Tears coursed down her face and her shoulders shook. Why did this one man have the ability to find her most vulnerable threads and rearrange them? She'd worked so hard to keep them in place and had grown so much since the day she'd run away from home. In fact, that girl no longer existed. Every hardship, setback and epic event—whether good, bad or sad—had led to this very moment. It'd taken a long time, but she finally knew what path to take. She just needed the strength to follow through with it.

"Hey, baby, what's up?" Margaret put her cross-stitch down and came over to wrap an arm around Kelly's shoulder.

Kelly swiped at her face and the motion caught William's attention. He joined them and they sat closely together, Kelly with her head on her mother's shoulder, waiting for the storm and her tears to abate. She didn't want to create a storm inside the cottage, but there was so much she needed to say and explain. She couldn't be in two places at once, but sometime during the past weeks her priorities had switched.

It was only a matter of minutes before the storm passed over. The rain had reduced to a light shower and the thunder sounded more distant by the second.

"Is this about Patrick?" Margaret asked when it was possible to hear again.

Kelly raised her face and nodded, her mother's perceptiveness not something she was surprised about. She'd shared all of Patrick's news with her parents and they'd discussed the progress of the new homestead on a daily basis. Had they seen a change in her?

William took her hand and squeezed it. "Tell us what's going on in that pretty head of yours."

Kelly managed a shrug. Her father was only trying to make her smile. Though he usually had the ability to do so, she couldn't quite manage it today.

"Let me guess. You want to move out to this property to be with Patrick?"

Her jaw dropped. This was exactly where her thoughts were headed, even though she hadn't admitted it to herself. She extricated her hand from William's and scraped it through her hair.

"The property is called Gem Springs. Patrick said he instantly thought of Gemma when he saw it. The name was one of the reasons he bought it."

William sighed loudly, his head bobbing as he took in the news. Tears glistened in his eyes as the three of them considered Patrick's gesture.

"Darling," Margaret said, "you've been through so much in your young life."

Kelly turned to face her mother as tears squeezed past her eyelashes.

"Your father and I are still very young. We love it here and don't want to leave. Why don't you visit Patrick and give things a go? Whatever happens, Kelrick Kastle will always be yours."

Something came alive under her skin. Every nerve ending sprouted wings. Leaving this place was her biggest stumbling block. She loved Kelrick Kastle, had invested so much time, energy and enthusiasm into the project. It was a part of her and she wasn't sure she could give it up. This was where most of her memories of Gemma had been made. Her parents would have to push her out the door for her to feel okay about leaving. Her mother's words sounded too good to be true.

"You mean that?"

"We're never going back to Sydney," William added. "This is the tree change we needed."

"But—"

"No buts," William scolded. "Your mother and I have been talking about this for weeks now. We all experienced the same pain and grief, but we feel you deserve something good." William wrapped his arms around her, giving her a hard hug. "Patrick loves you. There's never been any doubt about that, and if this isn't a sign that he's building that damn homestead for you, I'll eat my hat."

Margaret chuckled and Kelly managed a smile. "I miss him so much, Dad."

"Then go to him. What else did he say today?"

Overwhelmed at her parent's reaction, she picked up her phone and brought up the email. "I'll show you pictures of the entrance sign. He told me weeks ago he'd surprise me with the name when the sign was repaired."

"Well, you can't argue about the surprise factor," William quipped.

Once she'd shared the photos, she read the last paragraph aloud.

"'One last thing, Kel. I need to outfit the kitchen and bathroom and select tiles. Would you have some spare time in the following week or two to help me choose everything I need? I was thinking of shopping in Cairns for a few days before spending a day snorkelling on the reef. Darcy and Evelyn are coming too and I'd like you to come with us ...'"

Her heart raced. If she said yes, she'd see Patrick again—and soon. Her vision glazed over his words until her phone blacked out.

"Take the Landcruiser and surprise him first."

"What?" Kelly turned to her mum.

Margaret smiled. "Do something impulsive. Turn up on his doorstep and give him your answer." Taking her hand, she patted it. "Tell him how you feel."

Now her parents were acting weird. "Are you trying to get rid of me?"

William's laughter bellowed around the small cottage. "Too right we are. There's a man out there who loves my daughter and I want to see her happy. I'm not afraid of you being in the outback, because the outback made you a very capable girl. It's only a two-hour drive. You'll be there in the afternoon if you leave tomorrow at lunchtime."

Indecision gnawed at her. "I know you love this place as much as I do, but are you sure you want this? You don't want to slow down, take off and enjoy your life?"

"Of course we don't mind. We're having the time of our lives here and don't want to slow down yet. Now, move closer for a group hug. The next time we do this I want there to be four of us. Got it?" William demanded.

An orchestra played inside her chest, a symphony of beautiful music, her head swimming to its sound. By this time tomorrow she could be hugging Patrick. The thought warmed her from the inside out.

Her parents had figured her out too. Thank goodness for that.

⁂

Patrick heard the crackle of the two-way. He'd been so engrossed in the fencing he was working on, he'd barely stopped for a break all day. But it could be Darcy or Evelyn trying to contact him, so he didn't hesitate to straighten and stretch his back. When he turned away from the fence line and towards the utility, his mouth dropped open.

Where the bloody hell did those black clouds come from? Shoot, the storm looks close.

No wonder his back was dripping with sweat. The humidity was probably two hundred percent.

He swiped his sleeve across his sweaty brow and shoved his Akubra back on. As he headed to the vehicle, he heard Darcy's voice through the open window and swiftly opened the door.

"Reading you, Darcy. What's up?"

"There's a severe storm heading our way. Just heard the weather alert. You've got about twenty minutes, I reckon, before it hits."

"Just noticed the black clouds now. I'll pack up and head back straight away. Thanks, mate."

"They say that trough is movin' across. Could mean a few days of rain."

"Hope so. See you soon, Darce."

"I'll leave the shed gate open. Drive straight in and wait there if it's heavy."

"Okay, I'm on my way."

Within minutes, Patrick was driving back to the homestead. It would take him twenty minutes to get there, and the view outside the windscreen was dark and menacing. He cursed his stupidity for not seeing the danger earlier. Where was his head?

He grimaced, trying to push the utility faster than he would normally. The dirt road was rough in patches, so driving in these conditions required total concentration to ensure he didn't hit a pothole the wrong way. At least it would stop him thinking about why he'd never received an email from Kelly last night.

And that answered where his head had been all day.

He didn't need to be reminded that it had been two fucking days since the last email. Every minute leading up to last night had been agony. Every minute after, pure torture. He'd quickly checked his inbox that morning after breakfast, and seeing it empty had been difficult to swallow. Had he revealed the name of the property too early? Ruined his chances?

It'd been a long, cruel day. It was no wonder he hadn't seen the storm brewing; he'd been too busy concentrating on the one building inside his head.

About two hours ago, he'd torn skin off his finger through a tear in his glove. He'd sunk to the bare dirt and let his shoulders droop, releasing all the tension. It was time for a reality check. Thank God he was still capable of that. He urged himself to deal with the bitter disappointment. He'd done nothing wrong. If Kelly wasn't ready yet, he would try again another day.

At least I've found the real Patrick Van Der Meeliko.

This realisation calmed him a little. He'd found his place in the world, a place where he was finally content. As he'd sat under that hot sun, he'd revisited the positives in his life—how fate had led him to Gem Springs and having Darcy and Evelyn as mentors.

He swerved sharply to avoid another dangerous pothole and accidently bit his tongue. As the first spots of rain landed on his windscreen, he tried to push aside his frustration, needing to concentrate completely as the falling rain steadily increased. Jeez ... some days it wasn't easy.

With only the final kilometre to go, Patrick drove at a snail's pace. The dirt track was a muddied river of water and the utility slid dangerously from one side of the road to the other. The wipers swiped their fastest and he tensed when thunder shook the air around the vehicle. He could see the sheds. He was nearly home.

With the road improving slightly as he neared the sheds, Patrick began to relax. Finally, he could see the rain for what it was. *Hallelujah.* It might be the drought-breaking rain they'd waited on. The next three days could change things for Gem Springs. According to Darcy, it hadn't rained properly for nearly seven years.

Patrick drove the utility through the shed gate, switched off the engine and hurriedly got out, not wanting to miss a single second of this storm. Hastily he removed his boots and left them in the cab, then walked outside and looked up. The lightning didn't seem so bad, now that the initial storm had abated, and hopefully solid rain would follow. He raised his arms and let the soaking rain drench him completely, right down to his bare feet. He opened his mouth and drank in as much as he could, nourishing his dehydrated body.

Never had rain been so welcomed. He'd stood in the rain before, even danced in it, but he didn't want to revisit that memory now. Today was about Gem Springs and everything he wanted to achieve once the rivers and dams were filled to the brim. And boy, did he have plans.

A flash of light flickered in his periphery and he glanced towards it. A white Landcruiser was slowly making its way towards the homestead. He stood stock-still, his body frozen. He knew the vehicle, yet its presence didn't make sense. He knew the moment the driver spotted him—the lights switched off and the vehicle turned towards the shed.

Then the booming of his heart began a heavy thumping. He worked hard to remain calm and tried to douse any hope from building up. He wasn't prepared to believe anything until he saw her with his own eyes.

His eyes didn't disappoint. The vehicle stopped only metres away and Kelly climbed out. She was barefoot too, and the drenching, all-consuming rain coated her body in seconds, leaving her shorts and shirt stuck to her skin. Her midnight black hair was plastered to her face. She was the most beautiful she'd ever been, but still, he couldn't move, couldn't smile. Maybe he'd gotten too much sun and this was really some hallucination.

They stood staring at each other. His eyes filled with falling water; overflowed, and fell down his cheeks and inside his mouth. He swallowed.

Kelly looked wary, uncertain and possibly a little afraid.

Come on, mate, don't scare her away. She must be here for a reason.

He had to find the strength to make the first move. He'd regret it for the rest of his life if he didn't. He raised his arms and stretched them out, hoping it was the sign she was waiting for.

It was.

She ran the last few steps, careered into him and wrapped her arms around his neck. He lifted her easily, giving her an excuse to wrap her legs around his waist. She squeezed so tightly, he let out a loud chuckle, except it was barely audible over the heavy rain.

"Yes, Patrick," she shouted close to his ear.

He tightened his hold around her, not caring what question she was answering. Yes, she wanted to come shopping with him; yes, she'd take a day off for snorkelling; yes, she was ready to talk to him again. Yes, yes, yes!

A strong shaft of joy zapped across his body, and he spun around and around, laughing, the rain still coming down heavy. Kelly laughed with him, tilting her head back, allowing rain to gush into her open mouth.

He knew what to do in a situation like this. He'd done it before and he would do it again. He stopped spinning and cradled the back of her neck. Gently tilting her head forward, he found her lips and kissed her. He wouldn't stop until the rain did and he hoped it went on for hours. He was never letting her go again, and if this happened to be a dream, he didn't care if he never woke up.

EPILOGUE

Patrick slid off the makeshift bed and covered Kelly's shoulders with the blanket. She didn't wake, despite the pounding of the heavy monsoonal rain. He pulled on his pyjama shorts and crossed the room to the only window. In the light of dawn, he looked outside, but it was impossible to see anything. The thunderous rain fell in sheets, hit the glass and gushed down its smooth surface.

He smiled, memories of another morning in this exact room flooding back. It was hard to believe it had happened close to twelve years ago.

He leaned against the window frame and watched the rain, letting it lull him into a secure cocoon—it was the reason he enjoyed returning to Kelrick Kastle on its wettest days. They tried to visit at least four times a year and the three children always camped out in the small cottage with their grandparents. Patrick hoped his babies weren't scared by all the noise.

Seven-year-old Jarrod would argue he wasn't a baby anymore, and Patrick would have to agree. Always by Patrick's side on the station, Jarrod's raw talent with horses was becoming more obvious by the day. God alone knew where he got it from, but he had his Boston grandfather's tenacious streak and soaked up everything Darcy and the station hands taught him. Patrick was proud of him.

Five-year-old Finley was always one step behind his brother, but only because his stride couldn't keep up. Some days holding him back was a superhero's job. Patrick smiled often when he was in the company of his sons.

Three-year-old Sophie would be tucked in between William and Margaret. She would have crawled in with them at some stage during the night. She was a loveable child who delighted everyone with her cheeky smile and chatter, including her grandfather, Thomas. He travelled often from Boston and had managed to bond with his grandchildren as he'd never done with his children.

Some roads could be mended, Patrick mused.

During these visits to the castle, he and Kelly stayed alone in the left turret. A 'Private, Do Not Enter' sign was fixed to the door and the room was closed to visitors during their stay. The arrangement never changed and everyone was happy.

He ran a hand through his sleep-mussed hair—his dreadlock days were long gone—and found it hard to believe that barely three days ago they'd rested their dusty akubras on the homestead's hat rack. Their wet season hadn't quite started this year.

Gem Springs was their home, and in a lot of ways, it mimicked Samdarra. It was a working cattle station, but they also took care of troubled youths. Only a two-hour drive from the castle, it was close enough to share an outback life with a coastal one. These days they ran a tight ship and a successful business, and Gemma's memory lived on in the name.

Patrick peered outside again, towards the far right, past the falls, hoping to see a glimpse of the shrine he'd built all those years ago. The relentless rain wasn't going anywhere in a hurry, but there'd be plenty of time to spend near it in the coming days. He knew Kelly would sit by it each day and he liked to share that time with her too.

As each year rolled into the next, Kelly remained calm about being near the falls. Though these days, a latched gate prevented any child from venturing down the steep steps on their own.

With the wet season's arrival, William and Margaret, who were still very involved in the management of the popular tourist icon, enjoyed a more relaxed routine. For the next few months the castle would function with restrictions in place—the falls and swimming area would be off limits and the forest walks not available. The café and souvenir shop would continue to operate; the volume of water flowing over the falls, spectacular in its own right. Tourists experienced the magic of the place with a full stomach and a few trinkets to remember it by.

Kelly mumbled something in her sleep and Patrick turned towards her. She'd flung one bronzed arm over the blanket. Suddenly chilly by the window, he quietly padded back to the bed and slipped beneath the blanket. Warmth enveloped him, but he didn't plan on going back to sleep; Kelly didn't know it yet, but he had a gift for her.

He closed his eyes and rested his arm beside hers. Relaxed as he was, memories ignited and images played behind his eyelids. It still amazed him that his big adventure—his life, as he liked to think of it—had started with finding that stone in the road.

Now he was ready to start his own piece of history. So that in a hundred years or so, when someone discovered Kelly's diaries, which she religiously kept, they might talk about *their* magical love. Because charmed it was, and the dreams built into the earliest foundations of the castle would continue through the centuries.

When the right-sized emerald had become available, it hadn't taken Patrick long to make the decision. Inscribed on the back, he'd duplicated, 'All my love, P'. Kelly would freak out at the cost, but he would calm her like always. With a kiss ... a touch ...

She snuggled closer and mumbled again. He wound his arms around her and watched her beautiful face as she woke slowly. Her eyelashes flicked open and closed a couple of times as the fragrances of her body rose up to greet him.

Still sleepy, she said, "Wow, rain. So heavy."

"Mmm, yeah." He placed feather-light kisses on her mouth.

She pushed her legs against his until she found the spot, the way she always did, setting him off.

"Mmm, that's nice." She kissed him back. Nothing rushed. Just how they liked it. "Do you remember the time we were stuck in this room because of the rain?"

Boy, did he ever.

"And you insisted we drive to the roadhouse for a burger." She pulled back a fraction and kept her eyes open, defying sleep.

He nodded. *As if I'd forget.*

"And you insisted we dance naked in the rain?" She produced a sheepish smile.

He chuckled, reliving the memories, his body coming alive under her skilful hands. The emerald pendant, their stone in the road, could wait. This was more important, and anyway, his mind had already begun to switch off. His body was taking over and they had a few hours up their sleeve.

The pounding rain muted the heavy thumping of his heart, but it couldn't hide the pulse coming alive under his skin.

AUTHOR NOTE

If you'd like to read about North Queensland's real castle in the rainforest, search for Paronella Park.

Some historical facts in this story come from the fabulous history of this labour of love.

Opened to the public in 1935, it was a combination of genius engineering and a place for entertainment, refreshments, a museum, movie theatre, dancing, parties and swimming.

It still stands today as a testament to one man's hard work and the love for his family.

It remains a valued must-see attraction in beautiful North Queensland, Australia.

THANKS FOR READINGS

Thank you for reading **The Stone in The Road.** I hope you enjoyed it and continue reading the other stories in **The Australian at Heart Series**. Set mostly in Queensland, you'll recognise town names and places, along with our dusty outback and our refreshing rainforest.

There are many people to thank along the way when you sit down and write a book. Sometimes it's a word of encouragement you receive from someone unexpected, other times it's an idea they offer, which you foster and it becomes part of your story.

For this book I want to make special mention of the community where I live. Small and rural that it is, it's vibrant, alive and full of wonderful people. I'm in the public eye every day because of the business I own. As members of the community come to realise I'm an author, and with a published book (a surprise for many—who even has time to do this) they've been nothing but supportive and inspired. What's really funny, is how the majority of male customers who purchase hardware from our business shy away from the word romance. But let me tell you, one shy male customer at a time, I'm warming them up to the romance genre, and hoping to release a new generation of romantic men/husbands/partners out into the world. Nothing is impossible!

Of course, none of this would be possible without the constant support of my critique partner and friend, Lisa Stanbridge. We've taken every step on this journey together and continue to remain strong and committed. Cheers Lisa!

Then there are the following authors who I wish to personally thank. No question is ever too much trouble. Thank you, Phillipa Nefri Clark, Alicia Hope, Davina Stone & Sarah Williams. A special thank you is also in order for the fabulous FB group Indie Royalty. A wealth of information and assistance every time I ask.

And lastly thank you to my family who continue to let me do this, and you, my readers. I'm here because of you.

ALSO BY FRANCES DALL'ALBA

The **Australian at Heart Series** tells the stories of four interconnected siblings.

Little Blue Box – Book 1

Regrets, lies, and earth-shattering secrets. When Ella learns the identity of her biological father, nothing will stand in her way. Not even his power. When things don't go to plan, can one little blue box put Ella and Zane back on the same path? This second chance contemporary romance is filled with suspense, emotion and a life-changing sizzling romance.

The Stone In The Road – Book 2

Emotional, passionate and heart-wrenching. This suspense-filled captivating romance will have you dancing in the rain and smiling through your tears. Set in tropical northern Australia, we don't always get to choose our path.

The Silk Scarf – Book 3

An unravelling silken scarf ... mysterious gold ... a breathtaking romance.
An emotional and unforgettable contemporary romance set in Australia.

Rustic Denim Love – Book 4

Forgotten secrets ... blazing fires ... burning love.
She's busy and diligent, doing the best she can to save her crumbling family.
He's funny and witty, with a solution for every problem.
This one may just beat him.

Link to read more and BUY.

**https://francesdallalba.wixsite.com/francesdallalba/australianathe
artseries**

Sway of The Stars Series will share the stories of a group of friends.

The Shooting Star – Book 1

Hidden treasures ... broken spirits ... tangled love. A modern-day treasure hunt where hidden treasures will tangle their love and break their spirits. Duty or love, or can they have both?

The Glittering Star –Book 2

Shimmering waters ... towering giants ... buried mysteries. She's the no filters chick. Funny, full of life and always ready for a good laugh. Until her mother drops a bombshell. He's the environmental warrior. Passionate, driven and determined to save the world. Burnt once before, he's moving on and doing things his way. So how did they end up hand cuffed together on day one?

The Giving Star – Book 3

Endless roads ... timeless discoveries ... unbreakable love. She's packed up her life ready for change, with one regret still hanging over her head. He's working his way back from hell, adamant he's never going there again. But one stumble, one discovery, and one hotbed of attraction ... and the entire game plan changes.

The Priceless Star – Book 4

Forgotten treasures ... a perilous ransom ... shattered hopes

She's chasing answers long buried since the war.

He's content with a steady working life. Until he's not...

Sent to Far North Queensland to research a wartime mystery, Lucia Levorico escapes her privileged life and finds unexpected passion with reserved local, Theo Mather, under an outback sky – until a sudden goodbye and a devastating worksite tragedy tear them apart. When a ruthless ransom plot targets Lucia's wealth, their only reprieve will come from sharing the unravelling of a wartime mystery and its priceless treasure. Unless they're willing to fight for what they have.

Link to read more and BUY.
https://francesdallalba.wixsite.com/francesdallalba/swayof the stars

Eight Seconds, is a standalone story inspired by Australia's first female open bullrider. She pushed past the barriers and succeeded in a male dominated sport, creating a new legend showcased in two Australian halls of fame.

Triumph, hardship, true grit ... and one crazy dream.
An inspirational story about one woman, with one dream, and one almighty driving passion.

Link to read more and BUY.
https://francesdallalba.wixsite.com/francesdalla lba/eightseconds

Jack& Eva, is a standalone contemporary romance set in tropical North Queensland. It showcases our unique and adorable Lumholtz tree kangaroo and the valuable work done by Dr Karen Coombes in her care and continued research of them.

Broody meets bubbly ... and a bunch of cuddly tree kangaroos.
When the tempest blows over, will Jack and Eva be able to find a way forward, or are they destined for a train wreck with a bunch of furry animals caught up in the middle?
Fall in love with our adorable tree kangaroo while reading an emotional and passionate contemporary romance set in Australia.

Link to read more and BUY.
https://francesdallalba.wixsite.com/francesdallalba/jackandeva

ABOUT THE AUTHOR

As a contemporary romance author, Frances loves nothing more than losing herself in a good romance. She's all about helping you forget the housework, or the bus to work you're going to miss, if you don't put the book down now!

She's devoted to giving her readers an emotional, passionate, possibly some ugly-cry, fairly steamy love story, that'll melt your heart and have you fighting for the happy ending right until the end.

Frances sets her books in North Queensland. She makes no excuses if some of her settings include amazing lakes and waterfalls, stunning views from tops of mountains, spectacular outback scenes, or crystal-clear creeks shadowed by tropical rainforest.

When she isn't writing, Frances is climbing mountains, searching for waterfalls and swimming across lakes. She loves to exercise, would prefer it if someone else cooked dinner every night, and never notices dust on the furniture.

She lives with her husband in tropical Far North Queensland, Australia, and uses her great baking skills to tempt her family to visit home often.

Say hello to Frances

Visit her website: https://francesdallalba.wixsite.com/francesdallalba and subscribe to her newsletter. It will keep you up-to-date with everything happening in her author world.

Follow Frances on Facebook, Instagram, Bookbub, TikTok, and Goodreads. To do so, click on this link: https://linktr.ee/francesdallalba

Still have a question?

Ask her at: https://francesdallalba.wixsite.com/francesdallalba/contact

Leave a Review

Did you enjoy this book? The best favour you can do for an author is to leave a **review**. If you'd like to leave a review, go to your place of on-line purchase of the book, or search for the book on **Goodreads** and leave a review. Thank you.